Titles by Jennifer Ashley

Below Stairs Mysteries

A SOUPÇON OF POISON
(an ebook)

DEATH BELOW STAIRS

SCANDAL ABOVE STAIRS

DEATH IN KEW GARDENS

The Mackenzies Series

THE MADNESS OF LORD IAN MACKENZIE

LADY ISABELLA'S SCANDALOUS MARRIAGE

THE MANY SINS OF LORD CAMERON

THE DUKE'S PERFECT WIFE

A MACKENZIE FAMILY CHRISTMAS

THE SEDUCTION OF ELLIOT MCBRIDE

THE UNTAMED MACKENZIE
(an ebook)

THE WICKED DEEDS OF DANIEL MACKENZIE

SCANDAL AND THE DUCHESS
(an ebook)

RULES FOR A PROPER GOVERNESS

THE SCANDALOUS MACKENZIES
(anthology)

THE STOLEN MACKENZIE BRIDE

A MACKENZIE CLAN GATHERING
(an ebook)

DEATH IN
KEW
GARDENS

Jennifer Ashley

Berkley Prime Crime
New York

BERKLEY PRIME CRIME
Published by Berkley
An imprint of Penguin Random House LLC
1745 Broadway, New York, NY 10019

Library of Congress Cataloging-in-Publication Data

Names: Ashley, Jennifer, author.
Title: Death in Kew Gardens / Jennifer Ashley.
Description: First edition. | New York, NY : Berkley, 2019 |
Series: A below stairs mystery ; 3
Identifiers: LCCN 2019001011 | ISBN 9780399587900 (paperback) |
ISBN 9780399587917 (ebook)
Subjects: | BISAC: FICTION / Mystery & Detective / Women Sleuths. |
FICTION / Mystery & Detective / Historical. | GSAFD: Mystery fiction.
Classification: LCC PS3601.S547 D45 2019 | DDC 813/.6—dc23
LC record available at https://lccn.loc.gov/2019001011

First Edition: June 2019

Printed in the United States of America
1   3   5   7   9   10   8   6   4   2

Cover art by Larry Rostant
Cover design by Emily Osborne
Book design by Laura K. Corless

1

The Chinese gentleman ran from between the carriages that packed the length of Mount Street and straight into my path. I had no chance—he emerged so suddenly and without my seeing him that I barreled directly into the poor man.

My basketful of produce slammed into his narrow belly, knocking him from his feet. He landed on the cobblestones in a tangle of limbs and fabric.

I shoved my basket at my assistant, Tess, and bent over the unfortunate man.

"My dear sir, I do beg your pardon—you popped out so quickly." I thrust my hands down to him, intending to help him to his feet.

Instead of accepting my assistance, the man cringed from me, his face screwing up in abject fear.

"Come now," I said, softening my voice. "You can't stay on the cobbles—they're full of mud and muck."

The man hesitated, still afraid, so I firmly took hold of him and hauled him to his feet.

He was small boned and light, easily lifted, but I felt strength under his garments. Once he was standing upright, I saw that he was a few inches taller than I, dressed in a silk robe that fell to his feet, the sleeves so wide his hands would disappear if he folded them together.

His round cap had fallen to the ground, revealing a head that was quite bald from forehead to the top of his skull. As though to make up for the lack of hair in front, a thick braid hung down his back to his knees, and a beard curled to his chest.

His robe was a deep blue, with birds and vines embroidered on the hem in rich yellow and green. The colors were muted from dust, rain, and London grime, but the garment must have once been lovely.

The Chinese gentleman finally lost his agitation and looked at me directly. He was not a young man, middle aged perhaps, though his hair and beard held little gray and his face bore only a few lines. But his eyes, which were dark brown, nearly black, contained a weight of years greater than my own, an understanding that comes from experiencing life, all its tragedies and triumphs. He had an air of supreme confidence that even falling to a London street could not erase.

This gentleman stared at me a moment longer before he tucked his hands into his sleeves, dropped his gaze, and gave me a slight bow. "Forgive me, madam."

"Not at all," I said briskly. "I knocked *you* over, sir, so *I* ought to apologize. Do take care as you walk about. The drivers do not go as cautiously as they should, and they can't always stop their heavy drays in time. I would hate to think of you lying hurt on the street."

He listened to my speech without blinking, though he transferred that keen gaze to my left shoulder. I sensed Tess behind me, gawping at the man with no sense of her own rudeness.

"Please accept my many apologies, good lady," he said.

His manners were exquisite, such a refreshing change from those of men who had no intention of being courteous to a mere cook.

"No harm done," I said. "Now, you must excuse me, sir. I need to walk past you, and there is very little room on the road today."

The corners of the man's eyes crinkled with good humor. As he bent to sweep up his cap, I saw razor scars on the top of his scalp from many years of shaving back his hair.

He gave me a final nod and darted off, moving swiftly between the carriages, around the corner to Park Street. I watched until he disappeared from sight then I took my basket from Tess, and we walked on.

"Well, that was interestin'," she said in her cheery tones. "You don't see many Chinamen in *these* parts. I'm surprised he's allowed to walk in Mayfair."

I shrugged. "He likely works for a family here, as we do."

Even as I spoke, I felt a frisson of doubt. I'd been employed at the Rankin house on Mount Street long enough to have become acquainted with the servants in the homes around it, and none employed a Chinese gentleman.

Also, I did not believe he was a common laborer, as were many Cantonese who had come to London to escape poverty or war in their own country. While the gentleman had been afraid when I'd first knocked him down, he'd stood proudly on his feet, without the slumped shoulders of a menial. His faded robe had once been fine, the touch of the silk like gossamer.

"I'd never be Chinese," Tess said, swinging her basket. "I hear their women stuff their feet into tiny little shoes." She kicked out her long foot in its high laced boot. "Can't work if you do that."

"You couldn't help being Chinese if your parents were," I pointed out. "And the women in China from our walk of life work just as hard as we do."

"If you say so, Mrs. H.," Tess said. She crowded close and tucked her hand under my arm. "We're packed in tight today, ain't we? Her ladyship next door has no business inviting so many to her house for an afternoon. She's ruined the whole street."

Lady Harkness, wife of a knight of the realm, was holding a gathering today to show off her husband's exquisite and unusual garden, full of plants he'd brought home from his years in the Orient. As it was September, most families of note were off in the country, hunting foxes or shooting birds flushed out by their servants, but Lady Harkness still managed to fill her gathering. Her husband was decidedly middle class and possibly lower, said Mrs. Bywater, the mistress of my house, with a sniff. Sir Jacob had been given a knighthood for services to the Empire, but he'd been born a tradesman in Liverpool.

Regardless of his beginnings, his wealth had brought him much prestige. The number of fine carriages that lined Mount Street and wrapped around the corner showed that his humble beginnings had been forgiven.

Not only did the waiting carriages jam up the works, but

carts, wagons, and foot traffic served to clog the area further. Even the most elegant corner of London was a thoroughfare to somewhere else.

Mrs. Bywater was attending the garden party, in spite of her snobbishness about Sir Jacob and his wife. So was her niece, Lady Cynthia, with whom I'd formed a friendship. Both ladies wanted a look at the strange plants Sir Jacob had brought back from his many years in foreign parts. Lady Cynthia would tell me later about Lady Harkness's do, most likely how horrifically wearying it had been.

For now, I had to get supper on the table for the family when they returned and for the entire body of servants—a dozen of us—who kept the Mount Street house running efficiently.

I entered the kitchen, exchanging coat and hat for apron, and began to sort through the comestibles, my encounter with the Chinaman fading to the back of my mind.

While Lord Rankin, a baron, owned the house where I lived and worked, he allowed Lady Cynthia, sister of his deceased wife, and her aunt and uncle, the Bywaters, to occupy the house while he dwelled in Surrey. Cynthia's aunt and uncle had moved in to chaperone her, and also to keep her behavior in check—at least Mrs. Bywater considered this to be part of her duty. She and her husband wished to get Cynthia married off, out of harm's way, but Cynthia, so far, had resisted.

The family had remained in residence through the sticky, smelly, uncomfortable London summer. Mr. Bywater always had much business in the City, and Lady Cynthia refused to return to her father's house. Therefore, my duties had not eased during the hot months, and the kitchen had become like the devil's anteroom.

Tess and I and the rest of the staff had sweated and struggled, our tempers short. A walk outside had scarcely brought any relief, as the heat enveloped the entire city. At least we were mercifully away from the river and its stink.

September brought welcome coolness and abundance as farmers began to cart in the harvest. Potatoes and apples gradually dominated the vendors' carts, as well as walnuts and game from the countryside—partridges to venison. Mr. Bywater did not hunt or shoot, but he had friends who sent him whole birds or meat packed in paper and sawdust. Such a savings, Mrs. Bywater never failed to state.

One lesson the penny-pinching Mrs. Bywater learned, however, through the long, roasting summer, was that we truly needed a housekeeper.

Mr. Davis, the butler, and I had taken on much of the housekeeping duties, but I was too busy cooking, Mr. Davis too busy tending to the wine, silver, and service at table, to take care of much else. Discipline deteriorated among the maids and footmen, and tasks did not get done. I insisted on a large share of the household budget for food, but Mr. Davis wanted it for the master's wine and brandy. We quarreled frequently, and Mrs. Bywater lost her patience with us.

Mr. Davis told me, triumphantly, a week ago, that Mrs. Bywater had finally broken down and asked an agency to send her candidates for a housekeeper. She hadn't found one she liked yet, but at least she'd begun the proceedings.

Until then, it fell to me to go over the household accounts, keep inventory of the food, supervise the kitchen staff, and cook until my hands were sore, burned, and abraded.

Tess had proved to be quite capable, learning what I taught her quickly, and was beginning to master recipes and more complicated cooking techniques. She'd been scrubbing floors before I'd taken her on—a sad waste of talent. She'd make a fine cook after more training.

I did not muse on my encounter with the Chinese gentleman the rest of that day, as I had much to do. The next day was also particularly busy, and by the time I prepared the evening meal, I was short-tempered and exhausted. Mr. Davis blamed me for a missing bottle of wine—had I put it into my sauce by mistake?

When Charlie, the kitchen boy, spotted the wine behind a stack of greens, had Mr. Davis apologized and owned he'd been wrong? No, he'd sniffed, tucked the bottle under his arm, given Charlie a half-hearted clout on the ear, and stalked away.

I could only shake my head and return to my sauté pan, hoping I hadn't ruined my sole in butter sauce. The butter had to brown, not burn, or the entire dish was spoiled.

Mr. Bywater liked his supper the moment he returned home, and we were a bit behind with the soup and greens. I thickened the soup with flour instead of letting it reduce, tossed in some cream and a good handful of salt, and sent it up.

Then Emma, the downstairs maid, spilled half my perfected butter sauce on the floor, and fell to weeping. I plunked the rest of the meal onto platters to go up in the dumbwaiter, told Tess to see to the staff's supper, caught up a basket, and went out through the scullery.

Cool air touched my face as I walked up the stairs to the night, and I breathed a sigh of relief. I usually did not mind my life as a cook, but at times I found it trying. I reminded myself of the virtue of hard work and the fact that I was saving my shillings for the day I could reside with my daughter and run a little tea shop, the two of us living in bliss. Sometimes this vision helped, but tonight, peace eluded me.

In spite of my pique, I hadn't forgotten those in more need than myself. My basket held scraps I'd saved from the meal—greens too wilted for the dining room, trimmings of cooked meat or fish sliced off for symmetry, fruit too squashed to look fine in the bowl, and dried ends of yesterday's cake.

The few who gathered outside, knowing I would appear with my basket, swarmed to me with gratefulness. I handed out the food in pieces of towel that would have only gone into the rag bag.

A slim figure joined those in the shadows. I always met the beggars exactly between the streetlamps, where the darkness was greatest. The poor things feared the light, knowing they could be arrested for being unemployed and hungry.

I turned to the newcomer with my last bundle of scraps. "Now, sir, get that inside you, and you'll feel better . . . Oh."

I was surprised to see my Chinese gentleman from the day before. His long beard was a wisp against his robes, the blue of the silk black in the shadows.

He held out a box to me, a small wooden casket. "Please," he said. "A gift for you."

I held up my hands. "No, no, you do not need to give me anything."

"You did me a kindness, madam. Allow me to thank you by doing one for you."

"You are courteous," I said, softening. "And I thank you, but I cannot possibly accept it. A gentleman does not give gifts to a lady, especially one he is not acquainted with. I am not certain of your customs in China, but in England, I am afraid that is the case."

His eyes glinted as he raised his head, and I saw in them a flash of hurt. I felt contrite—I must have insulted him.

I gentled my tone. "Forgive me. I know it must be difficult being far from home." I'd never been farther than Cornwall, and though I'd found it lovely, I'd longed to return to London with all my might.

To my concern, his eyes filled with tears. "Indeed." The sadness in his voice tugged at me. "Very difficult."

I put an impulsive hand on his arm. "My dear sir, I am so sorry. Might you tell me your name? Then you would know at least one person in London. I am Mrs. Holloway."

He hesitated, gazing at my hand on his arm. I lifted it quickly, wondering if I'd just insulted him again.

"Li," he said after a moment. "That is my name."

"Excellent. Well, Mr. Li, now that we are friends, perhaps I can accept the gift you are so generously bestowing. As long as it is not too extravagant, mind."

The box was small and did not look very costly, but one never knew what was inside boxes until one opened them.

"It is, as you say, a trifle."

"If you promise," I said doubtfully.

A smile pulled at the corners of Mr. Li's mouth. "It is tea."

"Oh," I said, pleased. A good cup of tea was a fine thing. "Thank you, Mr. Li. You are kind."

"It is you who are kind, Mrs. Holloway."

I decided to end our effusion of politeness by taking the box. The wood was intricately carved but the box was light.

"There now," I said, not certain how to gracefully take my leave. "If ever you have need of a friend, Mr. Li, I am the cook in the house yonder." I pointed to it. "I am extremely busy most of the time, but if you do need help, do not hesitate . . ."

I trailed off, realizing I spoke to empty air. Mr. Li had

slipped into the shadows as I'd pompously waved at the great house. I glimpsed him walking swiftly along Mount Street toward Berkeley Square, but I soon lost sight of him in the lowering mist. The beggars had taken their food and gone, and I stood alone.

Chuckling at myself, I tucked the box into my basket and returned home.

I left the basket in the larder, but the tea I took upstairs to my bedchamber and locked into the bottom drawer of my bureau. It was *my* tea, and I would not risk Mr. Davis happening upon it, and my gift disappearing down his throat.

I n the morning, Sunday, as I was about to pour out the batter-like dough for the breakfast crumpets, Lady Cynthia rushed into the kitchen.

She did this often, as she found the company of her aunt and uncle stifling and many of their guests a bore. The accepted life of a spinster was not for her. She demonstrated this today by appearing in trousers—riding breeches to be exact—with boots to her knees and a waistcoat, long-tailed coat, and neatly tied cravat.

As she kept to her feet, I remained standing, as did Tess, Charlie, who tended the fire, and Emma, who'd come in to help convey breakfast to the dining room.

"I thought you'd like to know right away, Mrs. H.," Lady Cynthia said. "There was a death last night. Sir Jacob Harkness."

"Oh, dear." I'd never liked Sir Jacob—what little I'd seen of him—but I felt a dart of sympathy. Sudden death was always sad, difficult for the family. "Poor man. Was he ill?"

"No, indeed. Fit as a proverbial fiddle." Lady Cynthia's voice was as robust as ever. "That's why I'm telling you. He was murdered. Stabbed through the heart in his own bed-chamber. The police are even now swarming the house next door, questioning everyone in sight."

2

I stared at her in shock. The others froze in consternation, Tess behind me, Charlie poised with a shovelful of coal, Emma at the dumbwaiter.

"Good heavens," I exclaimed. "What happened? Were they robbed?"

"Don't know," Cynthia admitted. "I have my knowledge from Sir Jacob's valet, Sheppard, who came charging around to tell Uncle, most upset. Lady Harkness is in hysterics, and Aunt Izzie has gone to calm her down. Not the person I'd want with me if *I* were upset, but there was no stopping her."

Before I could ask more, the back door banged open, and one of the housemaids from next door burst in. "Oh, Mrs. Holloway, Mrs. Finnegan says, will you come?"

Mrs. Finnegan was the Harkness family cook, and she was disorganized on the best of days. She would be in a right mess now.

I glanced at the pots burbling on the stove, boiling the

eggs for the family's and servants' breakfasts. The crumpet dough rested on the table, ready to be poured into rings on the stove. "Tess . . ."

"Go on," she said, waving me off. "I can manage. I know you like to be in the thick of things."

"Not at all," I said coolly. "I'm certain their kitchen is at sixes and sevens, and I ought to help."

"Right you are, Mrs. H." Tess winked at me and moved to take over the crumpets.

"Not too long on the hob," I told her. "Or they'll burn on the outside and be raw on the inside." I called the last words as I hurried down the passage to the housekeeper's parlor, where I kept my coat.

"I know." Tess's voice rose behind me. "I do pay attention when ya teach me things."

I snatched my coat from its peg and put it on over my apron. I saw no sign of Mr. Davis in the hall or in his pantry—I guessed he was upstairs watching the footmen ready the dining room for breakfast.

Lady Cynthia waited for me at the back door and accompanied me out through the scullery to the street.

A small crowd had gathered before the house next door. They glanced with envy at Lady Cynthia and me as I walked around the railings and down the stairs to the kitchen. Cynthia continued to the front door, where she was quickly admitted.

I'd been correct about the kitchen being in chaos. Mrs. Finnegan sweated desperately over a stove that was nowhere near as well ordered as mine. She shouted commands at a kitchen maid who wept and paid no attention.

The table, strewn with flour and blotched with butter and grease, held a pile of kippers on its wooden surface. I suppressed my distaste. I would have put the lack of cleanliness down to the violent crime in the household, but I'd been in Mrs. Finnegan's kitchen before.

"Mrs. Finnegan," I said loudly over the fizzling stove and the maid's histrionics.

Mrs. Finnegan swung around. She was a large woman with greasy black hair stuffed into a soiled cap and burn marks on her cheeks. She was not an unfriendly woman, but now she glared at me.

"There you are, Mrs. Holloway. You took your time fetching her, Jane. Her ladyship wants breakfast for all the coppers rushing over the house, accusing the servants of stabbing the master to death."

"I've only just heard." I stripped off my coat, found a place to hang it out of danger of spattering fat, and took up a towel that looked somewhat clean. "Cease your crying, child," I said kindly to the kitchen maid. "Fetch a plate for these kippers, and scrub off the table. The best cure for an upset is hard work."

The kitchen maid obviously did not agree, but she hurried to obey.

While the maid cleaned up the mess, I looked over the boiling eggs, the bacon frying in an inch of grease, potatoes bubbling in another pot, and a basket of yellow onions starting to brown.

"If you're feeding policemen, make a nice hash," I suggested to Mrs. Finnegan. "They won't expect to sit down to a polished meal."

Mrs. Finnegan gave me a surly nod. "Best get to chopping those onions, then. I have pork from yesterday's roast, and plenty of scone scraps from the garden party."

The leftover scones proved to be in another basket, hard

and stale. But stale breads could be added to other dishes to give them body.

I moved the onions to the table, which the maid had finished wiping, picked out a few of the best ones, and fell to slicing.

"Tell me what happened," I said.

"I don't know, do I?" Mrs. Finnegan jerked a greenish copper pot from the rack above her head and slammed it to the stove, dumping in the bacon she fished from the frying pan. "I was starting the breakfast when Sheppard bursts in, shrieking the master was dead. Next thing I know, housekeeper is hailing a constable, and in they come, demanding us to tell them whether we'd killed the master. I never *see* the master, I say to them. I keep to my kitchen and my little cubby for sleeping. But you know what coppers are like. Everyone is a villain, in their minds."

I had encountered such policemen before, so I could not argue. "Jane—what do you know about it?"

Jane, the maid who'd retrieved me from next door, shook her head. "Nothing much, ma'am. I was on the upstairs landing, dusting as usual, when Mr. Sheppard comes rushing down, yelling his head off. When I peeked up the stairs, I see the mistress coming out of the master's chamber, Mrs. Redfern holding her up. I went down to the kitchen to find out what was the matter, and Mr. Sheppard is here, babbling that the master is dead. Cook had to give him brandy to calm him down."

Mrs. Redfern was the Harkness housekeeper. The household did not employ a butler—Mr. Sheppard filled the butler's duties.

"And now the police are questioning all of us," Mrs. Finnegan said sourly. "The master went out last night, so

Sheppard said, to that Kew Gardens place, which the master gives so many of his plants to. They're asking when he came home, who did he meet, did anyone return with him? As though we take all the master's particulars."

"Where is Mr. Sheppard now?" I asked.

"Policemen have him cornered upstairs," Jane said. "They think he did it. But he couldn't have, could he? Mr. Sheppard faints when he sees a mouse."

But a man afraid of mice might not necessarily be afraid to fight or kill, especially when threatened. I agreed, however, it was highly unlikely that timid Mr. Sheppard had decided to murder his master and then run downstairs to announce the fact.

"The house wasn't broken into?"

"No one has said that." Mrs. Redfern chose to enter the room as I asked the question. "Good morning, Mrs. Holloway."

"Mrs. Redfern." I gave her a nod. She and I were not on the most cordial terms, likely because we both knew our own minds and were not willing to retreat from our opinions.

Jane, who should have returned to her duties upstairs, curtsied stiffly to Mrs. Redfern and hurried contritely out.

"Very kind of you to assist us, Mrs. Holloway," Mrs. Redfern said. "But scarcely necessary." She gave me a sharp look from eyes that were intelligent and watchful.

"On the contrary," I answered. "Mrs. Finnegan is rushed off her feet. I have suggested a hash for the constables, since you need to feed them. Browned onions give it a nice flavor."

As I spoke, I chopped the onions into a careful dice, my knife making a *tick, tick, tick* sound on the table.

Mrs. Redfern folded her arms, the keys on her belt clanging. "Since I know you will be eager to learn all, I will tell you this, Mrs. Holloway. Sheppard entered the master's chamber early, as Sir Jacob likes to rise and breakfast at six. Sheppard found the master in bed, in his dressing gown and nightshirt, with a stab wound in the middle of his chest amidst a quantity of blood. Turned the white sheets quite red, he said."

I have a good imagination, and the description made me a bit queasy. The kitchen maid sank into a chair—a maid should never sit when senior staff is present, but I do not think the poor girl knew up from down at the moment.

Mrs. Redfern ignored her and continued. "Sheppard lost his nerve and bolted out of the room, shouting hysterically, which woke the mistress, who, I am sorry to say, ran in and saw her husband lying there, dead. I put Lady Harkness back to bed, she being upset, as you can imagine, and went out and found the constable on his beat. He fetched a sergeant, and *he* fetched a fellow from Scotland Yard, who is now investigating. One of the ground-floor windows was open, so it is likely the culprit entered and exited that way."

Mrs. Finnegan dumped cut-up pork into the pot with the bacon and scattered flour over all. I would have added some mushroom ketchup and cloves to give the hash flavor, but Mrs. Finnegan only poured in a handful of salt and mashed everything together.

"The police should stop accusing us of doing him in," Mrs. Finnegan said darkly. "Next thing you know, they'll cart the lot of us to jail."

The kitchen maid gasped again. I wiped my hands and patted her shoulder. "If it's an open window, they'll believe it an intruder." I longed to examine the window in question, but I would have to invent an excuse to go upstairs. "Stands to reason. Why would any of you murder Sir Jacob?"

Mrs. Redfern's lips pinched. "Nothing has been stolen, that we can find. Sir Jacob's watch and purse with his money were in their places, all as should be. But the master never made a secret that he left us each a small legacy in his will, so of course, one of us killed him for our fifty guineas. Or the mistress did it for all the money he'd leave *her*." Her icy stare told me what she thought of these theories.

Sir Jacob had certainly been generous—fifty guineas was a good sum, enough to ease a person's way in the world. I'd observed while working in great houses that often those who had little or started with little were more lavish and open-handed than those who were used to wealth. I'd known the cook to a duke who'd nearly beggared the woman while he lived in ease upstairs, while a man who started in the gutter paid his servants handsomely.

"That's as may be," I said. "But none of the servants would have reason to climb in through the window. And if you are like me, you prefer to be fast asleep in the middle of the night, not skulking about the house with a knife."

The kitchen maid nodded fervently, and Mrs. Finnegan looked relieved.

I returned to my task of preparing the onions and carried them to the stove to brown. I advised Mrs. Finnegan to add the meat and gravy she'd just made to the onion pan, and though she stared at me in puzzlement, she obeyed. We added the potatoes after that, stirring all together and letting the hash sizzle.

"Why did your master go to Kew Gardens in the middle of the night?" I asked Mrs. Redfern. "Surely, the place would be shut."

"It wasn't the middle of the night," Mrs. Redfern answered. "It was seven of the clock. Sir Jacob bade Sheppard fetch a hansom, and off they went. Sheppard accompanies him everywhere. He says that once they were there, he lost the master in the fog for a few minutes. He swears he saw him talking to someone off in the mist, but he can't be certain. They came home just before nine, and Sir Jacob went to bed."

"I see." I briefly wondered whether the person Sir Jacob met at Kew had followed him home and committed the deed.

Then again, the journey to Kew might have nothing to do with his death—if Sir Jacob shared his exotic plants with the gardens, he might have met with a person there to discuss such things when they wouldn't be disturbed by punters coming to gaze on the flora. Still, it seemed an odd time for a garden appointment.

Once we had the hash finished, I helped Mrs. Finnegan set it in a covered pan to be carried up to the constables. Mrs. Redfern departed, muttering that someone had to keep an eye on the goings-on upstairs.

The dumbwaiter in this house had ceased to work a year ago; Sir Jacob had never bothered to have it fixed, so the maids and footmen lugged the food up themselves.

I volunteered to help carry the trays and plates to the dining room so I might have a look about. I had never been anywhere but the servants' areas in this house, and when I emerged from the back stairs, I was astonished to find the main floor decorated with every part and parcel of China that could be fitted into a packing crate and transported on a steamer.

There were many-drawered cabinets of red polished wood, chairs with curved backs, screens painted with lavish scenes, and settees upholstered in red and strewn with tasseled cushions. Scrolls of silk, some with Chinese writing on them, others with pictures, hung on the walls.

Objets d'art crammed every available space the cabinets and tables provided. I saw carved wooden boxes, as well as vases, bowls, and pots of many shapes, sizes, and colors. One lovely bowl of translucent porcelain, a blue dragon dancing around its sides, caught my eye. It was exquisite, like a breath of air.

There appeared to be no organization for these things—they were simply jammed onto every shelf and surface or piled on the floor.

A long table of exotic wood filled the center of the dining room, surrounded by ordinary factory-made chairs. The sideboards held plenty of lacquerware and thin vases, but these were for decoration, not use.

We set our trays onto silver racks that had small candle burners beneath to keep the food warm. The plates the policemen would eat from were plain, not the exquisite Chinese porcelain the family used.

I had worked in houses whose owners had collected chinoiserie—furniture made in the Chinese style and lavishly decorated with black lacquer and gold paint. The Harknesses, however, had brought home the true China—or at least what the Chinese would sell to foreigners—with furniture in rich woods, lovely porcelain, and scrolls with beautiful calligraphy.

The wooden boxes reminded me of the one Mr. Li had given me, carved with curlicues and flowers. I admitted I valued the box more than the tea inside—I drank tea every day, but it was not often I was given such a fine container.

The Harknesses had piled up a treasure trove, and *pile* was the correct verb. The things sat haphazardly, as though we walked through a warehouse, not a home.

I peeked inside the room Jane whispered to me held the unlocked and open window. It was a drawing room, also filled with Chinese souvenirs and glass cases. One of those cases lay on its side, smashed, presumably where the thief had knocked it over while climbing into or out of the house.

A man with a thick golden mustache stood next to the window, scowling at a footman who babbled back at him. I recognized Detective Inspector McGregor, and beat a hasty retreat, hoping to heaven he hadn't noticed me.

I was to be thwarted in my hope, because Inspector Mc-Gregor strode out of the room a moment later. "I ought to have guessed I'd find you here, Mrs. Holloway."

His glare could make the most stouthearted criminal wilt, but I swallowed my trepidation and met his gaze. "Of course, as I live next door. I came to lend my aid to the cook and housekeeper, as you see." I indicated the dining room, where the food now reposed. "Policemen in the house means extra work for them."

His hazel eyes held a skeptical glint. "As long as you are here, tell me what you know of this. Did you see anyone lurking near the house last night or this morning?"

"I saw a good many people," I answered truthfully. "Mount Street is a busy thoroughfare. As for lurking, I could not say. What time did the crime occur? I could be more specific if you told me that."

"We don't know." McGregor might be a bad-tempered man—mostly from frustration—but he was an honest one. "The valet saw him alive at nine last night, and found him dead this morning at six."

"That is quite a long span. About nine last night I was outside in the street, handing the leavings of supper to beggars. They took what I gave them and went. None lingered or crept near this house. After that, I was attending my duties until I went off to bed, and I did not bother to look out any windows. So I am afraid I cannot help you."

I kept my encounter with Mr. Li to myself. I knew the moment a foreigner was mentioned, the police would fix on him as the most likely suspect, and I was quite certain Mr. Li had nothing to do with this. He was a polite, well-spoken gentleman, and after he'd given me the box of tea, he'd walked off in the opposite direction from the Harknesses' house, heading for Berkeley Square.

I knew full well that Mr. Li could have returned to Mount Street later in the night, but I had lived with the dregs of London in my youth, and Mr. Li was not at all the criminal type. He was also past his first youth. How easy would it have been for him to climb into a window, rush upstairs, and stab a rather hearty man like Sir Jacob?

The ground-floor windows lay behind railings, which would have to be scaled. A nimble burglar would have no trouble, but a middle-aged man in flapping robes might be hard pressed. Then he'd have to ramble through the house to find the correct bedchamber, avoiding servants and other members of the household. Not an easy thing, by any means.

The inspector looked disappointed with my lack of knowledge. "If you remember anything . . ."

"I will immediately send you word," I assured him. "Now, if you will excuse me, they will expect me home."

McGregor nodded a dismissal, but I felt his suspicious gaze on my back as I went.

I returned to the kitchen, told Mrs. Finnegan to send for me if she needed further assistance, and left through the scullery to the street.

As I made my way to the stairs leading to our kitchen door, two constables came out of Sir Jacob's house and hurried past me. I watched them, mystified, as a chill wind blew along the street, holding a note of coming winter.

I continued down the stairs and in through the scullery. As I entered my warm kitchen and slid off my coat, a man rose from the table where he'd been lounging. My heart skipped a beat and I stood with my coat dangling half on, half off, probably looking a right fool.

"There you are, Mrs. Holloway," Daniel McAdam said. "Did you find the murderer yet?"

Mr. Davis strode into the kitchen at that moment and snatched up the teapot to slosh tea into a cup for himself, sending Daniel a severe look as he did so. Mr. Davis did not approve of my friendship with Daniel. He believed Daniel too far beneath me.

If only Mr. Davis knew the truth. To be fair, I wasn't certain *I* knew the truth of Daniel. He was many people all jumbled up.

"Don't be silly," I said. A steaming cup of tea rested on the table at Daniel's place, which meant he'd charmed it out of Tess.

"I saw the police run down the street, likely to search for a culprit," I continued as I hung my coat on a peg and moved to the stove. "I suppose Inspector McGregor has already fixed on a poor unfortunate."

"A Chinaman," Mr. Davis said. He blew across his tea to cool it. "Sheppard told me a few minutes ago. Seems a gardener—at least a man helping Sir Jacob with his garden—claimed to have seen a Chinaman wandering the street nearby last night. Sir Jacob made plenty of enemies in China, so Sheppard says. Sheppard was in China with him, so he'd know."

"Oh," Tess said with interest. "I wonder if he means *your* Chinaman, Mrs. H.? Just fancy—you might have been talking so cozy to a murderer."

3

Silence followed Tess's remark, and I turned to find all staring at me—Mr. Davis in shock, Tess with curiosity, Daniel in growing concern.

"Mrs. H. was chatting with him like they were old friends," Tess babbled on. "Of course, she knocked the poor bloke over day before last, and I suppose she was apologizing again. Fancy, not long after that, he went next door and done in their master."

"He certainly did not." I resolutely returned to cooking, giving the potatoes Tess had put on to parboil a vigorous stir. "He walked in entirely the opposite direction—I watched him until he was gone. I will *not* tell the police to chase him down because he is Chinese."

"Would you if he were simply another Londoner?" Daniel asked, his voice holding a note of gentleness.

I sent him an irritated look. "No, I would not. Not only did he walk the other way, he did not seem the murderous sort.

He was very polite and well spoken. But I am not being senti-mental because he is foreign, if that is what you are implying. Even if he'd been a Cockney carter, I'd not set the police on him. He did not linger, I tell you, but went on his way. Once the coroner discovers the time of death, or as near as he can, I imagine the suspects will be narrowed down."

"How can they do that?" Tess asked as she chopped mush-rooms into a neat pile. "Find out when a man died, I mean? When he's been laid out for hours?"

I shrugged, relieved the topic had been changed. "Stiff-ness, I believe. I suppose coroners develop an instinct—the same as I can tell how long a fish has been sitting on a market stall. The fishmonger might claim it's fresh as a daisy, but I know he's had it for a day or so."

"Blood." Daniel took a noisy slurp of tea and lifted a flat crumpet from the platter in the middle of the table. "It pools in the bottom half of the body. How much blood has sunk can help the coroner guess how long the person has laid in one place."

Mr. Davis shuddered. "Gruesome. Well, Mrs. Holloway, I hope your conviction does not let a murderer get away. I shall certainly secure all the windows on this house quite rigor-ously tonight."

"Wise," Daniel said. "One never knows, Mr. Davis."

He spoke calmly, chewing his buttered crumpet like a man happy to have a few moments to do nothing. The tops of his work boots were muddy, but I could see from lack of mud on the floor that he'd scraped them well on the doorstep.

"You won't tell the constables, will ya?" Tess appealed to both Mr. Davis and Daniel. "Don't want to get Mrs. Holloway in trouble."

Mr. Davis gave her a freezing look. "I do not speak to the

police, young woman. Mrs. Holloway must follow her con-
science."

With that he strode out, turning in the direction of the
butler's pantry. I noticed another crumpet missing and a few
spots of butter on the floor where he'd stood.

Tess shook her head. "Some days I want to creep up behind
him and yank off his false hair. Wouldn't we all laugh?" She
cackled in delight.

"You will do no such thing." My admonishment was a bit
more forceful than need be, because I was at times tempted to
do the same. "Mr. Davis is butler here and deserves your respect. Now, say no more about it."

Tess had grown used to my chiding, and her smile did not
waver. She'd learned to discern when I shared her opinions.

Daniel came to his feet. *His* crumpet had vanished, crumbs
and all. "Perhaps we can have a word, Mrs. Holloway?" He
spoke easily, but a firmness underlay his tone.

"If you wish." I poked at the potatoes then used cloths
around the pot's handles to remove it from the burner and set
it on the back of the stove to keep warm. I'd sauté the potatoes
later—they fried up better if they were parboiled first.

Taking my time, I laid down the cloths, glanced approv-
ingly at Tess's heap of mushrooms, and told her to move on to
the onions. Only then did I lead Daniel to the housekeeper's
parlor.

I'd taken over this room as my own since the last housekeeper had departed. I'd made the place cozier with a few
more cushions and two framed prints I'd bought in a shop—
one of flowers, the other of a pleasant country landscape. I
kept my cookbooks and accounting books here along with
my kitchen journal and the few magazines I allowed myself
as an indulgence.

I waved Daniel to a chair. "As I see you have cleaned your boots thoroughly, I will allow you on the carpet."

"Good of you, Kat." He dropped his working-class accent for the more neutral one he used when we were alone. He waited until I'd seated myself on the Belter chair before he took the plainer, harder one. "Now, tell me about this Chinese gentleman."

"Do you know I believe no one would be interested in the poor man if there hadn't been a murder," I said. "He'd just be one more foreign face on the street."

"But there *has* been a murder, and Sir Jacob has a strong connection with China. You'd never seen this man before . . . When did Tess say? The day before yesterday?"

I told Daniel the story, ending with how Mr. Li had waited for me last night to give me a small token of thanks.

Even as I spoke, I realized Daniel was correct. It was strange that Mr. Li had been in the street near the Harknesses' house for me to run into, and also odd that he'd returned to give me so elaborate a present. I also had to wonder how he'd known I would emerge to give scraps to the beggars, though that could have been chance. He might have been waiting to go downstairs and knock on the door when I'd walked out. Or he could have asked the beggars, and they'd told him I would come appear.

"What was the token?" Daniel asked, his tone holding caution.

"I suppose you cannot help your suspicious nature. It is nothing grand. A box of tea. Kind, but hardly gold from the court of Peking."

"Did you look inside the box?"

"A quick peek. It is definitely tea. Brown leaves. Smelled fine—higher quality than what servants usually have, but that does not signify. Mr. Li might work in a tea shop or a tea ware-house. Not that I mean he stole it," I added quickly. "He might simply know how to purchase a better grade."

"I am not happy you are so close to a house in which there was a murder," Daniel said.

I laughed lightly. "You forget, my dear Daniel, there was a murder in *this* house earlier this year."

"And I was not happy about that either. You do seem to attract trouble."

"The murders we've stumbled across were hardly *my* doing," I pointed out. "This one does not seem as great a puzzle as the others—I wager a burglar climbed through the open window and made his way upstairs in search of riches. Sir Jacob woke and surprised him, and the burglar stabbed him in panic. He then fled through the same window, in too much of a hurry to steal anything, and vanished into the night."

"I would agree with you," Daniel said, "except for one thing. *You* live next door, and ordinary things do not happen around you."

I gave him a stern look. "Now you are being fanciful. Not everything is about antiquities thieves or plots to assassinate the queen. Sometimes it is an ordinary burglary and a frightened person in the wrong place at the wrong time. Unnerving, but not a grand conspiracy."

"Ah well." Daniel sat back. "It must be my suspicious nature that makes me believe otherwise."

"My apologies. I did not mean to insult you."

"No insult, Kat. I am teasing you."

"How is James?" I asked abruptly.

Daniel's eyes warmed. "Hale and hearty. Driving me to distraction."

"Good. As it should be."

James was Daniel's sixteen-year-old natural son who'd been grievously hurt in our last adventure. Daniel had taken a house in Kensington—very cozy; I quite liked it—and had moved James in to care for him.

James, with the vigor of youth, had recovered quickly. But instead of sending his son back to the boardinghouse where Daniel had been keeping him, Daniel had James remain with him.

I quite approved of the arrangement, but after a long, hot summer together, I knew both were chafing. Father and son were very much alike.

"And Mr. Thanos?" I inquired.

"Also hale and hearty, and has returned to his own rooms near Regent's Park. Has a bee in his bonnet about Maxwell's equations at the moment, but I am certain the fit will pass."

I did not know who Mr. Maxwell was or what his equations were about, but Mr. Thanos was a brilliant mathematician, and I was certain he'd solve them soon.

"You may tell Mr. Thanos," Lady Cynthia's voice came to us from the doorway, "that he could remember his friends and send them word occasionally. And that there are other things in the world besides mathematics."

Daniel came to his feet and made a servant's bow as Lady Cynthia strolled in and shut the door. He balled his large hands around his cap, which made him look like a laborer who'd been caught where he shouldn't be.

"I am not certain Mr. Thanos realizes this," he told her.

"Do sit down," Cynthia commanded, waving at us both—I too had come to my feet. She plopped into the remaining chair. "You do not have to play the lackey for me, Mr. Mc-Adam. I know too much about you. I've come to tell you more about the murder next door, if you are interested."

I was very much. Despite my dismissal of it as a simple crime, I admitted to curiosity. I felt a twinge of guilt at my morbidity, but I assuaged it by telling myself I could possibly help find the killer and make him pay for what he'd done. Sir Jacob, from what little I knew of him, had been pompous and boasted a bit too much about his adventures in China, but he no more deserved to die than if he'd been saintly and silent.

Cynthia crossed her booted feet. "It's all very well for Inspector McGregor to send his men to scour Limehouse for any Chinaman who happened to be west of Regent Street last night. But McGregor wasn't at the garden party the other day, was he? Harkness got into it with his botanist, the very one who is trying to throw suspicion on a Chinese man he claims he saw skulking about. Skulking, my foot. The chap's inventing things."

"Mr. Davis said the man who'd seen the Chinese gentleman was a gardener," I said in puzzlement.

Cynthia shook her head. "Mr. Chancellor is a botanist Sir Jacob quizzes every fortnight about his Oriental plants. Chancellor is installed at Kew Gardens and apparently has all the goods on anything that grows. Sir Jacob consults him, I suppose, about grafts and fertilizer and other things for growing his exotic blooms. At the garden party, the two were at it, hammer and tongs. Shouting and screeching. We all saw and heard. Lady Harkness hovered about, not knowing what to do, so I went over and told them to quiet down."

I could well imagine Lady Cynthia striding to Sir Jacob and explaining to him that he was ruining his wife's party. She had little patience with those who bullied others, and she had confidence in her own authority.

"Chancellor looked dashed embarrassed," Cynthia went on. "Though Sir Jacob snarled at *me*, the uncouth ass. Nonetheless, the two men went their separate ways. But I saw the look Chancellor threw Sir Jacob as he departed. Disgust, near to rage. Not surprised Chancellor wants to throw the blame onto someone else. I suspected *him* right off, especially as Sir Jacob had toddled out to Kew Gardens beforehand."

"But Sir Jacob was stabbed while he was in bed," I said. "I can understand Mr. Chancellor coming to visit and the two getting into a tussle, but if he'd lured Sir Jacob to Kew, why not finish him off there? Or lure him somewhere else entirely? Why follow Sir Jacob home then creep into his bedchamber and stab him?"

"Haven't the faintest idea," Cynthia said without worry.

"And why would Mr. Chancellor be in Mount Street to see a Chinese man lurking?" I went on.

"Don't know," Cynthia answered. "Only filling in what I observed. You are the expert on the whys and wherefores, Mrs. H."

"Many possibilities," Daniel agreed.

"I still believe a burglar is the most likely culprit," I said. "Unlocked window, the family in bed. Is Lady Harkness certain nothing was missing? I saw quite a lot of things in their house—I imagine it would be a job to inventory them all."

"No one believes anything was taken," Cynthia said. "At least not that they've discovered. What I do know is that the family was *not* in bed. Lady Harkness had a late-night visitor, Mrs. Knowles, a sort of companion and confidante. I know nothing about her—no one does, really. The woman seems respectable enough, if a bit smarmy for my taste. Hangs on Lady Harkness's every word, tells her how wonderful she is, that sort of thing. A sycophant."

"Is *she* likely to have stabbed Sir Jacob?" I asked doubtfully.

"One never knows, does one? *You* taught me that. Mrs. Knowles is a tiny woman, but a lucky blow, from above . . ." Cynthia demonstrated with her strong hand. "Could have done it. She's like a terrier, is Mrs. Knowles, protecting Lady Harkness. Sir Jacob might have been threatening Lady Harkness, or simply said the wrong thing to Mrs. Knowles."

"Have they determined the time of death yet?" Daniel broke in. "As Mrs. Holloway pointed out to me, that may be the deciding factor."

"Not really. Sheppard helped Sir Jacob dress for bed at nine, just after they returned from Kew. Sir Jacob believed in early to bed, early to rise—all that nonsense. It was Sir Jacob's habit to be put into his nightshirt and dressing gown, and then putter about his room, reading and whatnot, before he retired, usually at half past nine, or at ten if he felt particularly vigorous. Up again at six. Hell of a life."

"No one saw him after nine o'clock?" I asked. "He did not ring for the valet to fetch him tea or help him into bed?"

"Sheppard says not. The man's terrified though, so he might have lied about that. But Lady Harkness swears she heard no one go upstairs to her husband after Sheppard left him."

"I can always ask in the kitchen," I said. Mrs. Redfern no doubt would know every step every servant in the house took at every minute, though I was not certain she'd tell me. Mrs. Finnegan might, but her memory was less reliable.

Cynthia touched her fingers in turn as she summed up. "So, we have Lady Harkness, her friend Mrs. Knowles, Sir Jacob, and Sheppard all upstairs at nine. Mr. Chancellor I suppose somewhere nearby. Sheppard goes down soon after nine—or so he says. Mrs. Knowles did not depart until after twelve."

"Is there a *Mr.* Knowles?" I asked. "I mean, she did not feel the need to rush home to a husband?"

"None that I've met," Cynthia said. "He might be the meek sort, always in the background, or perhaps spends all his time at his clubs, paying no attention to what his wife gets up to. As I said, none of us know much about her. Lady Harkness has another sycophant friend, Mrs. Tatlock, but as far as I can find out, she was not there that night."

"Any other acquaintances?" I asked. "Or, I should say, anyone else who quarreled with Sir Jacob?"

"He has a friend called Mr. Pasfield," Cynthia answered. "Who, by the way, arrived moments before I departed just now, the man in such a state. Horrible thing to happen, says he, all aflutter. Poor Lady Harkness. He must go to her."

"Ah," Daniel said, brows rising. "The loyal friend come to look after the widow?"

"He's not a dashing Lothario, if that is what you are thinking," Cynthia said, mirth in her eyes. "He's middle aged, rotund, and conceited. What one calls an Old China Hand—a man who's lived and worked in China and purports to be an expert on it and the Chinese. Businessmen consult them about how best to approach the natives, and so forth. Sir Jacob was one too—they knew each other in Shanghai, or Hong Kong, or wherever they were. Sir Jacob was made a knight for grubbing about in the Orient and amassing a fortune, but Mr. Pasfield seems to be stolidly working class. They were great friends, the two of them."

I thought of Mr. Li and wondered how "expert" he'd consider these gentlemen.

And I hoped, I truly hoped, that Inspector McGregor would leave Mr. Li alone. They would not, I feared, if they found him. I would simply have to prove someone else had done the deed. It was the least I could do for the kindly gentleman with loneliness in his eyes.

I drew a breath to ask Lady Cynthia more about this Mr. Pasfield when Mr. Davis threw open the door.

He stopped short when he saw Lady Cynthia and made a quick and correct bow, but he looked a bit wild about the eyes.

"Begging your pardon, my lady," he said breathlessly. "But I need Mrs. Holloway to come with me at once. Our new housekeeper has arrived."

4

I rose in surprise. Mrs. Bywater had been conducting interviews for the past week, and according to Lady Cynthia, disliking all candidates she met, largely because their agency requested salaries higher than Mrs. Bywater wished to pay.

She'd said not one word about actually hiring a woman, and Cynthia looked as astonished as I.

Daniel faded out of sight as we went out. He had the knack of disappearing into the mist—sometimes quite literally—but I wasn't finished speaking with him yet. I'd hoped Lady Cynthia would keep him pinned down, but Cynthia was fast beside me as we hurried down the passage after Mr. Davis.

The woman in question waited with Mrs. Bywater in the servants' hall. The rest of the staff stood woodenly at attention—that is, except for Tess. While she stood as straight as the other servants, she sent the woman with Mrs. Bywater a belligerent glare.

The lady looked respectable enough, with iron gray hair in a soft bun and a black gown unembellished except for glittering buttons that marched up her bodice to her chin. Her high collar framed a face that was neither plump nor thin, pretty nor plain. An unassuming woman, with the bearing of the quintessential housekeeper.

She glanced at me without much interest in her faded brown eyes, but she schooled her expression as she took in Lady Cynthia in her riding breeches and coat.

"This is Mrs. Daley," Mrs. Bywater said in a bright voice. "Mrs. Daley, my niece, Lady Cynthia Shires, and Mrs. Holloway, our cook."

Mrs. Daley made a formal bow to Lady Cynthia and gave me a nod. "Your ladyship. Mrs. Holloway."

Although Daley was an Irish name, her accent spoke of the north—of the Yorkshire Dales or Lancashire; I was not familiar enough with the north of England to place it.

"I shall leave you to it," Mrs. Bywater said. She disliked to come below stairs, and was always uncomfortable in the servants' hall. "Mrs. Holloway and Mr. Davis will show you your duties. Cynthia, dear, will you join me upstairs?"

Cynthia clearly wished to stay below and assess this new member of the household, but she acquiesced. "Pleasant to meet you, Mrs. Daley. You'll find this an easy place, if dull as ditchwater."

She strode for the back stairs and ascended, boots thumping. Mrs. Bywater gave Mrs. Daley an apologetic look and turned to follow Cynthia.

"Well now," Mrs. Daley said as soon as the door at the top of the stairs shut. "Her ladyship's an odd duck, ain't she?"

"Lady Cynthia is a kind young woman," Mr. Davis, who had criticized Cynthia any number of times, said huffily. "Please do not call her odd."

Mrs. Daley raised her brows. "I never said she weren't kind,

Mr. Davis. I don't know the girl, do I? What the upper classes get up to has nowt to do with me. Now, Mrs. Holloway, be so good as to fetch me a cup of tea."

I would have to put a stop to *that* right away. "Tea will be brought by one of the maids, or Tess. She is my assistant." I indicated Tess, whose face had grown ever more sour. "The housekeeper's parlor is this way."

"Mr. Davis may show me," Mrs. Daley said. "You stay with your kitchen, Cook. That is your domain—the housekeeper's parlor is mine and Butler's."

I could already see I'd need to have words with Mrs. Daley. "Mrs. Holloway," I said to her retreating back.

She turned. "I beg your pardon?"

"I am called Mrs. Holloway," I said in a firm voice. "Not Cook. Not below stairs, anyway."

Her brows went up again. "Well, pardon me, I'm sure. Mr. Davis—I assume you wish to be called Mr. Davis and not Your Lordship?—will you escort me to my parlor?"

She held out her hand as though expecting Mr. Davis to lend her his arm. Mr. Davis only stared at her with an irritated expression and led the way down the hall.

I waited until they were shut into the housekeeper's parlor before I strode from the servants' hall to the kitchen. Tess dashed in behind me, skirts swirling.

"Well, ain't she a one? I ain't doing a thing *she* says. Hoity-toity, nose in the air—"

"You will follow Mrs. Daley's orders as you would mine, Tess," I interrupted her. "Housekeeper, butler, and cook are in charge below stairs, and you must remember that."

Tess gave me a sullen scowl. "I work for *you*, Mrs. Holloway. No other. If Mr. Davis and Mrs. Hoity-Toity say I must do a thing, then I'll do it, but I'll ask you first."

"Very well," I said, if only to keep the peace. "But you be on your best behavior around Mrs. Daley, no matter what. I do not want her telling Mrs. Bywater to dismiss you because of impertinence. I need your help."

I kept my tone stern, but the truth was, I'd miss Tess desperately if Mrs. Bywater turned her out. I was growing fond of the impetuous young woman.

Daniel materialized out of the shadows near the scullery. I was used to him appearing and disappearing by now, so I only jumped a little.

"You'll smooth her over, Mrs. H.," he said with his carefree confidence. "As for me, I think I'll pay a visit to the botanical gardens at Kew. Brush up on my gardening skills."

His tone was indifferent, but I understood the glint in his eye. He was off to look up Sir Jacob's botanist friend, Mr. Chancellor, as well as to try to discover whom Sir Jacob had gone to meet last night.

"Do *not* disappear for days on end, please, Mr. McAdam," I said. "I will want to hear every detail of your Kew adventure."

Daniel pressed his hand to his heart. "You wound me, Kat. Have I been disappearing of late?"

He had not, it was true. Since our adventure this spring, which had left James and Mr. Thanos hurt and me frightened out of my wits, Daniel had remained in London. He'd looked in on me nearly every day, if only briefly, but he'd made certain I knew all was well.

He had not yet found the frightening Mr. Pilcher—a more thorough villain I'd never seen—who'd revealed he worked for a man Daniel believed had long ago murdered his father. Daniel wasn't certain the man who'd raised him had been his true father, but he'd always viewed him so and had taken his death hard.

I'd learned much of Daniel's history, and how it had shaped him, the day he'd revealed this information to me, but still he remained elusive. For instance, I had no idea why the police sometimes asked for his help in catching criminals, when Daniel had made clear to me he'd been turned away by the police when he'd tried to join up. It was most puzzling.

"No, you have not been disappearing—much," I conceded. "You are looking after James, as you should be. Do tell me all about the gardens, Mr. McAdam, when you return."

Daniel gave me a warm look then waved to Tess, slapped his cap on his head, and departed the kitchen through the scullery, calling a cheery farewell to the scullery maid in passing. Elsie watched him go in admiration. When she caught my eye, she flushed and returned to her sink, but I did not admonish her. Daniel was a whirlwind.

I sometimes accompanied Mrs. Bywater to church on Sundays, but this morning had begun so muddled that I remained home to catch up with my cooking. I'd prepare the meals for the rest of the day, and make sure enough was set on for tomorrow, which was my half day out.

I saw almost nothing of Mrs. Daley, though Tess returned from delivering the woman's cup of tea with a scowl on her face and rage in her eyes. Tess opened her mouth, no doubt to begin a tirade about Mrs. Daley, but I shook my head. She settled for clamping her lips together and banging things about to make her feelings known.

I worked to prepare the Sunday roast, including a puffy Yorkshire pudding, which Mr. Bywater liked, stirred up from flour, milk, and eggs, flavored with drippings from the beef.

I showed Tess how to cut green beans to pretty lengths and boil them, and then to sauté them in butter with a smattering of onions and the juice of a lemon. The green beans had to be served right away, so the trick was finishing them just as the roast and pudding were ready to be sent up. Indeed, timing a meal correctly was an art in itself.

Cooking occupied my hands, freeing my mind to think. I worried greatly about Mr. Li. If the police managed to trace him, would they arrest him for murder?

In any event, I hoped Mr. Li was safe and would not be found. I also hoped he truly had nothing to do with Sir Jacob's murder. In spite of my protests to the contrary, I knew the fact that I liked the quiet Mr. Li did not mean he wasn't a villain.

But I was not so bad a judge of character as all that. I made myself remember that I'd watched Mr. Li walk down Mount Street toward Berkeley Square and disappear. He'd not returned, at least not when I'd been standing in the street.

Besides, why, if Mr. Li had planned to creep into the house next door and kill Sir Jacob, would he have drawn attention to himself by seeking me out and giving me a gift?

It was far more likely that this botanist had glimpsed Mr. Li outside and immediately decided a Chinaman had committed the crime—if Mr. Chancellor hadn't committed it himself. So much easier to shift the blame to an outsider.

Mrs. Daley did not emerge from the housekeeper's parlor even after I sent up the roast and made the staff a meal they'd consume once those upstairs were taking their Sunday rest. I had no intention of serving Mrs. Daley in her parlor as though she were the lady of the house, and I didn't have the heart to make Tess do it. Instead, I would tell Mrs. Daley she was welcome to fix herself a plate of something in the servants' hall if she wished.

I bustled to the housekeeper's parlor to inform her thus. I opened the door to find Mrs. Daley seated at the small table, an empty teacup and half-drunk glass of cordial at her elbow. She had my cookery books spread out before her.

I prized my books, which I collected, treasured, and carefully transported to each house in which I worked. Books were dear, so I purchased them secondhand and kept them as well as I could.

Not only did Mrs. Daley have my books wide open, in danger of breaking the spines, but my personal notebook as well, my notes and scraps of paper spilling out. She had a pen in her hand and an open inkwell next to the cordial. As I entered, she circled something in one of my cookbooks, spattering ink across its page.

"Mrs. Daley," I said in a near shriek. "Whatever are you doing?"

Mrs. Daley did not glance up. "Going through the mistress's receipts. She's got a funny way, don't she? By what's in *this* book, she's having you make them all wrong." She tapped my notebook with the pen, and a blotch of ink fell across my careful handwriting. "I used to be a cook, you know."

No, I hadn't known. "The books are *mine*, Mrs. Daley," I said stiffly. "Not the mistress's. I record in my notebook what I like or dislike about a recipe and modify it accordingly."

"Do you, now?" Mrs. Daley gave me an assessing look, but at least she laid down the pen. "I can see you like to get above yourself, Mrs. Holloway. Why shouldn't you be called Cook? I proudly bore the title. And though I learned my letters, I kept it to myself and didn't parade *books* about the downstairs.

You should let the mistress tell you what to cook and how. That way, if she's disappointed, it's her own fault."

Only if you are a bad cook, I wanted to retort, but dignity made me keep my silence. Mrs. Daley must have been the sort who resentfully slammed meals to the table and blamed everyone but herself if the family did not find it palatable.

The cook who'd trained me had been talented, better than any chef I'd known. She'd taught me that food wasn't simply sustenance, but should be a feast for all senses—sight, scent, and the feel of a morsel in the mouth, and those *before* one even thought about taste. Even the sound of a crisp pastry breaking should be satisfying.

I prided myself on my meals, each dish wrought with care. If this meant I was above myself, then so be it.

"Please do not mark my books, Mrs. Daley," I said coolly.

"Then you'd best not leave them in here." Mrs. Daley capped the inkwell and tossed the pen aside, splattering yet more ink. "This is the *housekeeper's* parlor, I believe. Cook has her kitchen."

I wasn't foolish enough to store my precious books where they could be ruined by flame, smoke, and grease. I'd always kept them in the housekeeper's parlor, where all was clean and neat, and copied out receipts to use in my kitchen. No housekeeper I'd worked with had objected.

The previous housekeeper here, Mrs. Bowen, whatever her faults, had at least not thought she was queen of the downstairs. This room had been a sanctuary for all the senior staff.

I pictured Mrs. Daley throwing my books on the fire if I did not take them away, so I stalked forward, collected them and the notebook from the table, and strode out of the room, my expression stiff. Mr. Davis stood in the doorway of his butler's pantry across the hall, his brows drawn in a grim line.

"Bloody woman," he whispered.

I gave him a nod and walked on, my arms full of books, and made for the back stairs.

When I reached the second floor and turned for the third, I realized I should have asked Mr. Davis, or Tess, or a footman, for help in carrying my load. Anger and pride had made me march off, and now I was flagging.

My room was at the top of the house, the fifth story above the ground floor. I climbed the last narrow flight of stairs, puffing hard and glad no one was near to observe me.

I had to set down the books to open the door, and then I carried them in, a few at a time, to stack on my bureau. I had no bookshelf up here—perhaps I'd ask Daniel to look out for a discarded one or find one secondhand for me, which I'd give him the money to purchase.

I'd lived in this bedchamber seven or so months now, and while my home under the eaves was plain and functional, I'd managed to soften it a bit. I'd spread a quilt my mother had made across the bed and found a few cushions to make the straight-backed chair, a relic from earlier years, inviting.

The top drawer of my bureau held treasures from my days out with my daughter—a feather she'd presented to me from a day in the park, paper flowers we'd bought at a stationers, tokens made from old ha'pennies, threaded on a cord to wear for luck. My underthings were tucked into the drawers below, and my Sunday best dress and my second-best one hung on pegs behind the door.

All in all, it was not a bad little room, more comfortable than some I'd lived in, and it was mine alone—I did not have to share it.

This house, which had once been two houses and knocked together at some point, was large enough that I, the housekeeper, and Mr. Davis had bedchambers of our own. The maids and footmen had only two to a bed, not three or four as in some other households. Male and female staff were kept quite separate, as should be, ladies to the left of the house, gentlemen to the right.

My room had a window that looked out over the back of the house and its little garden far below. I could see into all the walled gardens behind the Mount Street homes—tiny patches, it was true, but nonetheless soothing green space in the middle of the brick-and-stone city.

I rarely had the chance to see these gardens in daylight, but I glanced down now to enjoy the serenity of trees and neat shrubs, with birds flitting about.

In light of this morning's tragedy, I was especially drawn to the garden of the house next door. I'd always thought it an odd but pleasant design, with its curving walkways and clumps of trees and other foliage.

Whereas the rear of our house held one very straight walk cut at right angles by two others, and was bedded out with geraniums in summer, mums in autumn and winter, and bulb flowers in spring, the Harknesses' gardens were a riot of ever-changing colors. Even the greenery came in shades of yellow, deep green, and gray. I could not discern individual plants from above, but the overall effect was pleasing.

As I gazed down now, I saw a man in the Harknesses' garden.

This gentleman was on his hands and knees, crawling among a clump of plants. I lost sight of him a few times when he became obscured by the branches of a spreading tree, but he'd pop out again, still on all fours. His movements spoke of desperation as he scrabbled about.

At last he backed out of the bushes, climbed to his feet,

and dusted off his trousers. He had something clenched in his fist, though from this distance, I could not tell what.

The man had a shaggy brown beard, a balding head, and broad forearms protruding from rolled-up sleeves. I had a few times in the past seen this gentleman going into and out of Sir Jacob's house through the front door. A visitor, not a worker.

He glanced furtively about before he caught up the coat and hat he'd left on top of a bush, and made for the gate in the back of the garden that led to the mews behind it. I craned to keep him in sight, but he ducked out of the gate and through a narrow passage to the stables, and was gone.

I hurried out of my chamber and made for the stairs, ideas whirling through my head about how to get a closer look at the garden next door.

5

In the kitchen, I took up my basket, lined it with a fresh cloth, and told Tess I would be stepping to the Harknesses' kitchen.

Tess gave me a dark look as she shelled peas into a bowl. "I'll carry on with the dinner, shall I? If that bat asks me to do anything else, I'll say *you* gave me orders first."

"Of course," I said, hiding a sigh. "Only be civil when you say it."

Tess gave me a grave nod, as though she'd decided I was wise.

I walked next door and rapped on the scullery door before I stuck my head inside. "Mrs. Finnegan? Might I borrow some herbs? I want to serve a fresh vegetable soup, and I am all out of chervil."

Mrs. Finnegan did not question my glib excuse for rummaging in Lady Harkness's garden and opened a door at the top of the back stairs to usher me through.

I had many times suggested to Mrs. Bywater—obliquely and politely—that my kitchen could benefit from our having an herb garden. That way, I would have fresh herbs as I needed them, readily and cheaply. There would be an expense, at first, for tilling the earth and planting the rows, but the garden would pay for itself in time. Mrs. Bywater, however, typical of her, was loath to part with a lump sum or to ask Lord Rankin for it, which was why I or Tess went out for fresh herbs nearly every day.

Lady Harkness had a lovely knot garden, from which Mrs. Finnegan had her pick of herbs in season. Mrs. Finnegan did not bother with them much, she told me, as Sir Jacob seemed to subsist on boiled mutton alone. Though he'd spent much time in foreign parts, he'd retained his taste for plain English food, and in fact, preferred it.

I took scissors from my basket and crouched down beside the herbs. The knot garden was lovely, with its intertwined borders of parsley and chervil, purslane and dill. The scents as I snipped refreshed my senses.

I scanned the rest of the garden while I chose the best strands of chervil and bright green parsley.

The full garden had been cleverly laid out to convey a sense of space larger than it was. Brick paths led around clumps of bushes, many in flower, with trees strategically placed to heighten the feeling of being in a park.

The man I'd seen scrabbling about had been in the very center of the garden, twenty feet or so from where I knelt now. The dark-boled tree that had obscured my view of him shaded a bench on a bulging curve of walk. The shrubs lining the paths sported different flowers and leaves, no two bushes alike.

I'd been born and bred in the middle of the metropolis, and my knowledge of trees and shrubbery was somewhat limited. I thought the spreading tree was an elm, but I had no idea. I'd seen plenty of foliage in London's parks, where I walked with my daughter, but unless a plant was edible, I could not identify it by name.

I tried to contrive a reason to amble to the bench—perhaps my exertions harvesting herbs tired me and I needed a rest. However, this was a private garden of Mayfair, and a servant from the next house had no business strolling the walkways.

"Good afternoon, Mrs. H.," a voice sang out. "Lovely day. I hope those are for my supper."

Lady Cynthia, still in her breeches and frock coat, came down the walk to me. I straightened, letting her see the clipped herbs in my basket. "They are for a *potage printanier*."

Lady Cynthia did not blink. "Of course."

"I saw a man here from my window," I told her quietly. "He was searching, just there." I surreptitiously pointed at the spot. "He took something. I could not see what."

"Did he? Let's have a look, shall we?"

Cynthia moved down the walk in her manlike stride, fine leather gloves outlining her feminine hands. I followed a few paces behind, clutching my basket.

"Here?" Cynthia gazed into the shrubs.

"In the middle of that clump behind the bench. Crawled out on hands and knees, his trousers covered with mud."

"And he wasn't the gardener?"

"No, he was a toff," I said. "I beg your pardon. I mean, he was a gentleman. In gentlemen's clothes."

Cynthia did not look offended. "I comprehend you. A person who had no business scrabbling about in the dirt in someone else's garden."

"I have to wonder what he was looking for. And what he found."

"Curious." Cynthia walked around the shrubs, eyes sharp.

"What kind of plants are these?" I asked her.

She shrugged, shoving her hands into her pockets. "Haven't the foggiest. I grew up in the country—all rhododendrons, roses, and yew hedges in our gardens. These are none of those. They've got roses over there." Cynthia pointed to a line of green branches running across a wall, the last of the summer roses fading on their stalks. "But few of these plants are English. Or at least what we consider English. Roses and rhodies came from somewhere else in the first place."

"Are they shrubs Sir Jacob brought back from China?"

"From what I gather, yes. China, India, wherever he traveled. It's why Lady Harkness throws so many garden parties, to show off the plants. Orchids and things. Though these aren't orchids."

Cynthia stepped off the path and sidled around the bench. I remained where I was—the inhabitants of the house would never tolerate me treading anywhere but the path.

"Something growing in the middle here," Cynthia said. "Little spindly thing. Probably can't get enough sun with all these crowding it." She bent closer, her coat catching in a thick-leafed bush. "Looks like someone took a cutting—recently too." She pointed, but I could see little. "Unless the gardener trimmed this bush today, I'd say your man took a bit of it."

"Why?" I asked. "Is it a valuable plant?"

"Doesn't look like much to me. But as I say, I'm no botanist. However—" Cynthia took a knife from her pocket and sliced off a thin shoot or two. She straightened, showed me a few stems with green leaves, then tucked the knife and shoots into her pocket. "I can always ask another."

She flushed as she spoke, and I suspected she meant Mr. Thanos. The young man knew quite a lot about many things—

not only was he an expert mathematician, but he had interest in astronomy, chemistry, history, and much else. I would not be amazed if he had a catalog of the world's botany in his head as well.

"I would be interested in Mr. Thanos's opinion," I said. "It might help his recovery."

Mr. Thanos had been the unfortunate victim of a poisoner a few months before, and while he'd been purged of the poison, arsenic could have persisting effects.

"Yes, just the thing," Cynthia said briskly, though her cheeks grew still more red. "It'll jolly him along."

I scanned the garden to give her a moment to recover herself. "I wonder who the gentleman was?"

"I can find that out. The dragon Mrs. Redfern wouldn't let just anyone back here. Had to bludgeon my way past her, so to speak, to come into the garden myself. I saw you and was agog to know what you were up to."

"Snooping," I said. "Where I have no business to be."

"Nonsense. A man has died and another is raiding his garden—they likely are connected. The police are fools."

I did not agree. Inspector McGregor, though he could be unpleasant, had keen perception. I knew that if *he* fixed upon Mr. Li, the man would have little chance of escaping arrest. The gentleman I'd seen in this garden, however, had been decidedly English.

We looked about a little longer, but found nothing else. Cynthia led the way back to the house, and I followed a few paces behind.

A footman opened the door to admit us. Cynthia thanked him in her friendly way then strode down the hall crammed with settees and tables of Oriental vases to the front drawing room. I paused near the back stairs, next to a glass case full of tiny plants. I knew I ought to exit the house through the kitchen instead of lingering, but curiosity kept me in place.

"Auntie will be by later," Cynthia said into the drawing room, presumably to Lady Harkness. "Do you want for anything? Auntie and I would be happy to help."

I knew Cynthia did not like Lady Harkness, yet there was a note of sympathy in her voice, and her offer of assistance was genuine. Mr. Davis had been correct when he'd called Lady Cynthia a kind young woman.

Lady Harkness emerged from the chamber. She was dressed all in black, from her high collar to the undecorated hem of her skirt above severely black shoes. Her dark hair was pulled up and tightly curled in the latest complicated fashion, her skin made more pale by the severity of her clothing.

A second lady exited behind her, breathless and dithering where Lady Harkness was straight backed and regal. This lady was shorter, thinner, and less neat than Lady Harkness, wisps of her brown hair straggling from pins, though the hair had been dressed in an attempt at the same style. She too wore black, but her gown was plain cotton instead of bombazine, with no braid or trim.

A maid followed them both—a lady's maid by her dress. She bore a veiled hat in her hands, which she fixed to Lady Harkness's hair with long pins, then draped the black veil to cover Lady Harkness's face.

"Thank you, Griffin," Lady Harkness said. "And thank you, Lady Cynthia. You and Mrs. Bywater have been such a comfort to me. As have you, Amelia."

Amelia—I took her to be Mrs. Knowles, who'd been visiting in the night—flushed, pleased. She reached up to give the veil a helpful twitch, which endangered the hat coming off.

Griffin reached out a startled hand, but Lady Harkness adjusted the hat without fuss. "Do be careful, Amelia dear. Good afternoon, Lady Cynthia. Putter about as long as you like. I do not know when I shall return today. Nothing seems to matter anymore."

The last words were delivered in a listless tone that sounded more sincere than anything else the lady had said.

Neither Lady Harkness nor Mrs. Knowles noticed me in the shadows as they made for the front door, but Lady Cynthia signaled me to join her as she followed the two out.

It was not done for a cook to walk in and out of a house's main door, but on the other hand, I could not disobey a direct order from my employer. I ducked outside and stood with Cynthia on the walk as Lady Harkness, like a black ghost in her long veils, ascended into her carriage. She stepped in gracefully, barely touching the footman's hand.

Mrs. Knowles scrambled up behind her, having to clutch at the footman quite hard, the lad wincing when she squashed his hand. Griffin climbed inside with more dignity.

Cynthia shivered as the carriage rattled off. "God save me from widow's weeds. They make my flesh creep. Why bury yourself aboveground, I ask you?"

"To protect yourself from prying eyes?" I suggested. "No one wants to show a weeping face to the world."

"Ha. She hasn't shed a tear. Not saying she didn't love the old duffer or isn't sorry he's dead, but I wept more over my favorite hound when he went to the other side."

"We all show grief in different ways," I said diplomatically.

Cynthia shot me a skeptical look. "You're a kind soul, Mrs. H. I can't help being so pessimistic—my own family is frightful. Well, I'm off to look up Mr. Thanos."

My eyes widened. "Do not be foolish. You cannot."

Cynthia stopped in true confusion. "I thought you wished me to consult him."

"You cannot go unchaperoned, I mean. A young lady does not visit a gentleman on her own."

Cynthia started to laugh, then she scowled as she realized I was serious. "Damned nuisance. Lord help me if I am in the same room with a gentleman without some busybody watching over me. We all know Mr. Thanos would leap upon me and ravish me without restraint."

I had to smile at the thought. A more gentlemanly and proper young man I'd never met.

"Don't worry, Mrs. H. I know better than to visit him in his rooms. We meet at the pub near the British Museum—you know the one, off Bedford Square. Bluestockings welcome, and we're in the public reading room. Plenty of chaperones about."

I relaxed a fraction. "True, but if you meet him too often, tongues will wag. You must have a guard for your reputation."

"Rot that. My family has destroyed what reputation I ever could have. But I take your meaning. Fortunately, everyone knows Mr. Thanos is more interested in numbers than anything else. I am quite safe." She kicked out with one foot, as though laughing it off.

I said nothing, but I then and there determined to speak to Daniel on this subject.

But what then? I thought as Cynthia and I parted ways to enter our house through our respective entrances. Mr. Thanos was a gentleman but without much money. Cynthia had no money of her own and no hope of it. They might like each other quite a lot, but if they married, they'd starve together. I would have to speak to Daniel about that as well.

* * *

The next day was Monday, my half day. As usual, Tess and I worked to prepare most of the meals in the morning, so I wouldn't be missed in the afternoon.

Tess by now had mastered many techniques, and I worried less each week about leaving the kitchen in her hands. She was a bright young woman, which for some reason she felt she had to hide behind silly remarks and flashes of temper.

"Warm the leftover potage for the midday meal, then use any leavings of it to put into the rice soup." I showed Tess the Carolina rice I had rinsed and let drain in a sieve. "Once the rice is cooked, add the potage, then beat up an egg into warm cream and strain it into the soup. You must stir and not let it get too hot, because the eggs will cook—it needs to blend in smoothly to thicken. Can you remember that?"

Tess watched, focus intense. "I've been whisking up the eggs first and adding them in little bits to hot cream—keeps them from cooking, like you say."

"Very good." I warmed. This was the first time Tess had taken what I'd taught her and applied her own ideas.

Mrs. Daley chose this moment to enter the kitchen.

She'd kept mostly to the housekeeper's parlor since her arrival, but this morning, she'd met us early in the servants' hall to give the staff their orders.

I privately thought she'd piled too many chores upon them at once, nearly twice what Mr. Davis and I expected in the same amount of time, but I held my tongue. Mr. Davis did as well—the two of us had agreed the night before to give Mrs. Daley a chance before we condemned her. The well-trained maids and footmen forbore from arguing, but I could sense their dismay.

Mrs. Daley, after she'd given her orders, seated herself at the table in the servants' hall, ate a hearty breakfast, and then took her time over tea and a newspaper.

Now she stood in the kitchen door, hands folded, the keys I'd relinquished to her hanging from her belt.

"You have a half day out as well as a full one?" she asked me.

"I do," I said as I untied my apron and hung it on its hook. "A condition of my employment."

"Why?" she demanded. "Do you have a secret husband?"

Mr. Davis, who'd come up behind her, snapped, "Mrs. Holloway is a respectable woman."

"One can be respectable and have hidden depths," Mrs. Daley said complacently. "I only wonder why she has so many days out."

I kept my expression neutral, but my heart sped at her words. Her guesses struck too close to home.

"I am certain Mrs. Bywater would arrange for you to have a day and a half if you ask her," I said. "Now, if you will excuse me."

I had to move past Mrs. Daley to reach the back stairs so I could ascend to my chamber to change my clothing. I did not want to wear my drab gray cook's uniform to visit my daughter.

Mrs. Daley stepped aside without fuss, but I felt her watch me as I went.

Mr. Davis announced to her, "The wine merchant is arriving today. I see that you slashed my budget for port, and that will not do."

"What will do, Mr. Davis, is running this house efficiently," Mrs. Daley returned. "Mrs. Bywater has instructed me so. Far too much is spent on wine and spirits, she says."

Mr. Bywater liked his port, so that would be a short argument between man and wife.

I left Mr. Davis and Mrs. Daley to haggle, and their voices carried up the enclosed back stairs as I made for my bedchamber. When I descended again, the doors to both housekeeper's parlor and butler's pantry were shut tight, Tess looking amused.

"You go on," she told me. "Don't you worry. Mr. Davis and me will keep the dragon at bay."

I did not linger to admonish her.

Once on the street, hurrying for an omnibus, my cares fell away. I no longer worried about Mrs. Daley's intrusiveness or Tess with the soup, or even the murder next door.

I was on my way to see my daughter, and my heart was light.

"What shall we do today, Mum?" eleven-year-old Grace asked me after we'd embraced and I'd inquired about her lessons and the Millburns' children—my dear friends Mr. and Mrs. Millburn looked after Grace for me.

"I thought a journey to Richmond," I said. "On the train. Would you like that? I have a mind to visit Kew Gardens."

6

The train cost a bit more than I wanted to pay, and I disliked riding trains underground, but my curiosity was too great, and soon we were chugging in and out of tunnels on the Metropolitan Railway. Grace enjoyed the ride, pressing her face to the window to catch sight of the stations glowing through the darkness.

After about an hour, we descended at the station at Kew Gardens, in the light of day once more.

The Royal Botanic Gardens at Kew were not the same as the parks and tucked-away gardens in London, green refuges from the city. Kew was set aside for botanists and men of scholarship who collected and studied plants from around the world.

The botany of the British Empire had been harvested and brought bit by bit to this corner of England, to be put into the huge glass greenhouses. It cost a fee to enter those greenhouses, though one could stroll the park when the gates were open.

I had worked in nearby Richmond for a time last winter and liked the town with its narrow lanes, leafy trees, and the Thames snaking past through green banks. The river here was far less stinking, and I'd had many a pleasant walk along it.

I had enjoyed the park at Kew Gardens when I had a day to myself, and I'd brought Grace here once or twice for relief from the unhealthy air of London.

From the lane outside the gardens, all one could see were walls with trees towering over them. The gardens had been part of the monarch's residences long ago, but given over to scientific studies in the middle of the last century, open to the rest of us in the middle of this one.

Gates pierced the wall at intervals, all shut at the moment. We glanced through one to see wide parkland, stands of trees, and a corner of the enormous structure called the Palm House, a massive greenhouse that contained, as the name implied, palm trees and other tropical plants. A few people wandered the park, but not many were about on a Monday afternoon.

"It's ever so beautiful," Grace said beside me. "I liked visiting when you lived here."

"I liked it too," I admitted. I had left the post because the family had moved to the Lake District. They had asked me to accompany them, but I refused to go so far from Grace.

I had learned, during my visits, that Kew had its own constabulary. The park was so large and some plants so valuable it had to be constantly guarded. That fact came back to me as a constable peered through a gate and noticed us.

"Good afternoon, missus," he said politely, but he gave me a sharp eye, as though checking me for bags in which to stash purloined plants. "A fine day."

"It is indeed," I answered. "A relief from the rain we've been having."

He continued to watch me, probably alert for covert pruning shears and trowels.

"A lovely view." I gestured at the Palm House and the greenery around it. "I was showing my daughter."

The constable's eyes narrowed, and I took Grace's hand, preparing to beat a hasty retreat. I had no idea what he could arrest us for—it was not against the law to walk down a street or look into a public park.

"Good day to you, sir," I said, and led Grace away.

I heard the rattle of a lock and then the creak of the gate as it opened. "Oi!" the constable called. "Might you be Mrs. Holloway?"

I turned back, startled. "I might be."

The constable stepped out into the lane, one hand on the open gate. "Then come in here with me."

I remained where I stood. "Whatever for? Are you arresting me for peering through a gate?"

The constable looked amused. "Not arresting you, missus. Don't you want to come inside?"

"Can we, Mum?" Grace asked in eagerness.

She was not a spoiled girl, and never asked for much. She understood, even at her young age, that there was not much to be had. I hated to disappoint her.

Without answering, I walked back to the constable, my hand firmly around Grace's.

"Of course," I said to the young man. "If you promise to let us out again."

He grinned. "That's not up to me. I'll let *him* sort it out."

I did not like the sound of that, but I'd already stepped

through the gate. The constable closed it behind us, locking it with a key.

I intensely disliked being locked in anywhere, but I admitted that this was a glorious prison. The park spread out before us, a sea of grass studded with trees. Some walks were neat and groomed, others overgrown. A few steps from the gate let me see the Palm House in all its glory rising from the green.

To my left I glimpsed another vast glass building, the Temperate House, which looked uncannily like an ordinary manor house, but with walls and ceilings of glass. I could see the tops of trees inside. Beyond the Temperate House, just visible, was the spire of the famous pagoda.

"This way." The constable set off with a vigorous stride toward the Palm House.

The Palm House was very much a greenhouse, with a towering rounded roof, its iron girders supporting thick panes of glass. Bedding plants in neat, ordered rows led to its front door.

A man in muddy boots, dusty breeches, and a tattered coat and hat opened the door of the Palm House. He carried a box of gardening tools and a spade.

"Well?" he asked me. "Will you come in?"

I kept hold of Grace's hand but hurried into the wonder of the Palm House, afraid someone would stop us at any moment.

The gardener, who naturally was Daniel, nodded to the constable. "Thank you, sir," he said. The constable touched his fingers to his helmet and closed the door behind us.

I stepped into an amazing world.

The wind outside had been brisk, but it died into the warmth of the tropics. The enormous ceiling let in plenty of light, which flooded the profusion of trees and leafy plants lining the floor. These plants lived in generous pots, and the humid air clung to giant palm fronds, brilliant flowers, and my skin.

I opened my coat, seeking relief, and Grace fanned her hand in front of her face.

Daniel laid down his gardening box and stripped off his thick gloves. "What do you think, young lady?" he asked Grace.

Grace stared about, enraptured. "It is beautiful, sir."

The Millburns and I were bringing up Grace to be polite, without the strictness of some families who did not allow their children even to speak. She held tightly to my hand but looked about without fear, taking in the grandeur without shrinking from it.

"It is indeed," Daniel said. "These particular palms come all the way from Madagascar. Do you know where that is?"

Grace looked surprised, as though wondering why *he* did not know. "It is a large island in the Indian Ocean, on the east coast of Africa."

"Exactly," Daniel said. "Well done."

Daniel knew full well that Grace had a good grasp of geography, because I told him everything about her. He was giving her the opportunity to show off.

"Grace," I said. "This is my friend Mr. McAdam. Mr. McAdam, my daughter, Grace."

"How do you do?" Daniel held out a hand to her.

Grace took it and bobbed a quick curtsy. "Pleased to meet you, sir."

This was the first time Daniel and Grace had come face-to-face, though I'd conveyed to each much about the other. I held my breath as I watched the meeting of my daughter and the man who had become a dear friend.

I could not imagine anyone not taking to Daniel, but Grace was no fool. If she disapproved of him . . . Well, I would have to tell Daniel he did not pass muster.

Grace, my little charmer, smiled up at him. "You are the

Mr. McAdam who has adventures with Mr. Thanos and Lady Cynthia and my mum."

"I am indeed," Daniel answered. "Your mum is instrumental in these adventures. We would come to grief without her."

"She pretends she does not do much, but I know it isn't so," Grace said.

"You are correct." Daniel nodded gravely.

"Goodness, the pair of you talk such nonsense." I gave them an admonishing look, but I was much relieved. I could see they had taken to each other. "I believe you have begun a new post, Mr. McAdam. As what? A gardener? Or a botanist?"

"Gardener's assistant," Daniel said. "The botanists will hardly let me near their priceless specimens to muck them up with my incompetence. I am in training."

"Are they priceless?" I asked.

"As any jewel." Daniel became serious. "Explorers bring back cuttings, seedlings, and seeds from every corner of the Empire. Here they cultivate them, study them, experiment with them, stick them into pots, and let them grow happily under this roof." He waved his arm to take in the towering palms that rose to the ceiling, I'd say sixty feet or so above us.

I was entranced. I'd seen plenty of potted palms decorating halls and drawing rooms of the houses in which I'd worked, and orchids and the like in their back gardens. Sir Jacob's garden held plants I'd never encountered before, but this was breathtaking.

It was so intensely green I began to wonder if I'd ever seen any other color. The contrast to the gray brick world of London, coated in coal dust, was stark.

"The Temperate House is even larger," Daniel said. "It contains trees and flowering plants from as many places as this one does, but from cooler climes. For instance, from the foothills of the Himalayas, and the tea-growing regions of China."

Grace absorbed all this, her mind quick. As she looked about, enchanted, I said in a low voice to Daniel, "You were confident I'd come. You told the constable to look out for me."

"I did." Daniel gave me a nod. "I had thought it would take you a few more days to make the journey, but I knew you could not resist. One of the constables is a friend of mine, and I asked him to look for a curious young woman milling near the gates, dark haired and pretty, probably wearing a black straw hat with feathers, and most likely with her daughter."

"I see." I tried to decide whether I was flattered by this description. "Can you tell me what you have discovered?"

"Not very much, but I only started the post this morning." Daniel rested his boot on a nearby rock. "Sir Jacob did indeed return from his travels with many plants, carefully sealed into Wardian cases."

I knew what those were—miniature greenhouses on stands that decorated drawing rooms as much as potted palms did. These cases, named for Nathaniel Ward, the gentleman botanist who'd invented them, provided the perfect atmosphere for the plants. The water inside, warmed by the sun, filmed on the glass and then fell like rain, to be evaporated onto the glass again. A maid had only to dust the outside and never worry about watering the plants inside.

"Did he bring back orchids?" I asked. Orchids were costly, and collectors obsessed with them could hoard them as greedily as a miser hoarded gold.

"He did," Daniel answered. "As well as a good many temperate plants from the mountains of China. Some are in his garden at home, but most are here. He was rather a hero, according to Mr. Chancellor."

"So you have already managed to speak to your quarry."

"Of course. It was he who hired me on."

I could not be amazed. Daniel was expert at jumping directly to the heart of the problem.

"Is he here?" I asked.

Daniel steered me to a narrow path and pointed down the walkway. Grace, who had let go of my hand, skipped to catch up to us.

At the far end of the greenhouse, small in the distance, was a man with a shaggy brown beard and a sturdy body, a notebook in his hands. He wore breeches rather than trousers, and boots that ended at midcalf.

"I saw him," I whispered. "Yesterday. Rooting about the Harknesses' garden. He took something."

Daniel's expression did not change except for a flick of brows. "Interesting. Do you know what it was?"

"Lady Cynthia and I had a peek, but I don't know one shrub from another. Lady Cynthia said she'd show a cutting from the plant to Mr. Thanos."

"Wise. If Thanos doesn't recognize it, he'll know exactly where to look it up."

"That is what I surmised."

"Hmm." Daniel gazed at Chancellor, who appeared to be doing nothing more than staring at a plant. Once in a while, he made a mark in his notebook.

"What if Mr. Chancellor knew the value of a plant in Sir Jacob's garden?" I asked in a quiet voice. "And Sir Jacob refused to give it to him?"

"He might steal it—or a cutting of it," Daniel answered.

"But would he have—?" He broke off, glancing at Grace, who was listening avidly. "Could he not simply wait until Sir Jacob went out of the house?"

Instead of murdering the man, he meant. But who knew what made one gentleman stick a knife into another? A court judge would only need to know for certain the man *had* stabbed Sir Jacob to death in order to convict him. *Why* he'd done so would be fodder for the newspapers.

If I were to help Mr. Li, I would have to prove for certain he did not wield the knife that killed Sir Jacob. The whys and wherefores, as Lady Cynthia called them, would make no difference.

"He must have been near the house that night," I said, indicating Mr. Chancellor, "if he saw Mr. Li lurking as he claims. You must get him to tell you if he was present."

"I am trying, my dear Kat. I have to work my way around to it."

"I understand, but you must tell me as soon as you know."

Daniel looked exasperated, and I did not blame him, but before he could answer, Mr. Chancellor glanced our way. "Mc-Adam!" he bellowed.

"My master calls." Daniel slid on his gloves. "Do not worry. I will pry plenty out of him before the day is over. Wander the Palm House as much as you like—I arranged it. Save me a slice of your excellent seedcake in return."

He pressed my hand, winked at Grace, and moved at a smooth trot toward Mr. Chancellor.

"I haven't made any seedcake, ridiculous man." My words died in the humid air.

Grace watched Daniel go then looked eagerly up at me. "What has happened, Mum? Is it another adventure?"

"Yes, but we cannot speak of it here." I waved my hand at the stunning plants under the vast glass arch. "Let's have a look around."

I led her down the deserted walks, determined to enjoy our afternoon and ponder no more about the murder.

We found many delights—flowers as big as our heads, orchids growing up the sides of trees, palms so large they bent with their own weight. I'd read somewhere that one of the trees here had been brought to Kew a hundred years ago.

Explorers had carried all these here, whether commissioned to or of their own volition. Some men searched the world for gold or jewels, but these men had seen the value in nature. I admired the gentlemen—and ladies too—who ran all over the globe, risking their necks to harvest unique plants for our pleasure and instruction.

I sometimes thought I might like to be an explorer myself, but I knew they must lead very uncomfortable existences. Sleeping in a small tent in a rainforest sounds romantic when one is reading about it in a snug, dry bed before a fire. The reality, I imagined, would be full of stinging insects, dangerous animals, and natives resentful of one's presence.

"I'm afraid I would not make a very good explorer," I said. "I like to sleep indoors, out of the rain and the night."

"Mr. Millburn says there are hotels now in foreign parts, run by English people," Grace informed me. "We could go to Egypt."

"Only when we are very rich," I answered with a laugh.

"Is Mr. McAdam very rich? You could marry him, and we could go."

I squeezed her hand playfully. "I see, minx. You wish me to marry so you can visit a luxurious hotel. I do not believe Daniel is rich, so you will have to put that idea out of your head. He grubs for a living as I do."

In truth, I had no idea whether Daniel had money or not. He assisted the police in addition to his various jobs, but he'd never said whether he assisted them for pay. Daniel at present let a small house on the far side of Kensington, but while the house was comfortable and perfect for himself and James, it was hardly a mansion.

Grace's question troubled me in spite of my teasing, because it reminded me how little of Daniel I truly knew.

I spoke no more about it as we observed the astonishing palms in the very wet air, until I decided we had better depart. I spied Daniel as we exited—he had left the Palm House and was striding along behind Mr. Chancellor toward the Temperate House.

We made for the main gates. The constable who'd admitted us saluted us with a cheeky grin as we went out.

Grace and I turned to start for the train station. In the next moment, I stumbled, gasping, and nearly lost my footing.

"Mrs. H.? Good Lord, I didn't mean to knock you down."

She hadn't touched me. Lady Cynthia stood before me, in her man's clothes, her friend Bobby—Lady Roberta Perry—next to her, her femininity buried behind a fine tweed suit.

Lady Cynthia's gaze snapped to Grace beside me—Bobby hadn't been looking at anything else. Cynthia took in Grace, me holding her hand, and the obvious resemblance between us.

No one in the Mount Street house knew about Grace—no one knew of her but Daniel and the Millburns.

And now Lady Cynthia stood before me, her fair brows climbing, as she discovered my darkest secret.

7

I stood for a long moment, uncertain what to do. A respectable, unmarried cook should not have a child, much less an illegitimate one. The fact I hadn't known Grace was illegitimate until my husband, who'd proved to be a bigamist, had drowned, did not make her less of a by-blow.

I'd once worked for a house where a maid had been turned out when it was discovered she had a husband and a young son, because the mistress had wanted only unmarried misses in her parlor. That maid's marriage had been legal, but it had made no difference. Maids at another place had been dismissed for even a suggestion of a lover in their pasts.

If I'd been older, my daughter grown with children of her own, my illegal marriage and ignorance about my husband might be overlooked. But I was young for a cook, barely thirty, and any indiscretion would be held against me. I was acquainted with a few cooks who were not happy that I could walk into any post I wished because of my skills. If they knew my secret, they'd be pleased to use it to their advantage.

Lady Cynthia was not a traditional woman, by any means, but she did not actually employ me. My contract was with her brother-in-law, Lord Rankin, in whose house we dwelled. Mrs. Bywater now decided who stayed and who went.

Should I say nothing and pretend that Grace, who was clinging tightly to my hand, did not exist? Introduce her and admit I was not the unstained woman I was supposed to be?

Bobby made all points moot by stooping to Grace. "And who might you be, young lady?" she asked brightly.

Grace was a cautious child, not about to blurt information to a stranger. She looked to me for guidance, and I cleared my throat.

"This is my daughter, Grace." I paused, then added, "Holloway."

Bobby had taken on the fond look of those who dote on children. "Well, aren't you a bonny one? Did you like the gardens?"

"Yes, ma'am," Grace said courteously. "We saw the Palm House. It was very beautiful." She stared up at Lady Cynthia, far less apprehensive about her presence than I was.

"This is Lady Cynthia," I explained, keeping up the politeness. "And her great friend Lady Roberta Perry."

For the second time today, Grace executed her curtsy. "Pleased to meet you." She gazed unabashedly at Cynthia, having heard all about her from me. "You are very pretty, your ladyship."

Bobby laughed. "Cyn, you look poleaxed. Why shouldn't Mrs. Holloway have a daughter? And a lovely one at that. Here you are." Bobby produced a silver coin. "Buy yourself a dolly, or if you're too old for dollies, a hair ribbon or some such. A present from me. Your mum's a good egg."

Grace didn't much want to take the half crown from her—she had dignity and did not like charity. But my daughter was also polite and sensitive to others' feelings.

She closed her hand graciously around the coin. "Thank you, your ladyship. You are kind."

Cynthia finally found her voice. "We came to have a look at the gardens. And Mr. Chancellor. And to see if we can discover what he stole."

In the back of my mind, I wondered if she'd had the chance to speak to Mr. Thanos about the cuttings, but I did not like to ask her for particulars on the street, in front of Bobby.

"Sleuthing hard," Bobby said. "Such fun. Good day to you, Mrs. Holloway. Cynthia sings praises about your meals, but she won't invite me to partake of one."

"That's entirely down to Auntie," Cynthia said, her briskness restored. "She doesn't approve of you, Bobby, and you'd have to wear a frock."

"Botheration to that," Bobby said. "Nice to meet you, young lady. You do your mother proud."

So saying, she strode in through the gates, leaving Cynthia behind.

Cynthia and I studied each other. I, the servant, was not supposed to look her full in the eyes, but these were extenuating circumstances.

Cynthia at last gave me a nod. "Never fear, Mrs. H. See you at home."

She breezed past me to the gate, calling for Bobby to, for God's sake, wait for her.

I silently led Grace away, and to the train, shaking so hard I could barely hand the conductor our tickets.

* * *

When I reached home, Tess was in a foul temper. She threw greens into a pot along with so many cloves of garlic I had to fish most back out.

"She came in here, sweet as you please, and told me I was using too much foodstuffs," Tess growled. "She'd tell Mrs. Bywater, she said, and Mrs. Bywater wouldn't like it one whit."

Tess banged a bunch of carrots to the table and viciously chopped off their tops. I stopped her before she threw the greens into the bin—carrot greens made a fine addition to a salad.

I did not need to ask who "she" was. "Ignore her, Tess. Mrs. Bywater agreed I was to have full command in the kitchen. We discussed it when she first came to live here."

Mrs. Bywater had at first wanted a full accounting of every scrap and every drop used below stairs every day, from Mr. Davis and me both, but we soon persuaded her otherwise. She agreed on an accounting once a week, and quickly learned that on some expenses, Mr. Davis and I were adamant.

Tess's knife rammed through the carrots. "Well, I don't want her standing over me watching me measure flour and scolding me for dropping a grain. Telling me it's not the way *she* used to cook. If she were so good at cookery, why ain't she still doing it?"

Why not indeed?

"I will speak to Mrs. Daley," I said. "But your annoyance at her is no reason to abuse the vegetables. I want an even slice on the diagonal."

Tess heaved an aggrieved sigh, but at least she calmed her knife. She began cutting more neatly if viciously.

The rest of the kitchen staff were subdued. Elsie scrubbed

dishes in the scullery, but her cheeks and neck were flushed, and she didn't sing. Charlie, who usually played quiet games in the corner, hunkered there with his arms around his knees. Sara, the upstairs maid, stalked in, fetched a basket from the servants' hall, and stalked out again without a word. Mr. Davis never appeared from behind the closed door of his pantry.

I resumed my apron and fell to helping Tess prepare the evening meal. I tried to let the mundane tasks of rubbing the simmering beef with pepper and salt and creating a potato and cheese dish calm my agitation. I was less worried about Mrs. Daley's minute inspection of the kitchen than I was about the fact that Lady Cynthia now knew about Grace.

She had hinted before she'd rushed into Kew Gardens that my secret was safe with her. I believed her, though I was not so certain about Bobby. Though that lady had appeared to see nothing wrong with a cook having a child surreptitiously tucked away, would she spread the tale? Not deliberately perhaps, but she might mention it to an acquaintance who might find the story too delicious not to repeat.

I would have to lie, of course. I'd believed with all my heart I'd been married lawfully, so I would claim widowhood and be done. I'd say I left Grace with friends because I could not look after her while I worked in a kitchen. Every word true.

Cynthia would not betray me, I was certain. But she would expect to speak to me about it.

Tess and I finished preparing the meal in silence. I was not happy that Mrs. Daley, as welcome as help in the house would be, had disturbed our tranquility. We worked hard, Tess and I, with Elsie and Charlie assisting, but we also chatted and argued, laughed and were silly. I did not mind Mr. Davis sitting at the table in his shirtsleeves, reading interesting bits from the newspapers while I chopped and sautéed, diced and basted.

Tonight we were sullen and out of sorts, talking little except for me to give instruction or for Tess to ask a brief question.

This could not continue. You cannot let a difficult person gain the upper hand, or you will be checking your behavior every second, even when that person is not in the room. Once that happens, you will be in thrall, your own mind trapped. It was best to nip such things in the bud.

Once Tess and I had sent up the dinner and carried food into the servants' hall for their much-needed meal, Mrs. Daley wandered in and sat down.

Tess made a face but said nothing. She kept her gaze on her plate and shoveled in her food, as though afraid Mrs. Daley might at any moment yank it away.

Mrs. Daley, clad in serviceable black, sat up straight in a chair and folded her hands on the table.

"I've left your meal in the kitchen," I said. "It's on a covered plate on the back of the stove. Have it here or in your parlor, as you like."

"Nothing for me," Mrs. Daley said. "A biscuit perhaps, before bedtime. I take little in the evening."

Tess coughed, but Mrs. Daley didn't notice. "Did you enjoy your half day, Mrs. Holloway?" Mrs. Daley asked me.

"I did. Very much. I went to Kew Gardens. Did you know they have a palm tree that was brought to England in the 1700s?"

Tess looked up. Any other day, she might make a comment or a joke, but today she only sent me a glance and returned to eating.

Mrs. Daley looked uninterested in *Palmae*. "I spoke to Mrs. Bywater at length today, about my duties and about the staff here. I told her that a day and a half out for a cook was excessive. I had no more than one afternoon a week at my last place. You wouldn't be so run off your feet and shorthanded if you took only your Monday afternoon and not the other day. You were able to have a nice holiday today in only a few hours, weren't you? There is no reason you could not do so every week."

Tess jerked her head up. For a moment, all was silence.

"Mrs. Daley," I said crisply, "my days out are my business. They were agreed upon when I first took employment here, with Lord and Lady Rankin. My acceptance of the post was contingent upon it."

"Lord and Lady Rankin ain't here anymore, are they?" Mrs. Daley said. "Mrs. Bywater is mistress of the house, and she's got her hands full dealing with that hellion, Lady Cynthia. Mrs. Bywater don't need an absent cook as well."

I laid down my fork. "Perhaps it was different in your other places, but in *this* house, the kitchen is up to me, and my days out are a condition of my employment. I am an excellent enough cook that any number of ladies would leap at the chance to employ me. That is not a boast—I work very hard, have learned much, and take great care in preparing meals. Lord Rankin wanted my skills enough to grant me my wishes, and Mr. Bywater agrees that my abilities are worth my expense. Since Mrs. Bywater needs to please her husband's stomach, I *will* continue my days out, and we will speak no more about it."

Tess listened in awe, and when I finished, she shot me a look of triumph.

Mrs. Daley pushed back her chair and got to her feet. "Well, we shall see what the mistress decides, won't we?"

"Indeed," I said. "I shall speak to her myself."

Mrs. Daley looked down her nose at me. "See that you do."

She walked out, not hurrying. We watched through the doorway as she entered the larder, scraped and banged through a cupboard, then walked out with a few water biscuits on a plate.

When the door to the parlor thumped closed, Tess turned to me. "*She takes little in the evening*, my foot. It's because she were in and out of the kitchen all day, sampling this and that, slicing off a big piece of cold meat pie, and that after she ate a hearty meal at midday. She's a glutton, she is, even more than me."

"Hush," I said, but I had already noticed the lady liked her meat and drink.

When Mr. Davis descended with the rest of the footmen after dinner, chiding one of the lads for some discrepancy, he paused in the kitchen, where Tess and I had returned to prepare bread and other things for tomorrow.

"The mistress has sent for you," Mr. Davis said, both a warning and apology in his tone.

"What for?" Tess asked. "I bet that harpy has been filling her ears with tales."

"Never you mind," I said to Tess, but not unkindly. "Finish here, and I will be back down to say good night. Thank you, Mr. Davis."

Mr. Davis hesitated. "I can go up with you, if you'd like."

I was touched by his offer, because Mr. Davis severely hated any conferences with the Bywaters. He considered them hoi polloi and lacking taste, and Mrs. Bywater's parsimony upset him. I declined, declaring that I had no fear of our employers.

I removed my apron, dusted off my sleeves, and climbed

the stairs to the main floor. The others watched me go, a bit like fellow Christians in Roman days as one of their own was sent to the lions.

I did not often venture beyond the green baize door in this house, preferring to keep to the downstairs. I used the scullery door to go into and out of the house, and the back stairs for journeying to and from my chamber. I was satisfied with my domain, in large part because it was under my rule, and I would not allow Mrs. Daley to change that.

Mr. Davis had told me Mrs. Bywater awaited me in her private sitting room on the second floor. I climbed to it, remembering my first day when I'd emerged onto that floor with much indignation to beard Lord Rankin in his den. Many unexpected things had happened since that encounter.

To my dismay, I found Mrs. Daley ensconced with Mrs. Bywater in the warm room, Mrs. Daley standing stiffly upright while Mrs. Bywater reposed on the sofa, teacup in hand.

"Thank you for coming, Mrs. Holloway," Mrs. Bywater said as I entered and curtsied politely. "I will come straight to the point. Mrs. Daley tells me you are unhappy with my decision to limit your days out."

I was not pleased that Mrs. Daley remained for this interview, and not pleased at all that she'd rushed up here to split to Mrs. Bywater when I'd told her I would speak to the mistress myself.

"I always have a day and a half in any place," I explained, forcing my voice to remain calm. "I am quite capable of maintaining the kitchen, as I have shown since I began here."

Mrs. Bywater's mouth pinched, and she set her cup and saucer on a dainty table. "To the contrary, you and Mr. Davis complained all summer that you are overworked, which is why I hired Mrs. Daley." She shot the housekeeper a conspiratorial look, which alarmed me. "Mrs. Daley has come up with the perfect remedy—if you take fewer days out, you will not fall behind in your work. We might be able to do away with your assistant as well, now that we have a housekeeper, which would be a savings."

Send Tess away? I switched my gaze to Mrs. Daley, knowing full well Mrs. Daley had suggested sacking Tess because she did not like her—nothing to do with economies. Mrs. Daley must have recognized she could not bully Tess, who would never grovel to one she did not respect.

"Nonsense," I said heatedly. "I need Tess. Me spending an extra day in the kitchen will not make up for all Tess does. Things have run much more smoothly since her arrival, and it would be foolish of me to agree to do without her."

Mrs. Bywater frowned. Had she expected I'd meekly capitulate? That I'd agree to cut my days out and toss Tess on the rubbish heap?

"Tess works for *me*," I went on. "I will keep her in the kitchen and out from underfoot of Mrs. Daley if necessary."

"That is all very well," Mrs. Bywater said. "But I agree with Mrs. Daley that your days out are excessive. Maids have half days. Cooks, housekeepers, and butlers have one."

Mr. Davis did have a full day out a week, though he rarely took it. His obsession over the wine and silver made him not want to let it out of his sight for long, so he said. He showed no interest in or ever spoke about meeting friends at a pub or walking out with a young lady. In some ways, Mr. Davis was as enigmatic and mysterious as Daniel.

"Perhaps," I countered. "But my agency has down in their books that I have a day and a half. They search for places that will expressly agree to this."

Mrs. Daley wanted to respond, I could see, but a house-keeper could not speak as though she were an equal to the mistress. She folded her lips, her eyes on Mrs. Bywater.

"I am surprised you find places, then," Mrs. Bywater said. "Ladies of my acquaintance would not stand for such things."

Ladies of *her* acquaintance, Mr. Davis would sniff, were middle-class nobodies with no idea how to treat servants.

"On the contrary," I said. "I am one of the best cooks in England. I never have to wait long for a post. Lord Rankin did not object to my requests when he employed me."

"Lord Rankin has retired to Surrey," Mrs. Bywater reminded me, echoing what Mrs. Daley had said downstairs. "He pays your salary but left *me* in charge of decisions about the staff. My decision is that you will retain your Thursdays out, but not Monday afternoons, and we will keep Tess. That way you will not fall behind in your duties."

That verdict was slightly better than what Mrs. Daley wanted, but it was still unacceptable to me.

If I were unattached, like Mr. Davis, I doubt I'd leave the house much. This was an agreeable place, for the most part, and an evening with an entertaining book was enough to relieve my mind.

But I had Grace, and from the moment I'd realized I had to work hard to keep her from starving, I determined that she would not grow up out of my sight. I'd do anything I must to both earn our keep and make certain we could be together as often as possible. I would not be one of those mothers who made her painful way to the Foundling Hospital to set her baby on their doorstep, and tear out her heart as she walked away. My friends the Millburns had come to the rescue, but even so, I did not want my daughter to not know me.

I cleared my throat. "In that case, Mrs. Bywater, I must give you my notice."

Mrs. Bywater blinked at me. "I beg your pardon?"

"A day and a half are the terms of my employment. If you take them away, I must give my notice."

Mrs. Bywater's brows climbed. "Well, I never, Mrs. Holloway. You would give *me* your demands?"

"Not at all," I said. "But if my work has been unacceptable to you, then I must seek employment elsewhere. I ask leave to spend the night, but I will go tomorrow if you wish."

Mrs. Bywater's jaw went slack, but I saw a smile of victory hovering on Mrs. Daley's lips.

"A week will do," Mrs. Bywater said once she regained her composure. "Thank you, Mrs. Holloway."

I curtsied and turned away, my heart heavy. Behind me, Mrs. Daley said, "It will be for the best. You will find a better cook than that one."

Mrs. Bywater didn't answer. I shut the door behind me and descended to the kitchen, the echo of my footsteps loud in the silence.

8

"You can't give notice!" Tess wailed. "You can't leave me here with that old witch!"

I wasn't certain whether the old witch was Mrs. Daley or Mrs. Bywater, but I chided Tess to watch her tongue.

Those in the kitchen crowded around me: Mr. Davis, Elsie, Charlie, a couple of the footmen, Tess, Emma.

"I had no choice," I told Tess. "Though I admit, I will be sorry to leave."

This was a comfortable house, thanks to Lord Rankin's wealth. When I'd first arrived, he'd had the despicable habit of dallying with the maids in return for his generosity, but now that he was far away in Surrey, this no longer worried us. He'd been bowed with grief the last time I'd seen him, and my disgust for him had turned to some pity.

I had made friends here—Mr. Davis in spite of his foibles, Tess, Lady Cynthia. I knew I could see them again—we'd visit—but it would not be the same. Mr. Davis might not remain much longer, in any case, with Mrs. Daley wedging herself in, and who knew where he would go?

Tess faced me in true fear. She had difficulties in life, including a simple brother she looked after, and she'd found a refuge here. I could not guarantee that refuge would remain once I was gone.

"I will find a way to bring you with me," I told her. "To my new post."

"Ye can't promise," Tess said, tears in her voice. "Ye can't make them hire me."

That was a point, and I could not lie and tell her otherwise.

Mr. Davis glowered. "All was fine until *she* came poking her big nose in. Well, if you're off, Mrs. Holloway, I am too. I'll give my notice as well."

"Don't do that, Mr. Davis," I said quickly. "You'll fare better than I would if you stay—a butler need have no fear of a housekeeper's whims."

"Ha. Until she dissolves my budget for decent wine and persuades the mistress to take away *my* day out. No, thank you."

"We can't *all* give notice," I protested.

"Yes, we can," Tess said. "We can be like the people in the factories who stop their work until they get better wages."

"Good Lord, do *not* compare me to a factory worker," Mr. Davis said in indignation. "But she is right, Mrs. Holloway. The mistress cannot sack us all."

"Oh, I'd not put it past her," Tess said darkly. "Mrs. Dragon might convince her."

I held up my hands. "Stop," I commanded. "I have given notice. No one else needs to, and that is all we should say about it."

"Who is giving notice?" Lady Cynthia's question cut through our babble.

She'd come in through the back door, as she often did when she'd been out with Bobby. She must have dined with her, because she'd missed supper here, or else they'd gone to one of the secret clubs of like-minded women where they smoked cigars and drank brandy.

Mr. Davis answered. "Mrs. Holloway. Mrs. Bywater tried to cut her days out, and Mrs. Holloway won't stand for it. Quite right too." He lifted his chin, as though expecting Cynthia to contradict him.

Before this morning, Cynthia might not have understood why I was being so stubborn, but now she looked me up and down, a frown in place. Her gaze moved to the house above us, and determination lit her eyes.

"Right. You stay where you are, Mrs. H." She pointed an aristocratic finger at me. "I'll sort this out with Auntie."

"Please, do not, your ladyship," I said worriedly. "The mistress is already unhappy that you speak to me as much as you do."

"Absolute rot. Auntie has no business being so high handed. If Uncle doesn't have his daily dose of your sausages he'll fall dead of apoplexy. Worse, he'll rail like a fishwife. I am only saving myself, Mrs. H., believe me. Now move out of my way, or I'll have to bodily shift you."

I couldn't speak. I stepped aside, trembling, not because I thought Cynthia with her far slighter build could lift the plump mountain of me, but because her compassion had drained me of strength.

I groped my way to a kitchen chair and sank into it as Cynthia marched out and up the back stairs. The door at the top slammed loudly.

"Oh my," Tess said excitedly. "Better than a panto." She smiled broadly and scuttled out the door.

"Where are you going?" I had just enough wherewithal to demand.

"To listen at the keyhole."

"Tess!" I protested, but she was gone.

I shooed the others out of the kitchen after that, telling them it was high time they went to bed. Mr. Davis said good night and disappeared, but Mrs. Daley never returned below stairs.

Tess bounced in again as I was sharpening my knives. I'd doused the lights until only one candle flickered, barely piercing the darkness, but I found the absence of light soothing.

Tess whirled around before she ended up in a chair, facing me across the table. "She gave them a right ticking off, did her ladyship," she said happily. "Told the mistress she had no business changing things up from what Lord Rankin wanted. That she, her ladyship, knew more about the running of a house than her aunt, and that a good cook was more precious than a diamond necklace or a fine carriage. Lady Cynthia said the household was lucky to have you and they should give you yet another day out if you wanted it, *and* a rise in wages, and an apology."

"Oh dear," I said in alarm.

Mrs. Bywater had once chastised me for being too friendly with Lady Cynthia. If Mrs. Bywater convinced herself that Cynthia needed to be under her father's control, she could tell her husband to cart Lady Cynthia home to her parents, break up the household, and send us all packing. My stubbornness, and Cynthia's, might mean we were all out a place.

"Mrs. Bywater tried to argue," Tess went on, "but Lady Cynthia said she'd take it up with *Mr.* Bywater, who likes your cooking, and Lord Rankin, on whose charity her aunt and uncle are staying in this luxurious house. The mistress backed down, I can tell you. She don't want to go back to their poky village in Somerset when she can live like a fine lady in London."

I tried to laugh. "Mrs. Bywater never agreed to give me a rise in wages."

"No," Tess admitted. "But she said your days out would stand where they were and no more would be said about it. Mrs. Daley was that furious, but gave in, in a voice that froze my blood. But what could she do? Mrs. Daley's as much a slavey here as we are, the old trout."

"That's enough, Tess." I was so weary I could barely give her the admonishment. "Listening to a private conversation is bad enough, but you must curb your tendency to speak so about your betters."

"Fing is," Tess said, sliding into her street cant, "Mrs. D. ain't my *better*, is she? Not in my opinion."

Not in courtesy or human regard, no, I agreed. "Nonetheless, she has more experience and is older than you are. That accords her some respect, whether you like her or not. If you disgrace yourself, you also disgrace me, and then Lady Cynthia's speech on my behalf will go for naught."

Tess took my chastisement good-naturedly. She came to me and gave me an impulsive embrace, mindful of the knives.

A wet kiss landed on my cheek. "I'll not disgrace you, Mrs. H., don't you worry. What I say about the old harpy will stay between you and me."

"I despair of you," I said.

"I know. But you like me and think I have the makings of

a good cook. You've said. You want me to do ought else to-night? If not, I'm off to bed."

I knew the days were tiring for her when I was not here, though she didn't complain.

"Off you go," I said. "But you are not to repeat what you overheard to anyone. Is that clear?"

"Aye, aye, Captain." Tess saluted me. "I told ya, between you and me. Good night, Mrs. H."

Another quick hug, and she danced out again.

I dragged the blade of my carver over the whetstone, reflecting on what Cynthia had just done for me. I was humbled, and grateful. Cynthia had understood *why* I wanted the days out, and instead of being shocked and angry, she'd made certain I could continue seeing my daughter.

I wiped tears from the corners of my eyes. It would not do for my vision to be blurred while my fingers were so near the sharp blades.

I heard a soft tapping at the back door, in a rhythm I'd come to recognize. Setting the knife aside, I hurried through the scullery and unbolted the door to let in Daniel and the scent of the night.

"I was hoping you'd come," I said.

He lifted his brows and started to smile. I'd never expressed this sentiment before, though he'd taken to visiting me after the household had gone to bed so we could speak privately.

Daniel's mirth faded as he took in my expression. "What has happened?"

I fluttered my hand as I led the way to the kitchen table. "Oh, nothing really. Lady Cynthia saw me with Grace, is all, and I had a row with the mistress."

As he studied me in concern, I quickly related the tale,

including Mrs. Daley's challenge, and Cynthia's championing of me to Mrs. Bywater.

Daniel seated himself at the table, his strong brown hands lying on its top. He'd changed out of his dusty gardener's clothing and now wore a plain shirt and coat, a black cloth tied around his neck.

"Lady Cynthia is a fine young woman," Daniel said when I finished. "She will keep things to herself, I imagine, and think no less of you. She is generous, and all for women being unconventional."

"I did not set out to be unconventional," I protested. "I wanted a husband and child, like every other woman. I thought that is what I had. Imagine my surprise when I learned I did not."

"Not your fault."

"No, but you know how the world is. I ought to have found out all about Mr. . . . . Holloway . . . before I walked up the aisle with him."

"Why are you reluctant to tell me his real name, Kat?" Daniel asked with a frown. "He is dead, and out of my reach. I can't be arrested for wanting to throttle a man long gone, can I?"

I shook my head. "Least said, soonest mended. I believe that is the saying."

"It is." Daniel fell silent, but I sensed his annoyance that I hadn't bared my soul to him. I would—perhaps—whenever he bared his to me.

"When I said I was hoping you'd come . . ." I began.

Daniel shot me a smile. "Yes, I heard you. I am delighted at the sentiment."

"It is because I had a notion to try Mr. Li's tea after my rather vexing evening. I believe it will taste better if I share it with a friend."

"Ah. Very kind of you."

I knew it was not what he'd wanted me to say, but I rose to fetch the kettle which I'd left simmering. I warmed the teapot with a splash of water, discarding that and carrying pot and kettle to the table.

I had retrieved the box of tea from my chamber before I'd started on my knives, and now I took it from my apron pocket.

The box was small, and as I'd observed, wonderfully carved with beautiful flowers, some like the ones I'd seen at Kew today. I opened it, inhaling the tea's lovely fragrance, and carefully measured spoonfuls into the pot.

There was enough in the box for three or four brewings, I calculated; that is, three or four if I shared it, more if I kept it to myself. I filled the teapot with the water then returned the kettle to the stove.

Daniel told me as the tea steeped that he'd made Mr. Chancellor admit he'd been near the house the night Sir Jacob died. "I pretended I was morbidly curious about the stabbing and heard he'd been friends with the murdered man. Asked all kinds of interested questions." He took the empty mug I handed him and turned it absently on the table. "Chancellor seemed to find my eagerness amusing. He said he'd been on his way to speak to Sir Jacob around nine that night, but upon arriving had been told the man had retired, and so he departed. He'd seen a Chinese man wandering about the street, which he reported to Inspector McGregor. When I asked why he'd assumed the man had anything to do with the murder, he turned red and started to mumble. Finally told me to mind my business."

"Did you find out who Sir Jacob went all the way to Kew Gardens to meet that evening? If it was Mr. Chancellor, then why did Mr. Chancellor try to call on him?"

"I did not. Chancellor claims he had no idea Sir Jacob had come to Kew that day at all. He hadn't had an appointment with him."

"Hmm. Mr. Chancellor *might* have seen Mr. Li when Mr. Li came to visit me, and decided that if anyone was to be caught for a murder, it might as well be a Chinaman. But does that mean Mr. Chancellor did it himself and is shifting the blame? Or simply decided it was easiest to fix it on a foreigner?"

"Or did he fix on Mr. Li for another reason?" Daniel mused. "Sir Jacob spent many years in China—perhaps Mr. Li was one of Sir Jacob's acquaintances there."

"Why should he have been?" I lifted the pot to pour out the tea. "China is a vast country with many people in it. Why should Sir Jacob have met Mr. Li, or any other Chinese person now in London, for that matter?"

"That is not to say they *didn't* know each other," Daniel said. "The world is a strange place. I once met a man in Paris and then saw him again a few years later in Amsterdam, entirely by chance. He's from Cornwall, and I'm from London, and yet we only came together in countries not our own."

"But you know everyone in the world," I said with conviction. "So the comparison is not apt."

As Daniel chortled, I lifted my cup, blew on the tea to cool it, and drank. Daniel did the same.

The tea swirled across my tongue like silk, and my world stopped.

I tasted flowers and fruit, and a smoky note . . . But no, that evaporated in a whiff of anise, which turned to honey.

Daniel looked at me across his teacup, our gazes locking as we both realized we were drinking something extraordinary.

I did not want to swallow the beautiful nectar, but my

instincts took over, and the exquisite liquid flowed down my throat.

I drew a breath. "Goodness, I do not believe I've ever tasted a better cup of tea." My voice came out all wrong, the words tumbled. I gazed longingly at my cup, wanting nothing more in life than another taste.

Daniel set down his mug and stared at it. "Where did Mr. Li find this?"

"I really have no idea." I took another sip, closing my eyes. I tasted wet breezes, cool mountains, and a tang of green, growing things.

"May I?" Daniel reached for the box and opened it. He took a pinch of the dried leaves between his fingers, sniffed them, rolled them, and let them crumble back into the box.

"This is hideously expensive tea, Kat," he said reverently. "It's the finest blend, from the best leaves. What's sold to servants and the working class is called the 'dust,' the broken leaves and stems shaken out after the lot is dried. The best whole leaves are for aristocrats, the nouveau riche, and the Queen."

"I do know that," I said. "I purchase the comestibles for the house, including the tea. Ours comes from Twinings, and I mark the tins for upstairs and those for down very carefully. But how do *you* know? Have you worked in a tea warehouse?"

Daniel shook his head. "Elgin Thanos is a mine of esoteric information. He told me all about how tea is processed years ago—over a cup of tea."

"Mr. Bywater will spend some money on good tea, but nothing like this . . ."

It was as though Daniel and I drank the finest brandy France produced, or ate the most elegant chocolate from Flanders, or tested the most magnificently flavored Stilton. With some foods there was no mistaking quality, even to the untrained palate.

"It is certainly a special gift," Daniel said, imbibing another sip.

"I hope you are not implying Mr. Li stole it," I said. "He has not adopted Western dress, which might mean he has not been long on these shores. Perhaps he brought the tea with him all the way from China. Maybe Chinese men and women drink tea this fine all the time."

"I imagine their classes of tea are divided up much like ours." Daniel planted his elbows on the table so his steaming mug could rest close to his mouth. "Tell me more about Mr. Li. I am becoming very interested in him."

I'd already related most of what I knew about him, but I went over the encounter again, including every word Mr. Li had said.

"His robe was blue?" Daniel asked when I'd finished. "You are certain?"

"I did not take particular notice when I knocked him down, as I was more worried about breaking his limbs, but yes, blue. And silk. Very fine and soft but sturdy."

"And his English is excellent, you say?"

"Indeed. He must have studied very hard or worked for an Englishman for some time—"

"Or was born in England," Daniel broke in. "Children of foreigners often learn English without an accent—that is to say, they take on the accent of the place they are raised."

"Mr. Li wasn't quite as comfortable with our tongue," I answered after contemplation. "I will keep to my opinion that he studied very hard."

"I think you are correct." Daniel took another sip. "I believe I will scour Limehouse and other Chinese enclaves to learn what I can about Mr. Li." He paused. "*After* I finish this wonderful tea."

"What about Mr. Chancellor and Kew Gardens?" I asked. "There's more to be learned there, surely."

"Never worry. I have my ways to do both at once. He gave you no other name than Li? It is a common one."

"We did not have time to exchange family histories. Our conversation was brief, and I have told you every word of it."

Daniel smiled. "Never mind. You have a splendid eye for detail, and your description will be very helpful."

"Do not lead the police to him, please."

His amusement faded. "You are very convinced of his innocence, Kat. Everything this Mr. Li has done can be seen as suspicious—his being in Mayfair at all, his choice in time to visit you, his gift of extremely high-quality tea . . ."

"I know. But I liked him. I want him to be innocent. Of course, I am fond of you, and you are a thorough villain, so perhaps my judgment is not to be trusted."

Daniel let out a heavy sigh. "Ah, Mrs. Holloway. All I've ever tried to do is please you."

The twinkle in his eye made me want to laugh. "Don't be silly," I said.

We fell silent after that, enjoying every drop of the ambrosia in the teapot.

In the morning, after breakfast, I was startled to see Mrs. Redfern, the housekeeper next door, arrive at the back door and apologetically ask for admission.

"I'm unsettled in my mind, Mrs. Holloway," she told me as soon as I had her seated at the kitchen table, tea at her elbow— not Mr. Li's tea. That was back upstairs in my bureau drawer.

"What about, Mrs. Redfern?"

While Mrs. Redfern and I hadn't become great friends over the months, I did respect her intelligence, and now she appeared to be quite troubled.

The kitchen was empty except for Tess, as the rest of the servants were upstairs, desperately trying to complete the tasks Mrs. Daley had handed out today. Elsie was in the scullery, dishes clattering. Mr. Davis had retreated, and Mrs. Daley, as was her habit after haranguing the maids like a sergeant major, had shut herself into the housekeeper's parlor.

"Goings-on," Mrs. Redfern said. She gave Tess, who was peeling apples in the corner, a guarded look.

"Tess has learned to never repeat any of my conversations," I said. "Please tell me what is upsetting you."

Mrs. Redfern did not relax, but her agitation obviously outweighed her worry about Tess. "Mrs. Finnegan said you were a reassuring person to speak to. That you seemed to fix things. I am growing worried, but I'm not certain there is anything you can do."

"Is it to do with Sir Jacob's death?" I asked gently.

Mrs. Redfern looked surprised. "No, no. The police have said a burglar did that. We're not safe in our beds—quite literally. Sheppard and I have made very certain the windows have been closed and locked tight ever since, believe me. Not that Sheppard will be at the house long. He's been given the sack, but the mistress is allowing him to stay until he finds another place."

A valet whose master had died was a useless appendage in a widow's household, unfortunately. "Could she not pension him off?" I asked. "He served his master a long time, I hear. He was with him in China, was he not?"

Mrs. Redfern's mouth pinched. "Sheppard is not being pensioned off because *she* won't hear of it."

"Lady Harkness?"

"No, indeed. That is what is troubling me. Mrs. Knowles. She and the other woman, Mrs. Tatlock, hover and murmur, and her ladyship does exactly what they say. She listens to Mr. Pasfield too—he was Sir Jacob's greatest friend. Knew him from childhood. Her ladyship is not a stupid woman, but she is uncertain."

"The ladies give her counsel out of hope for reward?" I asked. "Or do they believe they act from kindliness?"

"That is the thing, Mrs. Holloway. I do not know." Mrs. Redfern heaved a heartfelt sigh. "They might mean well, only trying to help a friend in her bereavement. But they whisper, they close doors in my face, they don't trust any of the servants." Her hesitancy fell away, and she gave me a level look. "I'm afraid they mean to rob the mistress of all she has."

9

"What has made you think so?" I asked in concern. "Specifically, I mean. If you have evidence, you ought to go to the police."

"I have none. Which is why I came to you. You seem to find out things." Mrs. Redfern lifted her tea but set it down without drinking. "I can point to nothing specific. However, Lady Harkness has decided to sell some of the things in the house. Most of it is worthless—horrible stuff—but some is not. The master, according to Sheppard, accumulated whatever he liked without bothering about its worth. There is treasure among the dross, and I am certain Lady Harkness's friends want to get their hands on it before she can sell anything. Lady Harkness allows the ladies and Mr. Pasfield to roam the house, and they are picking it over like a pack of crows on a corpse. I believe they are taking things, but I can't be certain, and when I mention this to Lady Harkness, she does not listen."

I recalled the fussy Mrs. Knowles, pale and hollow beside the regal Lady Harkness. She seemed a harmless and rather foolish woman, but that did not mean she was not greedy or would not take advantage.

"Who is this other lady?" I asked. "Mrs. Tatlock?" Lady Cynthia had mentioned her but had not painted a full picture.

Mrs. Redfern took on an expression of distaste. "A social climber if ever I saw one. Has no connections, is a widow of a shopkeeper or some such, and latches on to Lady Harkness to be pulled into her circle." She let out another sigh. "If only one kept to one's place, this would be a happier world."

I was not certain I agreed. If I'd kept to my place, I'd be scrubbing floors and emptying slop pails for a living instead of sitting comfortably in a kitchen I ruled, sipping tea with a housekeeper. But I understood her gist. Ambition could make people do ridiculous things, and break their hearts when they did not succeed.

"How would you like me to help, Mrs. Redfern?"

She gave me a grateful look but shook her head. "I do not quite know. Find out if they are stealing from her, I suppose, and make Lady Harkness believe it."

"You are in the best position to do that. You know everything about the house, can go anywhere you like in it."

"I have tried. I asked Jane to keep an eye on Mrs. Tatlock and Mrs. Knowles, but Mrs. Tatlock caught her, claimed Jane was spying on her, and Lady Harkness nearly dismissed the poor girl. I had to speak swiftly and defend Jane's behavior before she relented. They are quite watchful, the two ladies. Pretending to be solicitous of their dear friend."

I thought about how Mrs. Knowles had fluttered around Lady Harkness, getting in the way and nearly knocking Lady

Harkness's hat from her head. Lady Harkness had been wearily patient, Mrs. Knowles panting and apologetic. But even a helpless-seeming woman could hold others under her thrall. I'd known ladies of the house who were too weak to leave their beds but who nonetheless ruled with an iron hand.

I of course could not simply wander about next door and investigate—I could not keep pretending I needed herbs or some such. But Mrs. Redfern intrigued me.

Mrs. Knowles had been in the house the night of the murder, and I was not as convinced about the burglary story as the police seemed to be. Perhaps Mrs. Knowles had been snooping about, hoping to find a most valuable piece from Sir Jacob's haphazard collection, and Sir Jacob had seen her. She might not have had the strength to fight him and kill him on the spot, but she might have convinced him to wait until morning to sort this out, and then crept in when he was in bed and silenced him. Then, in a weak attempt to cover up her crime, Mrs. Knowles opened the window to suggest a break-in. I wondered if the inspector had found any evidence that someone had actually gone in or out of the window.

If Sir Jacob had brought something truly valuable back with him from China or India, perhaps it had been costly enough to be worth killing for. Mr. Chancellor had been digging for plants—or he might have been looking for something buried *under* the plants. More could be put into a garden than trees and shrubs.

Even if I could not investigate the Harkness house myself, I could render assistance.

"Thank you for coming to me," I said to Mrs. Redfern. "I would be happy to help. You go home, and I will see what I can do."

* * *

Once Mrs. Redfern had gone, I rolled out sweet dough for the apple tart while the apples Tess had peeled simmered on the stove to render their juices. I sprinkled the crust with a dusting of sugar mixed with flour and set it aside while I rolled out the next crust.

"I can have a butcher's if you like," Tess volunteered. *A butcher's hook—Look.*

I folded my dough into quarters and lifted it into a pan. I'd planned to ask others to traipse about the house next door for me, but not Tess.

"And have Lady Harkness send for a constable when she catches you nosing about?" I asked. "What excuse would you have for being in her home?"

Tess finished with the apples and began to scrub potatoes. "I don't have to go in myself if you don't want me to. I'm friends with a couple of the maids, and one of the footmen fancies me. I can have them tell me what's happening above stairs."

"Do you fancy this footman in return?" I asked with a small amount of worry.

"Naw," Tess said breezily. "But he don't need to know that."

I was both relieved and disapproving. "You ought not toy with his affections so you can spy on Lady Harkness's friends."

"Don't see why not. If these friends murdered old Sir Jacob, they need to be arrested. Who knows when the ladies might take it into their heads to murder Lady Harkness as well?"

Tess had a point. "Very well, but do not hurt that young man's feelings," I said. "It isn't fair to him."

"Oh, he'll do all right. So many of the maids fancy *him*, I wager he'll console himself well enough when I give him the elbow."

I shook my head. "Whenever you do fall in love, Tess, I hope that man is kind to you."

"I already told you. I'm never falling in love. Married life ain't for me."

I was pleased to hear it. While I'd never stand in the way of Tess's happiness, marriage could be fraught with peril, and only the stoutest hearts should attempt it. I did not want to see her heart broken, or her life become one of drudgery to a brute.

"Shouldn't keep you and Mr. McAdam from jumping the broomstick," Tess went on. "That would be a different thing. You'd be two birds in a nest, you would, you keeping him and James in fine food while Mr. McAdam pretends to be all sorts."

I thumped my rolling pin to the dough with unnecessary force. "Birds in a nest, indeed. Do not be impertinent, Tess."

Tess looked in no way admonished and continued with the potatoes, humming a little tune.

"Her ladyship wants to see you, Mrs. Holloway," Mr. Davis called to me an hour later as he slung his coat onto a coatrack in the servants' hall and proceeded to spread a newspaper across the table there.

I paused between larder and kitchen. "Do you mean Lady Cynthia or our new housekeeper?" I asked him.

Tess, in the kitchen, laughed uproariously, and a passing footman snickered.

Mr. Davis did not change expression. "Lady Cynthia. She requests that you speak to her in the drawing room."

"Upstairs?"

I knew full well where the drawing room was, but the exclamation was one of trepidation. Lady Cynthia thought nothing of coming to visit me in the kitchen, and a summons above stairs sounded ominous.

"Where is Mrs. Bywater?" I asked.

"Gone out." Mr. Davis smoothed the newspaper and began to read, as though he had no curiosity about what Cynthia wished to say to me.

Swallowing, I set my load of tomatoes and mushrooms in the kitchen and made for the back stairs, so agitated I forgot to remove my apron.

I knew I'd need to face Lady Cynthia and her knowledge about Grace sooner or later, but I'd hoped she'd pretend the encounter had never happened. However, that was not Lady Cynthia's way.

I reached the main floor, Emma pausing her dusting in the hall to eye me in curiosity. I made myself walk straight to the drawing room without vacillation, but my hand trembled as I clasped the door handle and let myself in.

Tall windows admitted plenty of light, bright after my dark kitchen. A wide mirror above the fireplace reflected a room with ivory-colored paneled walls and furniture from the previous century, refreshingly free of the clutter that littered the house next door.

A glittering chandelier hung from a plaster medallion in the exact center of the high ceiling. It took the labor of one footman and two maids to clean all the prisms on that chandelier, which had to be done at least once a week.

Lady Cynthia wore a gray frock and looked out of temper. She'd seated herself on a cream and gold striped sofa, directly in a beam of sunlight that touched her fair hair and gave her an ethereal appearance.

"For God's sake, sit down," Cynthia said as I curtsied and waited for her to speak.

I remained standing. I hardly wanted Mrs. Bywater to return home unexpectedly and find me sitting in her best chair chatting with her niece. I also knew that though I'd shut the door behind me, any of the staff might grow curious and attempt a peek inside. I thought of Tess and her keyhole yesterday.

Cynthia scowled when I did not move. "Very well, fix yourself in the middle of the carpet if you must, but I want you to tell me the whole story."

I moved closer to her, bunching my hands in agitation. "Please, your ladyship, I beg you to keep the secret, and please, please ask Lady Roberta to do the same."

I spoke in a whisper, fearing being overheard. Cynthia glanced at the closed door and seemed to understand, because when she replied, her voice was quiet.

"If you think I condemn you for having a child, I do not. Neither does Bobby. She likes children, soppy about them, as you could see. What I'm unhappy about is that you never told me. I take a leaf from Mr. Thanos's book and like a person—or not—for herself, not her station in life. I dared hope we'd become friends."

She spoke in the manner of one disappointed. I too had hoped we were friends, but I knew a bit more of the way of the world than she. "You have been very good to me."

"Don't bleat to me about goodness, like I'm a queen scattering largesse. I mean what I say. If we'd been born monkeys or some such animal, there would be no difference between us at all. We'd share space on a branch without thinking a thing about it. I'm willing to forget I'm an earl's daughter—would love to, actually."

"I understand. But I can't forget I'm a domestic who needs her post, and who will be hard-pressed to retain that post if she is anything but respectable."

"Having a daughter makes you not respectable?" Cynthia's brows rose. "My aunt believes it's the only thing that would make *me* respectable, though producing a son would be ten times better, in her opinion. Is it your husband that's the problem? Where is he? *Who* is he?"

"Dead and gone, and who he was doesn't matter," I answered quickly. "He was not a kind man, and I was foolish. That is the end of it."

"Not quite," Cynthia said with perception. "A widow is not shamed—hell, in this day and age, she's glorified. Look how Lady Harkness's friends bow down and worship her, never mind whether the poor woman is grieving or not. Were you never married? Is that the trouble?"

"We were married. At least, I thought so." The words nearly choked me. It had been long ago, more than ten years now, but I'd never spoken of this to anyone but Daniel and the Millburns.

"The man tricked you?" Sympathy filled Cynthia's light blue eyes. "Blackguard. I am surprised though. You're usually such a wise woman. I can't imagine anyone pulling the wool over *your* eyes."

"If I am wise now, it was because I was quite naïve when I was young," I said, my throat tight. "I thought myself married by a vicar, and everything aboveboard. But it turns out he'd already been married, and his wife was still living."

"He'd left her? Believed that to be the end of it?"

"No. He kept her all along. She did not know of me, and I did not know of her. Until his death." I cleared my throat. "There you have it."

"Good Lord."

Cynthia looked me over. She could go on about us being monkeys on the same branch, but her assessment was one of an aristocratic lady.

"I quite understand why you kept silent about it," she said. "Priggish women like my aunt would condemn you. When a man does something horrible to a woman, the woman is blamed for letting him—so common opinion goes. My aunt agrees with this. However, I am not one of those priggish ladies, if you hadn't noticed."

"I did notice. But it is a difficult subject to broach."

"I don't doubt." Cynthia gave me another allover look then rose in a rustle of taffeta. "What about this other woman? The one he married previously. Did he leave her starving in a gutter?"

"Indeed, no. He had a pension, if a tiny one, and her family looked after her." I'd discovered everything I could about my husband's other wife—the one he'd married legally—when I'd found myself alone and penniless.

"Did you approach her?"

I shook my head. I'd wanted to, longing to demand she give me what he'd stolen from me with his promises, but I could never bring myself to do it. I do not know whether cowardice or prudence stayed my hand, but I never acted.

"I decided to go into service and earn my keep," I said. "I was lucky—I'd been trained by an excellent cook." Partly luck. My mother, before she'd died, had made certain I had received the training, which I'd nearly thrown away when I'd run off to be married.

Cynthia watched me in sympathy. "It is too bad the blasted man is out of my reach. I'd teach him a thing or two."

"He was quite large and strong." I allowed myself to be

amused picturing Lady Cynthia craning her head back to shake her finger at my tall husband.

"Doesn't matter. I'd have others give him a thrashing for me. Does McAdam know?"

"Yes. Everything."

"Good. And *he* has obviously not condemned you. Why did you believe *I* would?"

"Daniel is not the most traditionally minded man," I reminded her.

"And I am not the most traditionally minded woman. I go out of my way to convey this. Am I not convincing?"

I had to smile. "No, indeed, you convey it quite well."

"Excellent. Then you will trust me to keep my mouth closed and not think the less of you because some damned fool tried to ruin your life. I told Bobby to keep quiet as well. She was surprised that anyone would make a fuss about it, bless her. She quite admires you."

I had not thought highly of Bobby when I'd first met her, and I flushed, ashamed of that assessment. "I am flattered."

"Now, if you kicked over your traces and lived openly with young Grace and perhaps McAdam at the same time, Bobby would fall down and worship you. I had to remind her of the practical side of life—one must have cash to survive. She hasn't got any of her own, and because she grew up in luxury, she doesn't realize where it comes from. Bobby is a wonderful woman, but she can be obtuse."

Bobby had once asked Cynthia to run away and live with her, but she'd wanted the sort of intimacy Cynthia had not. I was pleased they'd obviously managed to remain friends.

"I will forgive you," Lady Cynthia continued. "For not telling me, I mean. In time. I am easily hurt." She sent me a smile to imply she was teasing, but I saw the injured look in her eyes. "You need have no fear that my aunt will not give you your days out—I told her she ought to go down on her knees and thank God every day you decided to stay and cook for her. After my father squandered all his money, we had to put up with the most incompetent cooks imaginable, and I've learned to appreciate a nice meal. Auntie, the silly cow, has no idea what talent you possess."

"I thank you for speaking for me. I don't much want to leave, in truth."

"Yes, well, we'll say no more about it." Cynthia bunched a fold of skirt in her fist. "I put on this dashed uncomfortable frock for a reason—I intend to go next door and find out what's what."

"I meant to ask if you would," I said. "I am most curious about Lady Harkness's friends." I briefly repeated what Mrs. Redfern had told me.

"Never liked that Knowles woman," Cynthia said when I'd finished. "Though I could swear she was harmless. Those who have nothing in life often cling to a friend of wealth or position to at least make people notice them, even if they're derided for it."

I nodded. "Mrs. Redfern said such a thing about Mrs. Tatlock. Both she and Mrs. Knowles may be completely innocent of anything but being lonely, you know."

Cynthia huffed a laugh. "You're a brick, Mrs. H. And as I've observed before, too sympathetic for your own good. I will ooze my way into the house and find out all I can."

"Thank you, your ladyship," I said sincerely.

"Don't be so damned formal. I won't embarrass you by telling you to call me Cynthia, but leave off with the *my lady* and *your ladyship*, at least out of my aunt's hearing. I'm trying very hard *not* to be a lady. And if you have any more startling revelations about your past—if your grandfather was Lord High Admiral or something—do tell me, won't you?"

I returned to the kitchen but set to pacing, the encounter having unnerved me. Tess watched me as she chopped parsnips for a soup.

"You all right, Mrs. H.? What did her ladyship want a chat about?"

"Never you mind," I said abruptly. "It was a private conversation."

Tess lifted her hands, paring knife in one, parsnip in the other. "Don't bite me head off. I were only asking."

I deflated. "Forgive me—I am out of sorts. Shall we get on with things?"

Tess gave me a curious glance but returned to her parsnips.

I forced myself to plunge into the tasks of cookery. I had set plans in motion—Cynthia and Tess would ask questions next door, Daniel had his eye on Mr. Chancellor at Kew, and he would look for Mr. Li. I had nothing to do but wait.

I joined Tess with the mundane chore of chopping vegetables. I'd add these to the broth from beef I'd boiled yesterday to make a tasty stew. I'd hoped the task would soothe me, but it only let my mind churn with questions.

If one wanted to put one's hands on a Chinese gentleman in London, where would one look? Chinatown in Limehouse was the most likely place, as many came from China to work in the docks there and in nearby Canary Wharf and the Isle of Dogs. Those were the docklands, where huge ships pulled in from all over the world—the Orient, India, the Near East, the Americas, the Antipodes. The sun never set on the British Empire, so the saying went.

From the four corners of the earth, vast wealth poured into London via the freighters. Human beings came too—why would they not? In many countries, they hadn't a morsel to eat or a place to sleep. In London, most found hard labor and hovels in which to dwell, but perhaps they'd believed it would be better than what they'd left behind.

I'd never ventured as far east as Limehouse, but when I went to the markets in Covent Garden, I sometimes saw Chinese men selling food, displaying wares, or shopping. These men either wore dark robes and had their hair in long braids, like Mr. Li, or they'd adopted Western clothing and dressed no different from Daniel.

Mr. Li did not seem to fit with these men and women who were clearly working class. I wondered if he'd hidden himself in the crowds in Chinatown or lived somewhere entirely different.

Or perhaps he'd already stepped on board a merchantman and was rapidly steaming back across the seas to his native land.

Curiosity did not let me remain in my dim kitchen for long. I'd put things in motion, yes, but I liked to be in motion too.

"Gather your basket, Tess," I said. "We're going to the market. Covent Garden today. I need rather a lot."

10

·⟡—⟡·

Mrs. Daley emerged from her hideaway before Tess and I could depart. She observed us with coats, hats, and baskets, and narrowed her eyes.

"Note down your purchases with care," she said. "I want a full accounting when you return."

Tess muttered under her breath, but I nudged her sharply and gave Mrs. Daley a nod. "Naturally. Come along, Tess."

We emerged into a wind that charged down the street, whipping our skirts and coats. Tess and I linked arms and trotted into it, heading to Piccadilly and an omnibus.

We rode on this conveyance and descended in the Strand at Waterloo Bridge, linking arms again to walk to Covent Garden. The wind, which had not died, poured up the narrow streets from the river, pushing us toward the wider space of the crowded market.

Tess had learned much in the past months, and already knew how to tell wilted vegetables from fresh, and two-day-old fish from that caught this morning. She also knew how to drive a hard bargain. I had not taught her this skill; it was natural talent.

As we bartered with the vendors, I kept a sharp eye out—I knew it was unlikely I'd stumble across Mr. Li himself, but I might meet someone who knew him, or who knew the best place to begin looking for him.

Most of the vendors were Londoners, jealous of the spaces they occupied. They'd not let in foreigners without a fight. Indeed, most Indian, Chinese, and African immigrants had their own markets elsewhere. However, a few managed to squeeze in around the edges, and I found several enterprising souls with carts surrounded by black-robed men buying their dinners.

I neared one cart, hearing clucking chickens from cages beneath. I could tell from the odor that the soup being dished out contained the unfortunate creatures' fellows, but the chickens below seemed oblivious to the fact.

As I craned to peer into the pot, I saw that what the Chinese vendor industriously ladled into bowls was not soup, but noodles dripping with sauce. The gentlemen purchasing backed away to sit against the nearest wall, slurping up these noodles with chopsticks. I'd never seen anyone eat with chopsticks before, and I admit I stared a long while before I realized I was being rude.

"You going to try that, Mrs. H.?" Tess asked me in trepidation.

"Yes, why not?"

When I reached the front of the line, the vendor began to absently ladle out the noodles. Then he realized who stood before him, and stared at me, openmouthed, ladle frozen.

Like Mr. Li, this man had a long braid trailing from under his cap and wore a beard, but there the resemblance ceased.

His beard was a mere wisp or two hanging from his chin, and his robes were a severe black cotton fastened with worn, cloth-covered buttons. The vendor didn't have many teeth, which I could observe because his jaw continued to sag.

"May I have some of that?" I asked him politely.

"I don't think he speaks English, Mrs. H.," Tess whispered to me.

"That doesn't matter. Food is food. A language of its own, as it were. Please?" I pointed to his ladle, still frozen in the act of dipping into the vat of noodles.

The vendor snapped his mouth shut, snatched up a plain porcelain bowl from a pile, and plunked a good-sized serving of noodles into it. I handed my basket to Tess and accepted the bowl in my gloved hands, the heat of it warming through the fabric.

"How much?" I asked. A placard hung on the front of the cart, marked with what I assumed were the prices, but they were in Chinese. I pulled out a few coins and held them out. The vendor grabbed one penny from the lot and whisked it out of sight.

I dropped the remaining coins into my pocket and was about to turn away, when the vendor waved a ha'penny at me. My change.

"Thank you," I said. "Oh, I suppose I need some of the chopsticks."

The gentlemen who'd been eating had their own, I noted, as I watched one tuck his into a little lacquer box. How convenient, I thought, to carry your utensils with you.

I had gathered a crowd. The men who'd purchased the noodles and other passersby paused to stare at the strange Englishwoman and her assistant who had decided to taste Chinese noodles.

One of the younger men said something to the vendor, who plucked a pair of wooden chopsticks from his cart and held them out to me with a bow.

I took them, bowing back, and then studied the chopsticks, mystified. The gentlemen had made using them look easy, but I fumbled the chopsticks between my fingers, nearly dropping one to the pavement.

"Like this, missus." The younger man, who couldn't have been much out of his teens, held his hand out for me to observe. He'd wedged one of his chopsticks between his thumb and palm, steadying it with his ring finger. The second stick was held above this, between his first two fingers, which let him pivot it on his thumb.

I copied the movements until I thought I could hold the chopsticks correctly, then I scooped up some of the noodles. I dropped more than I held, but I managed to shove a few into my mouth.

A savory, hot flavor flowed over my tongue, and my lips began to tingle and my eyes water. The sauce contained chicken broth, as I'd suspected, but much else, including a bite of spice that heated me to my belly. The slippery noodles went down easily, but the heavenly taste lingered.

"This is lovely," I exclaimed. "What is in it? Ginger, I believe. And garlic? What is that hot spice? Curry?" I'd eaten Indian curry before, but this flavor was not quite the same.

The young man translated for me, and the vendor said a few words in response.

"You are correct, missus," the young man explained. "Ginger and garlic and star anise. Also some peppers and a fish essence. He won't tell me exactly what is in it though. It is an old dish, he says, passed down through his family."

"I understand." I spoke loudly, as though that would help

the vendor comprehend my words. A foolish thing, but we do this thoughtlessly. "I will not demand your recipe."

The young man translated. The vendor rewarded me with a smile, which crinkled his eyes. I nodded in response then backed away to finish my noodles.

I remained the object of much interest, which meant I had to finish every morsel of noodles and then return the bowl and chopsticks to the vendor. It was not a hardship for me to eat them—I hadn't enjoyed a dish so much in a long while.

I thanked the vendor again, but the young man stopped me before I could go. "He has a gift for you."

I decided not to insult the vendor as I had Mr. Li by immediately refusing. The vendor thrust a small round cake covered with icing sugar into my hands, speaking as he did so.

"A specialty of his wife," the young man told me. "She sells them on her cart. Very good, he says."

"Tell him that he has been most kind."

The young man translated, we exchanged a few more bows, and I at last turned away.

I must have attracted every Chinese person in Covent Garden. The curious crowd dispersed as I went, many of them laughing, their merriment clear. I didn't mind. If my foolishness brought a smile to someone today, well and good.

"Ye never cease to amaze me, Mrs. H.," Tess said as I took my basket from her. "Fancy eating foreign food like that. Hope it don't make you sick."

"Nonsense. The dish was plenty nourishing and quite good. I will try to replicate it."

"I'd like to see you try to serve Chinese noodles to the master," Tess said with a laugh. "I wager he wouldn't even know what they were."

Mr. Bywater liked traditional English dishes and little

else. I made plenty of French recipes, but Mr. Davis knew to serve them as "chicken with port sauce" or "beef and Burgundy." I could not even use the term *ragout*, which was only a simple mixture of chopped meat and vegetables.

"I might save it up as a treat for myself," I said. "Or perhaps for Daniel and James."

"You could cook it for Mr. McAdam at his house," Tess suggested with eagerness.

The thought of cooking a meal for Daniel in his kitchen, as though I belonged there, made my breath catch.

I stifled the thought before it took hold. I tucked the cake into my pocket to enjoy later and started for Southampton Street, my other destination for the day.

A man stepped in front of me. He was a fishmonger I never used, and now was joined by a man who must be his brother. Both were beefy, and neither looked friendly.

"You leave them be, missus," the fishmonger growled. "They have no business here."

"Who? You mean the Chinamen?" I glanced at the noodle vendor, who looked to be closing up for the day.

"They steal our custom," the fishmonger went on, while his brother stood silently, arms folded. "Can't even speak English. Should go back where they belong."

"I believe where they belong is full of war and starvation," I answered. "Their homes were wrecked, and they had nowhere to go." I had heard that some parts of China were torn by disease and internal wars, though I had no idea if the vendor or his customers came from those parts. However, I was trying to stir any sympathy that might lurk deep inside these two, though I surmised it would be a hopeless case.

"Not my lookout," the fishmonger said. "You stay away from them, missus. Don't want them touching our women too."

"Oh, for heaven's sake. They aren't stealing your custom—the vendor is selling to Chinese men like himself. I had a very nice conversation with him. He was far more polite than *you*."

The fishmonger's lip curled. He was quite large, but I'd learned much about bullies in my youth, and more still when I was married to one. If you wavered before a bully, it only made him worse. A firm word and a pinning gaze was much more helpful.

Both men showed no shame, but they were finished with the conversation. "Well," the fishmonger said. "We've warned ye."

"If you like to think so." I gave them a nod to show them I knew my manners if they did not. "Good afternoon, gentlemen."

I walked past them, Tess scurrying at my side, keeping the wall of my body well between her and the two fishmongers. I felt them watch me go, but I did not give them the satisfaction of looking back.

As we left the market for Southampton Street, Tess let out a breath. "You're a brave one, ain't ye? Put those two right in their places. Will you teach me to be like you, Mrs. H.?"

"If you learn how to behave well and expect others to do so, there is no need for bravery," I said. I did not tell her that my knees still wobbled and my breath hitched. It's all very well to stand up to a bully, but sometimes they respond with a blow. "Now, I want to look in on Mr. McAdam's rooms, on chance that he's there."

Tess skipped a few steps. "That would be a fine thing. Mr. McAdam always makes me laugh."

"Yes, he is seldom serious." Whenever Daniel was somber, things were in a dire state indeed.

Before long, we stopped before the pawnbrokers on Southampton Street—the door beside it led into a boardinghouse.

I wasn't certain Daniel still hired the rooms there, as he'd been living in the small house in Kensington, but I suspected he kept bolt-holes all over London. I knocked and pushed open the door into the clean stairwell.

Mrs. Williams, the landlady, bustled out from a room in the back. Her gray frock was as severe as ever, but her new apron sported five rows of ruffles. "Mr. McAdam isn't in, dear," she said. "But his friend is upstairs. Studying."

I brightened. "Do you mean Mr. Thanos?" I climbed the stairs with eagerness.

"And—" Mrs. Williams's word cut off behind me as I opened the door to Daniel's front room.

Mr. Thanos was indeed there, his spectacles on the end of his nose, his dark hair as awry as his coat. He was waving his hands to make some point, not seeing me in the doorway.

The second man in the room was almost as young as Mr. Thanos, in his thirties perhaps, a shock of red hair giving him the look of a friendly dog. This man caught sight of me and rose in surprise from the desk where he'd been sitting, proving himself to be unnervingly tall.

Mr. Thanos looked around in bewilderment, observed me, and rushed at me in delight.

"Mrs. Holloway, how wonderful to see you!"

What I liked about Mr. Thanos was that when he said it was wonderful to see a person, he truly meant it. He advanced on me, hand outstretched, and I had no choice but to clasp it.

"Good afternoon, Mr. Thanos." I glanced behind him, uncertain of the welcome I'd receive from the second gentleman.

"Good Lord, my terrible manners." Mr. Thanos released me from his squeezing grip and waved at the second man. "Mrs. Holloway, this is Mr. Alastair Sutherland. Southy, this is

Mrs. Holloway and Miss Parsons. Southy is an expert on China—the absolute authority in the world."

Mr. Sutherland contrived to look modest. "Well now, I don't know about that."

"He is," Mr. Thanos insisted. "We were up at Cambridge together, and he's still there—one of the youngest chaps ever to be made a fellow."

One would hardly think to look at the gentleman that he was a professor and a scholar of all things Chinese. He was rawboned and a bit ungainly, though his suit fitted him well. The clothes were not costly, but not shabby either—he obviously had a good salary but not an ostentatious one. His eyes were light blue, which highlighted his rather bony face.

Mr. Sutherland made a courteous bow but glanced curiously at our baskets filled with produce.

Tess grasped my basket and had it off my arm before I realized. "I'm off to the kitchens to have a chat. Sing out when you're ready, Mrs. H."

Her words were cheery as she banged her way out, but I knew Tess was uncomfortable with strangers of the above-stairs world. She didn't mind Mr. Thanos or Lady Cynthia, but anyone else made her uncertain.

"Mrs. Holloway is McAdam's friend," Mr. Thanos said after Tess had gone. "She's uncommon clever."

Mr. Thanos did not add "for a cook," or "for a woman," or any other caveat, because it would never occur to him to do so.

"Mr. Thanos is quite flattering," I said. "How do you do, Mr. Sutherland?"

"Very well, and don't I know it. Mr. McAdam was looking for a Chinese fellow, Thanos tells me, and my name came up in connection. If he is the Mr. Li you describe, I do know him."

I forgot any shyness as my interest piqued. "Oh yes? Of all the Chinese men in London, you happen to know him?"

"It is not as far-fetched as it sounds," Mr. Sutherland said with a faint smile. "My Mr. Li is Li Bai Chang, a scholar from Peking. He has been working as a translator here in London, and I hired him to assist me with texts that have never been rendered into English. I speak Chinese fluently, but getting the exact context correct needs a native speaker who understands the nuances."

I tried to stem my excitement. If we indeed spoke of the same man, I had been right that Mr. Li was a scholar and not a laborer. I did not much know about professors in China, but in England, they could be rather threadbare, even if they were gentlemen. This could explain why Mr. Li's clothes looked costly, if worn at the seams, rather like Mr. Sutherland's suit.

What it did not explain was why Mr. Li had been in Mayfair. An errand runner or carter would not be an unusual sight, but a translator from China's imperial city? Why should he be diving between carriage wheels on Mount Street?

"Did your Mr. Li know Sir Jacob in China?" I asked, not really wanting to hear the answer.

"No idea if he knew him at all," Mr. Sutherland said. "But the odd thing is, about a month ago, Li asked if I could strongly hint to one Sir Jacob Harkness that he would do well to consult with Li about markings on the ancient pottery Sir Jacob had brought back from China. I could approach Sir Jacob as one Chinese expert to another and suggest a translator go through his pots and ancient writings. I suppose Li thought a Chinaman approaching Sir Jacob directly wouldn't be welcomed, but I could smooth the way. I tried to tell Li that a Chinese scholar from Cambridge and an Old China Hand like Sir Jacob were not the same thing, and besides, I'd never met the man. But Li insisted, and I promised to look into it. I did manage to make an appointment, but when we turned up for it, Sir Jacob was out. Dashed annoying."

Annoying, but interesting. "When was this?" I asked.

"Weeks ago," Mr. Sutherland answered. "Last month, anyway."

Which might have nothing to do with Sir Jacob's murder—or everything to do with it. "Don't most Englishmen go to Shanghai?" I asked. "Not Peking?" I was a bit fuzzy on the geography of China, but I'd heard that Shanghai was a notoriously wild city full of foreigners—that is, foreigners to the Chinese. "What I mean is that if Mr. Li worked in Peking, he's not likely to have met Sir Jacob there, is he?"

Mr. Thanos answered. "You are quite right—the trading ports are Shanghai, Hong Kong, Fuzhou, Canton, and a few more. Traders can move freely throughout China now, but they do most of their business in these cities. But that does not mean Sir Jacob's and Mr. Li's paths would never have crossed."

I thought of Sir Jacob Harkness, a tradesman who'd made a great deal of money, and Mr. Li, tall, dignified, and learned. I could imagine that in China, Mr. Li would not want much to do with someone like Sir Jacob, Old China Hand or no.

In London, however, so many from all over the world mixed with those they'd never have contact with elsewhere. I had to wonder why Mr. Li had been so adamant to reach Sir Jacob, and if he had, in fact, succeeded, even if the appointment Mr. Sutherland had set up had not been kept. The possibilities made me worry.

"We must ask him," I said.

"We must indeed," Mr. Thanos agreed. "Would he come here, do you think? Neutral ground, so to speak."

"I haven't seen Mr. Li for some weeks," Mr. Sutherland said. "Not since the failed appointment. We finished the last text, and we weren't due to begin another for some time. I could write to him, I suppose."

Mr. Thanos looked disappointed. "Would it be too rude to arrive at his rooms and thump on the door? Or—"

He never completed the thought because the door banging open interrupted him to admit a lad with windblown hair, the new coat he'd already grown out of exposing colt-like wrists. James McAdam glanced around at us in both surprise and relief.

"Mrs. Holloway," he said politely, but it was clear he hadn't come looking for me. He fixed on Mr. Thanos. "Dad thought you might be here, sir. He wants you to come. Inspector McGregor has arrested a man called Mr. Li, and he wants you to bring Mr. Sutherland around to find out if it's the right Mr. Li."

11

James did not include me in the invitation, but I was not about to go meekly home while the gentlemen rushed to Scotland Yard.

I gave Tess the fare for an omnibus back to Mayfair and asked if she minded carrying my basket as well as hers. She agreed readily when she discovered where I planned to go—Tess had a healthy dislike of the police.

James volunteered to see Tess home, and I left them running for the omnibus, James with my basket of produce over his arm. I was a bit surprised James did not want to accompany us, but I had a feeling Daniel had admonished him not to return. Daniel had become even more protective of James since the lad had been hurt this spring.

I thought the gentlemen would fetch a conveyance, but Mr. Thanos started off in a robust stride to the Strand, Mr. Sutherland falling into step with him. I hurried to keep up.

The Strand was packed with carriages and horses, carts

and wagons. The odors of horse and human melded with that of the river, the wind bringing the stench on top of us all.

Not far along was the pawnbrokers in which Daniel had once lurked, waiting to catch criminals. Beyond that was the great expanse of Charing Cross Station, and around the corner, toward Whitehall, lay Great Scotland Yard.

Mr. Thanos led us through the arched doorway of the brick building of Scotland Yard to the counter beside the stairs. A sergeant greeted us listlessly, asking in a monotone what our business was. Only when Mr. Thanos announced we were here to see Inspector McGregor did he show a bit more courtesy.

"Oi, constable—show these gents and the lady upstairs to the inspector," he said to a young man at a tiny desk behind him. "Look sharp."

The lad, in a creased uniform, every hair in place and his boots shined, rose hastily and gestured us to follow him.

We ascended several flights of stairs before the constable ushered us into an office, behind which was a room for interrogating prisoners. This chamber was not as stark as the one in which Daniel had interviewed the terrible villain Mr. Pilcher months ago, but it was still not a pleasant place.

Inspector McGregor and Daniel waited inside this room, gazing down at a dispirited-looking Mr. Li. He was indeed my Mr. Li, with his long beard, shaved forehead, and dark eyes, which were now quiet with resignation.

They'd shackled Mr. Li's wrists, but hadn't chained him to the table. I hoped that the lack of severe restraints meant they weren't certain he was a murderer, but more likely, Inspector McGregor did not worry that such a frail-looking man could escape him.

When we entered, Mr. Li blinked in surprise and began to

rise. He stared at me, then at Mr. Sutherland, and then bowed his head, as if ashamed, and sank back down.

Inspector McGregor gave me a cold eye. "I did not send for *you*, Mrs. Holloway."

Mr. Thanos indignantly began to speak, but Daniel cut over him.

"Let her stay," he said. "She knows this man."

McGregor's neck above his collar turned a fine shade of red. He did not look at Daniel but pointed a long finger at a chair in the corner. "Sit there and do not speak," he said to me.

Daniel gave me a reassuring nod as I took the seat. I wondered anew that Daniel could give a command, which an inspector obeyed, if churlishly. Assisting the police and giving them orders were two different things.

The room became rather crowded once we all squeezed in. Daniel sat beside Mr. Li while Mr. Thanos and Mr. Sutherland took the ends of the table. McGregor waited impatiently while they settled themselves before he sat down across from Mr. Li.

"I asked McAdam to fetch you, Mr. Sutherland, because he tells me you have worked with Mr. Li, and that he assists you to translate books. I have difficulty believing that, as Mr. Li will not respond to me in English. Will you tell him, in Chinese, that we know he was an acquaintance of Sir Jacob Harkness. He was seen arriving at the house a few weeks ago by the valet and the botanist, Mr. Chancellor, who also saw him outside the night of the murder."

Mr. Sutherland launched into a speech of fluid syllables. I knew full well Mr. Li spoke perfect English, but I could sympathize with him not wishing to directly answer Inspector McGregor.

When Mr. Sutherland paused, Mr. Li, after a moment's

hesitation, spoke, also in Chinese. He had such a gentle, pleasant voice that I wanted to close my eyes and enjoy it.

Mr. Li trailed off softly, and Mr. Sutherland cleared his throat.

"I should explain, Inspector, that I have been working at the British Museum for the last few months translating Chinese documents," Mr. Sutherland said. "That is how I met Li." He then told the inspector what he'd conveyed to me and Mr. Thanos—that Li had asked if Mr. Sutherland would contrive a meeting for him with Sir Jacob. "Li told me Sir Jacob had some ancient pottery he wanted a look at, purely for scholarly reasons. I wrote to Sir Jacob and managed to arrange an appointment one evening last month."

McGregor scowled at Mr. Li. "How were you going to ask Sir Jacob about his pottery if you don't speak any English?"

"Sir Jacob spoke fluent Chinese," I said from my corner. "He was tiresome about it."

"As do I," Mr. Sutherland said. A smile pulled at his thin lips. "Though I hope I am not tiresome. And I agreed to attend with Mr. Li, to smooth the way. In any case, when Mr. Li and I arrived for the appointment, Sir Jacob was not at home. Mr. Chancellor was there, and we spoke to him briefly, but Sir Jacob did not come. We waited for a time then departed."

McGregor turned his keen stare on Mr. Li. "You were seen the night of the murder, my friend. Why were you in Mount Street *that* night, eh? Ask him, if you will, sir."

Mr. Sutherland gave Mr. Li an apologetic look and began to speak.

Mr. Li answered in his soothing voice, his long fingers moving restlessly on the table.

"He does not remember," Mr. Sutherland said. His high forehead wrinkled as though doubting the words he spoke.

"He was walking, Li says—he misses his home and often simply walks until he is tired. Mayfair and St. James's remind him of the more beautiful places in Peking, and the emperor's palace in the mountains."

McGregor glared at Mr. Li. "The hell—" He broke off, flushing as though remembering one of the fairer sex was in the room. "Tell him that such a flimsy excuse will only get him convicted. I believe I have enough evidence now to charge him."

"He was there to see me," I broke in.

All eyes turned to me, including Mr. Li's. His held a pleading for me to be silent, and Daniel's look was warning. I ignored them both, deciding that truth was needed to end these games.

"Mr. Li came to see me that night," I said. "I had run into him on the street the day before and knocked the man over. He came to give me a gift—for helping him up, I suppose—a small box of Chinese tea. Which is excellent, by the bye," I said to Mr. Li. "It was generous of you."

Mr. Li shook his head. "Do not listen," he said to McGregor in broken English, still playing his part for whatever the reason.

"Of course you should listen, Inspector," I said. "Mr. Li gave me the tea, and then he went away. It was shortly after nine of the clock, and he walked in the opposite direction from Sir Jacob's house and was gone. If your coroner can determine the time Sir Jacob was killed, I am certain there are witnesses, besides myself, who can place him elsewhere."

"I doubt the coroner can fix the time at exactly five past nine," McGregor snapped.

"Well, if it is near enough to nine, then I am his alibi. I will swear Mr. Li did not go to Sir Jacob's at nine in the evening and climb through a window, which I imagine would be difficult for him, in any case. It is a long way to Limehouse from Mayfair, and I am sure others saw him on his journey."

"Or witnesses who saw when he doubled back to commit the deed," McGregor said in a hard voice but then let out a resigned sigh. "Would you be prepared to swear in court that you saw him clearly at nine o'clock, Mrs. Holloway?"

"Of course I am prepared," I said. "Because it is the truth."

Daniel's gaze held approval, and Mr. Thanos watched me in admiration—I half expected him to erupt into a cheer. Mr. Sutherland looked surprised at my vehemence, his pale forehead remaining wrinkled. Only Mr. Li was distressed, shaking his head.

"No one will take the word of a Chinaman," McGregor muttered.

"Which is why I will speak up for him," I said. "They may take *my* word."

I knew Inspector McGregor wanted to explode, but he was at heart a fair-minded man. Unlike some policemen, he wanted the correct culprit to be caught, not just any person so he could close the case.

"Do you have any reason to hold him?" Daniel asked. "Between eight and ten is indeed the time the coroner puts the death down to, Mrs. Holloway, and we have the word of Sheppard that Sir Jacob went to bed at nine. If there is a witness that can prove Mr. Li was elsewhere at nine, and then walked in the opposite direction, it narrows that window considerably . . ."

McGregor scowled. "My chief inspector will wonder why I've released the most likely suspect. The *only* suspect, damn—er—dash it all."

"Hardly the only suspect," I said. "I can think of six others. More, possibly."

McGregor's mustache quivered as he glared at me, but Daniel didn't bother to hide his grin.

"Swear in Mrs. Holloway as a detective constable," Daniel said jovially. "Explain to your chief inspector you could hope for none better."

"Don't be silly." I rose to my feet. "I already have employment, and now I must rush home to it. The clock will not wait for me. Mr. Sutherland, please ask Mr. Li, after he is released, to call upon me. He will have to knock on the kitchen door, I am afraid, but if he will stand the indignity, I will give him a cup of tea. Good afternoon, Inspector. Gentlemen."

Mr. Thanos leapt to his feet—all the gentlemen did when I stood, with the exception of Mr. Li, who looked uncertain about what had just happened.

"I will see you out, good lady," Mr. Thanos said. "Sutherland and McAdam should stay with this poor chap until he's set free."

Daniel said a brief farewell, pleased with me. Mr. Sutherland courteously, if a bit awkwardly, said good-bye, and McGregor muttered something that was likely supposed to be polite. I trusted that Daniel would take care of Mr. Li, and left the room in some relief.

Mr. Thanos and I walked downstairs and out to the street. The wind continued, buffeting the passersby, imperiling hats and skirts. Mr. Thanos waved down an empty hansom.

The driver was not pleased to halt on the busy road, and he waited only until I was settled before he put the horse into a brisk trot. Mr. Thanos, caught precariously on the step, more or less fell inside and landed next to me.

"Are you all right, Mr. Thanos?" I asked as I pulled the door in front of us shut.

"Perfectly well. Chap is in a bit of a hurry, isn't he? You are plucky, Mrs. Holloway, standing up to the inspector like that."

I warmed under his praise. "I was only speaking the truth. I refuse to let the wrong person be arrested for Scotland Yard's convenience."

"I agree." Mr. Thanos dusted off his trousers. "Poor Inspector McGregor is in a bit of a bother about this case, McAdam told me when he recruited me to find Mr. Li."

"Inspector McGregor needs someone to arrest," I said. "Sir Jacob was a knight of the realm, after all. It will be most shocking if someone is not arrested immediately."

Mr. Thanos burst out laughing. "Good heavens, Mrs. Holloway, do not sound so cynical. Perhaps Sir Jacob was a very important person—brought about treaties or some such."

I shook my head. "He seems to have gone on a rather long shopping expedition instead. His house is full of things from China. The housekeeper there has a theory of hidden treasure among it, and believes the family's hangers-on are searching for it. She could be right."

"How exciting," Mr. Thanos said. "Though that might be a mare's nest. One can buy jade and ancient pottery by the dozen in shops in the Burlington Arcade. A piece would have to be astonishingly unique to be worth stealing."

"Not to someone without much money of their own. For some thieves, anything they can possibly flog would do. Though perhaps the value of whatever they are looking for is historically significant," I suggested. "Or so rare none know much about it."

"Then its value would be relative. How would one go about proving it was unique or significant? One would need a trained specialist, an Orientalist . . ." He trailed off, unhappy.

"Like Mr. Li," I finished glumly. "He did wish to consult Sir Jacob about ancient pottery."

"If Mr. Li is telling the truth."

"I do not see why he would not. The appointment can be easily confirmed by Sir Jacob's valet or the housekeeper or Lady Harkness. But then, why wasn't Sir Jacob home when Mr. Li and Mr. Sutherland arrived?"

"Unless it was a ruse by someone else in the house to get Mr. Li there, and Sir Jacob never received Mr. Sutherland's letter at all. Why they'd go to such lengths though, I have no idea. Sir Jacob wasn't killed that night, in any case."

"Or perhaps Sir Jacob decided he had better things to do that evening, and an appointment with a Chinese man was not important to him," I said.

"All I know is that McAdam asked me if I could locate a man from China, probably a Confucian scholar, who went by the name of Mr. Li," Mr. Thanos said. "He asks this of me, calm as you please, as though I can scour the globe for this person in ten minutes. But I thought at once of Sutherland, who is the foremost expert on Chinese writing and scholarship in Britain. And, of course, he knew Li Bai Chang. Named for, Sutherland told me, a famous poet of old. Mr. Li's parents had ambition for him, it seemed. I was excited to meet the man. I would love to speak with him at length." His eyes shone in anticipation.

I hoped Mr. Thanos would have the chance, that McGregor wouldn't change his mind and arrest Mr. Li for the murder after all. "What is a Confucian scholar, exactly?" I asked. I was not certain what *Confucian* meant either, but I did not like to say so.

"Quite a fascinating person," Mr. Thanos said. "It means he has read and studied ancient texts and not only knows them inside and out, but can expound upon them, debate them, and write eloquently about them. It means he's sat through excruciating rounds of exams that make those at Cambridge seem like a punt on the river. Men who do well at these tests are given posts in the government—anything from unimportant accounting tasks up to advising the emperor himself."

"Then I was right that Mr. Li never was a menial."

"Indeed, no. He'd be from a highborn family, or at least a middle-class one. Any young man can sit the exams, but of course his parents must be able to afford the books and the tutors and the time for him to study. A lad who is needed to work on the farm doesn't have much chance. These boys study all the young years of their lives, but if one passes the exams and is rewarded with a post, he can do well for his family. Ergo, parents push their son into a corner and load him with books. Must be the devil of a life."

"British parents send their sons off to frightening schools when they are very young," I remarked.

I'd worked briefly for a family whose firstborn son had been packed off to Rugby School by his proud father. The lad had been terrified, and his father had snarled at him, calling him soft and mollycoddled. The boy had gone, weeping, taken in the carriage by the butler, because the father had rushed off to his club after he'd said a perfunctory good-bye.

"No need to tell me that," Mr. Thanos said with a shudder. "I was at Harrow—a spindle-legged, knock-kneed chap who needed spectacles, trembling among sons of the first men of the nation. I learned to use my fists quickly. And also that a bit of maths rattled off at high speed impressed others. I became quite the show-off."

"In self-defense," I said. "Clever of you."

"Not really. I have a first from Cambridge, have written

volumes that only other scholars read, and am still the knock-kneed boy who needs spectacles." He sighed and peered mo-rosely at Piccadilly unrolling around us.

"Lady Cynthia does not think so," I said.

Mr. Thanos turned sad eyes to me. The spectacles in ques-tion were tucked away in his pocket, and his gaze was a bit unfocused.

"Does she ever speak of me?" he asked wistfully.

I gave him a puzzled look. "Did she see you about cuttings from Sir Jacob's garden? At the pub in Bedford Square?"

"Cuttings?" he asked, equally bewildered.

"I saw Mr. Chancellor take some from a plant. Cynthia said she'd ask you what they were." Though Cynthia had not men-tioned anything of this to me, and I'd forgot to ask her in my agitation about her discovery of Grace.

Mr. Thanos's moroseness returned. "I have not heard a word from her. You see? She does not think of me, does she?"

"Of course she does. You are friends."

Mr. Thanos let his head thump to the cab's padded wall. "I hope she speaks of me as a bit more than that."

I sympathized with him, but I also had no patience with forlorn lovers. "Why not tell her how you feel, Mr. Thanos, instead of pining away? Lady Cynthia is a reasonable young woman. She likes things out in the open."

"Because she might kick me with her well-polished boots. She has such splendid ones, from a chap in Bond Street." His gaze went remote, Mr. Thanos no doubt picturing those boots on Cynthia's shapely feet. Then he sighed again. "She has made clear how she feels about marriage—dead against it. I dare not bring up such a subject. But what else can I offer a respectable lady like her, daughter of an earl, no less?"

"She is against marriage when it comes to the foolish

young sprigs her aunt and uncle thrust at her," I said. "Most are slow witted and not worth her attention, and she knows this. But do not give up, Mr. Thanos. I suggest you court her honestly, but content yourself with friendship if that is all she can give you."

"I can't afford a wife in any case," Mr. Thanos said, resigned. "I suppose friendship will have to suffice."

I had reflected before that they'd starve together unless they had a windfall. Daniel and I were not stupid people—surely, we could think of something to help them.

"Do not despair yet," I advised him. "It is early days."

Mr. Thanos gave me a look of such mixed hope and worry that I could not help patting him on the shoulder.

When we arrived in Mount Street, Mr. Thanos gazed up at the house as he helped me alight, his expression longing.

"You could knock at the front door," I told him. "Pay a call."

"No." Mr. Thanos stepped up on the hansom again. "It might alarm her aunt and uncle, and they'd send me away with a flea in my ear. I believe their ambition is for a rich and handsome gentleman for their niece."

"They should be glad to have such a gentleman as yourself for Lady Cynthia," I began, but the cabbie, an impatient man, abruptly started the horse.

Mr. Thanos was caught on the step again, and he scrambled into the seat, managing a wave before the hansom sped away and was gone.

I walked downstairs and into a kitchen in an uproar. Tess looked up from the stove with a scowl, but it was Mr. Davis who bellowed and waved his arms, while footmen watched in consternation. Elsie cowered beside her sink, holding a dripping dishrag like a soldier's shield.

"What on earth has happened?" I called over Mr. Davis's raging.

Mr. Davis swung on me. He'd lost his hairpiece somewhere in his harangue, and the bald patch on the top of his head shone.

"She stole a bottle of the master's best brandy, that is what has happened," he snarled. "I intend to throttle her, but no one knows where the bloody woman has got to."

12

"Mr. Davis!" I shouted as Mr. Davis turned to storm away. He swung back to me, the cords on his neck tight. "She stole it, Mrs. Holloway—do not tell me she did not."

I wanted to believe Mrs. Daley was a thief, but caution made me question him. "Not long ago, you thought I'd taken a bottle of claret. Then it was discovered, cleverly hiding behind a pile of leeks. Please look more before you run to the mistress."

"I *have* looked. I remember how utterly foolish I felt about the claret, and I made certain to search. High and low. Mrs. Daley has the keys to the wine cellar, and she's gone in and helped herself."

I believed him; however, I also knew we'd better be very, very certain before we made any accusations.

I strode down the hall to the housekeeper's parlor, which was locked. I had surrendered my key to it, but Mr. Davis had one, and he opened the door.

I stopped in astonishment, and Mr. Davis nearly ran into the back of me. Tess ducked under my arm to peer inside.

"S'truth," she exclaimed.

The cozy room was a cluttered mess. Not only was a decanter of brandy sitting in the middle of the table, half gone, but books, newspapers, and other flotsam were scattered about the room. On the desk, I saw a pile of hair combs, several buttonhooks, a jumble of handkerchiefs, spools of thread, a small dish with a spoon resting in it, picture postcards of Brighton, and other odds and ends.

Mr. Davis's mouth hung open. "What the devil?"

I shared his bewilderment. I'd known of mad collectors who gathered bits and bobs obsessively, but they collected jade, miniature paintings, ivory carvings, coins. Nothing in this mess was anything of worth. The items were strewn about the room, covering desk, table, and bookcase. One chair was piled high with lady's magazines.

"Those are the mistress's," Sara, the upstairs maid, said over my shoulder. "And her ladyship's newspapers."

"Snooping, Mr. Davis?" Mrs. Daley's imperious tones rang down the hall. All the maids but Tess scattered.

Mr. Davis and I turned to face Mrs. Daley. "You drank half a decanter of the master's brandy," Mr. Davis snapped.

Mrs. Daley's brows climbed. "Do I look tipsy, sir? My eyes bloodshot? Nonsense, I found it upstairs in Lady Cynthia's bedchamber, where it had no business being. I thought I'd better hide it before she came to some disgrace. Her aunt obviously cannot keep her from nipping down and taking what she likes."

Mr. Davis swelled up, ready to shout, but I spoke before he could. "What about all these other things? Where did they come from?"

Mrs. Daley's cheeks went pink. "Left about, carelessly, hither and yon. The maids do not tidy well, do they? I gather the things here to return to their proper places, and also, if need be, to prove to the mistress that slovenly work is being done."

What she said was plausible—the maids were to put away what Mrs. Bywater and Cynthia left lying about. Mrs. Daley might have picked up what the maids hadn't tidied to teach them a lesson.

But her explanation was too glib, I thought, and this was a lot to have been collected in a couple of days. Mrs. Daley's chest rose with her breath, and though she looked me in the eye, her gaze flickered.

"Very well," I said. Mr. Davis swung on me, outraged, but I did not let him speak. "Mr. Davis, take your brandy and lock it up. Have the maids return the things to Lady Cynthia's and Mrs. Bywater's chambers. No harm done."

"I am so glad you agree, Mrs. Holloway," Mrs. Daley said. "Now, I'm sure you have cooking to do. It is getting late, and you were a long time at the market."

I bit the side of my mouth to keep from a tart reply. As I herded Tess from the room, Mr. Davis stalked to the table, snatched up the decanter, and retreated to the butler's pantry across the hall, slamming the door behind him.

"She's a liar," Tess whispered to me once we were in the kitchen. "She stole those things. I know a tea leaf when I see one."

"I know," I said calmly.

Tess gave me an astonished look. "You do? Why'd you let her think you believed her?"

"Because we can't accuse her without proof. Lady Cynthia does leave things lying about rather carelessly, and the mistress, while she is neater, expects the maids to straighten up after her. And if Cynthia sneaked her friend Bobby into the house, she'd have offered her brandy."

"She's an odd one, is Lady Roberta Perry." Tess pronounced the name with exaggerated care. "If I did such things as she does, me dad would take a strap to me. God rest him."

"Who knows? Bobby's dad might have taken a strap to her too. But more likely, he ignores her. A girl child isn't much use to the aristocracy."

"Lord save me from being posh. Which is why our new housekeeper makes me blood boil. She ain't posh, not any more than you are or Mr. Davis. Why does she think she can lord it over us?"

"Housekeepers can be rather grand," I said. "But I admit, she's let it go to her head. If I ever become a housekeeper, I will thank you to keep me down to earth."

"No worries." Tess's nose wrinkled. "Me and Mr. McAdam will tame you. I still think you should go off and marry him. Then I can be *your* cook."

"None of that," I said. "I need those potatoes scrubbed. Mrs. Daley is right about one thing. We're behind."

Tess and I managed to get the meal prepared and served. Mrs. Daley remained shut in her room, and Mr. Davis, his hairpiece restored, presided over service in the dining room.

I fed Tess and the staff, taking a small meal on my own after Tess went up to bed. I lingered at the kitchen table to make notes about the rissoles I'd prepared tonight, made from leftover beef, which I'd coated in breadcrumbs and fried, to accompany stuffed hens in mushroom sauce.

I lingered because I hoped Mr. Li would accept my invitation to visit. I had no way of knowing whether Inspector McGregor released him as Daniel instructed, because I'd heard no word from Daniel. Or James, or Mr. Thanos, for that matter. *Botheration to the lot of them*, I thought, my pencil jabbing at the page.

Near to midnight, a soft knock came at the back door—two taps and then three. Daniel's knock. I tossed my notebook aside and hurried to admit him.

Daniel gave me a warm smile as he pressed my hand. Some nights he'd kiss my cheek, but not this evening—a shadow slipped down the stairs and followed him inside.

"Mr. Li," I said with pleasure. "I am glad to see the inspector listened to me."

Mr. Li gave me a stately bow, his formality out of place in this cramped scullery.

"Come in, please." I led the way to the kitchen table, clearing off my notebook and dishes. I had brought down the box of tea Mr. Li had given me, and now I warmed the pot and brewed up. I fetched some seedcake I'd held back from supper, and carried it along with cups to the table.

Mr. Li seated himself with some reticence as though he feared someone would find him there and eject him. I could not blame him, but he seemed to find Daniel's presence and the quiet of the kitchen reassuring.

Both men waited as I poured out the fragrant tea. Mr. Li lifted his cup in both hands and drank deeply.

"This tea is most excellent," I told him. "A matchless gift. I fear I don't have much to offer you in return but seedcake."

"Which I highly recommend," Daniel said, laying a large slice on his plate. "Mrs. Holloway is the finest cook in England."

"Mr. McAdam is a flatterer," I said. "As you've no doubt guessed. Now, Mr. Li, I do want to know all about you."

"That is her other talent," Daniel confided to Mr. Li. "She will have your life story out of you before you know it. But fear not. She is discreet, fair-minded, and kindhearted."

"And Daniel has a silver tongue," I said, trying not to be pleased by his words. "Please, Mr. Li, will you tell me why you were in Mayfair the day I ran you down?"

Mr. Li took another sip of his tea, the few lines on his face smoothing as he relaxed. He set down the cup, let out a little sigh, and then raised his dark eyes to me.

"I will tell you the truth, Mrs. Holloway. I was seeking Sir Jacob Harkness, because I had been thwarted from speaking to him before. I wanted to confront him and demand he return what he stole from my father. From my family."

My mouth popped open, but truth to tell, I was not terribly surprised at the accusation. According to Mrs. Redfern, Sir Jacob had run through China helping himself to all and sundry.

"I imagine Sir Jacob took a good many things," I said. "He returned from China a very wealthy man. What he stole from your family must be quite valuable if you've come all the way from China to find it."

"He is not the only one who took from us," Mr. Li said, lines of bitterness about his mouth. "They steal, they cheat, and they hire Chinese with no honor to be go-betweens, to help them. I was born in the mountains you call Wuyi. My family sacrificed much so I could read many books, study under great masters, and sit the exams. You see, in my country—"

"You take tests based on ancient writings and are given certain posts depending upon the results," I interrupted. "Mr. Thanos told me all about it."

Mr. Li looked surprised but rearranged his expression

and continued. "I was lucky and blessed. I had wise teachers, and I was a determined student. I did very well on the exams and was asked to work for the emperor himself." He smiled, his eyes filling with true amusement. "It would be dull to tell you about my duties. At court, I spend much time hunched over a desk. As some of my work concerns British dealings with China, I found a tutor of English and learned your language. I wanted to trust my own understanding of documents and agreements and not those of a translator or interpreter, who can be paid to write what a British merchant wants them to. I began to read many books in your language—poetry, drama, and novels—and to enjoy the activity for its own sake. You were amazed at my command of English, Mrs. Holloway, when I first spoke to you."

"I was, rather," I admitted, my face heating. "We are raised to be convinced that no foreigner can master our tongue, not really."

"The world is changing," Mr. Li said. "Not all of us like the change, but it will be so whether we accept it or not. My countrymen have been forced in the last forty or so years to bow to the wishes of Britain. I saw benefit in learning your language."

"You make me feel quite ignorant, Mr. Li. I am proud of myself for learning to read simple books and speak my *own* language correctly. I gave over most of my effort to learning cookery and little else."

Mr. Li sent me a smile. "We do what we must to fit into our worlds."

A good way of putting it. "Well, we have you happily ensconced in Peking, working away learning languages and doing much reading," I said. "What happened to tear you from all that?"

"A letter from my father." Mr. Li took another sip of tea and set it down, the bitterness in his expression deepening. "He is an elderly man now, but very astute and alert. He informed me that a party of Englishmen came to our village. The monks of the mountains gave them shelter, but my father, as the oldest and most prominent man in the area, offered his hospitality. Not only to be cordial but to keep an eye on them."

"Very shrewd of him," I said.

"The Englishmen were quite courteous, and they did not go to any areas we asked them to leave alone. Not until they were gone, however, did my father discover the theft. It was far too late to catch them by then, but he wrote of it to me, in case I could help."

"But you could not, I presume," I said.

Mr. Li shook his head. "I went to my superiors and explained what had happened, but they told me there was nothing to be done. I knew they were right. Once the British men reached the trade cities, they were safe from us. If an Englishman in China commits a blatant crime—whether against another Englishman or a Chinese—he is tried by a British court, not a Chinese one. If found guilty, he is sent home, out of our reach."

Daniel absently poked at the seedcake with his fork. "One of the men on that expedition to Wuyi was Sir Jacob Harkness?"

"Indeed." Mr. Li nodded. "My father told me the names of all the visitors. Three of the men returned to Hong Kong, and as far as I know, remain there. They do not have the item—I wrote to an emissary in Hong Kong who inquired for me. Sir Jacob Harkness and his friend Mr. Pasfield went to Shanghai from Wuyi and almost immediately left for London. Then I received a letter from a Chinese man in London telling me that Sir Jacob had purchased a large house and lived like a king, and so I concluded he must have brought the treasure with him. I decided to come and see for myself."

My eyes widened. "Just like that? You left your job to rush halfway around the world to look up Sir Jacob? Why couldn't this Chinese friend in London do that?"

Mr. Li leaned across the table, as though he feared someone listening in the shadows. "Because I dared not tell him too much. As I grow older, I trust only myself. I had to find out for certain."

"How did you arrange the journey?" Daniel asked. "What I mean is, in spite of the flood of immigrants pouring into the British Isles and America, it is no easy thing to leave China, especially for a scholar who works for the emperor."

Mr. Li bowed. "It is true. I obtained permission."

He folded his lips closed. I wondered at the significance of his statement, but I could see he had no intention of giving us further information about his travels.

"Will you tell us what this treasure is?" I asked. "I might be able to help you find it. There is quite a jumble in Sir Jacob's house, but I'm certain Mrs. Redfern can direct the servants to look for it—without letting on how valuable it is, I assure you. Is it porcelain? I have seen a number of beautiful pieces."

Mr. Li studied us for a long time, as though wondering whether he dared tell us. His eyes held the loneliness of a man who had given his entire life to a pursuit, forgoing earthly pleasures to obtain it.

As he assessed me, I had the feeling he could see straight into my true self, uncovering all my worries, hopes, and petty faults, as well as my fears and my love.

At last Mr. Li bent his head in a nod, as though giving himself permission to speak. He lifted his cup, and the corners of his eyes crinkled as he looked over it at me.

"It is tea, my dear lady."

I gasped and stared into my empty cup, at the bottom of which lay the long, curled leaves of damp and fragrant tea. Daniel, likewise, peered into his mug and then quickly set it down.

"Not *this* tea," Mr. Li said, shaking with silent laughter. "This is some of what I brought with me on my travels, as I feared I'd not find any palatable here. I have discovered that I *can* buy fine tea in London—as it came from China itself—but it is very expensive."

"It is indeed," I said faintly. "Are you saying, Mr. Li, that Sir Jacob stole *tea*? Do you mean bushels of it?"

"No, no," Mr. Li said. "The original bushes themselves, or at least cuttings and seeds from them."

Daniel gave his cup a reverent glance. "The British wrested the secret of Chinese tea from your country thirty-odd years ago. Why are you so interested in this crop?"

"Because it grows nowhere in the world but in our village," Mr. Li answered. "When Chinese tea was wrested away, as you say, to be cultivated by the British in India, it dropped the price of tea in China disastrously, beggaring many in my country. Much of what you drink in England is a result of that theft."

"Oh." I glanced guiltily at the dresser on which rested a tin of tea I'd recently purchased. "I never knew that."

"*This* tea, however, eluded capture," Mr. Li went on. "Our valley is hidden and difficult to reach, and the tea is delicate. If any was taken in that earlier theft, it must not have survived the journey, because none of it can be found in the West."

"I see," I ventured. "And if Sir Jacob managed it . . ."

"It would be the end of my village, my family, possibly the tea growers in the entire region. Our tea is some of the most valuable in the world, and if it is taken, replicated, and grown far from China, the price of it will fall dramatically. There will be more hunger and more poverty, while men like Sir Jacob will grow richer. More of my countrymen will flee their native land in search of a better life, and end up in the slums of cities around the world, shunned and scorned."

He fell silent, his sorrow weighing heavily.

Daniel and I exchanged a look. I saw mirrored in Daniel's eyes what I felt—pity for this man and fascination at his story.

"I must ask, Mr. Li," I ventured, "why are you revealing this to us? If the tea is that costly, Daniel and I might knock you on the head and rush next door to tear up the house and garden until we find it. You are trusting us much."

Mr. Li gazed at me unwaveringly. "Because I am wise enough to understand when I need help. I managed, as I told you, to set an appointment with Sir Jacob. But as I say, when I arrived that night with Mr. Sutherland, Sir Jacob was not there, only Mr. Chancellor. I do not know why. And now I am suspected of murdering the man. I was not certain at first if I should confide in you, as you are only servants, but then Mr. McAdam freed me from the clutches of the police, aided by you, Mrs. Holloway. And I remember how you spoke to me with such kindness and courage the day I met you. I looked into your eyes and saw that you had a good soul." He gave me a smile. "I hope I have not offended you."

"By dismissing me as a servant?" I asked, amused. "I am one, though *domestic* is the term I prefer. I am a cook, a rather different thing from a housemaid."

"Servants in China are not the same as here," Mr. Li said.

"For one thing, you are much more . . ." He trailed off as though fearing to offend me further.

"Impertinent?" I supplied. "Rude? Brash?"

"All of those." His teeth flashed in a smile. "I beg your pardon for my rudeness."

"No, indeed," I said. "You are quite right. Well, Mr. Li, I believe I can help you. I suspect Mr. Chancellor knows exactly where the tea bush is in Sir Jacob's garden. I saw him steal cuttings from it, which he might have taken with him to Kew Gardens. Should we start there? Or in the garden next door?"

13

—◆———◆—

"The tea is there?" Mr. Li said, rising. "You are certain?"

"Not certain," I said. "Though I strongly suspect. But as it is the middle of the night, we can hardly go rushing either to Kew Gardens or next door this moment. Let us have another cup of tea and think about this calmly."

Mr. Li sat back down, though he looked as if he wanted to dash next door immediately and begin crawling through the garden as Mr. Chancellor had. I knew, however, that we had to go carefully in order not to alert the world to this theft and the tea's value.

"How did Inspector McGregor know where to find you to arrest you?" I asked Mr. Li as I poured more tea for him and set down the pot. "He didn't send constables running up and down Limehouse and the docklands until they chanced upon you, did he?"

Daniel answered before Mr. Li could. "Chancellor gave McGregor his name, as he met Mr. Li the night he came to call on Sir Jacob, and told McGregor that Mr. Li was a translator. Chancellor didn't remember Sutherland's name, but Mc-Gregor was wise enough to ask at museums and Oriental societies until he was directed to Mr. Li's lodgings. I did the same, which is how I found out about Mr. Sutherland. Because Sutherland is a Cambridge man, I knew Thanos would know him—being Thanos, he is naturally acquainted with everyone who ever attended."

"You went to Cambridge," I said, lifting my teacup. "Or so you told me."

"I was there, yes." Daniel's gaze was steady, giving nothing away. "But no one knows the place and its people like Thanos."

"I lodge with another Chinese gentleman who works as an interpreter," Mr. Li finished. "Near the British Museum."

"I see. At least the inspector let you go," I finished in relief.

Daniel and Mr. Li exchanged a glance. "He didn't," Daniel said. "Not really. Mr. Li is under a sort of house arrest. He can go to his translation jobs, but if he leaves his lodgings for anywhere else, I must accompany him. I barely convinced Mc-Gregor to agree to the last bit."

"But we ruled you out as a suspect," I said to Mr. Li.

Mr. Li gave me an amused look. "Your Inspector McGregor does not want to lose sight of me. In case he can find no one else who committed this deed."

"Blast the man," I muttered.

"If McGregor truly thought you the culprit, Mr. Li, you'd even now be in Newgate," Daniel said. "The inspector isn't the sort who'd send you to prison and a trial without evidence, but I admit he's hedging his bets."

"I agree Inspector McGregor is careful," I said. "And, I must allow, fair." I pushed back my chair and rose. The two men did as well, but I waved them to sit down. "While it is far too late to skulk about the Harknesses' garden, and Kew is closed for the night, I might be able to show you what Mr. Chancellor took from the garden next door. Do enjoy your tea, gentlemen. I will return shortly."

Daniel gave me a puzzled look, but Mr. Li did not look hopeful. Resigned, rather, as though uncertain I could help.

I ascended the back stairs through the main house, very quietly opening the door to the second floor. All was silent and dark, with only the street lighting outside trickling through the windows on the landings.

I tapped softly on Lady Cynthia's door. She rarely went to bed early, unlike her aunt and uncle, but tonight her room held no lights. I peeked inside, but the bedchamber was silent, felt empty. Lady Cynthia was not at home.

Slipping in, I closed the door, then fumbled with matches on the mantelpiece and lit a lamp.

Lady Cynthia's chamber was neither feminine and frilly nor stiffly masculine. The decor was restrained, more fitting for a guest chamber than one belonging to a member of the family.

The bed's plain blue coverlet matched the draperies at the window, and a bookcase held books next to an upholstered chair. A dressing table contained a brush and comb, a box of pins to hold Cynthia's hair in its unadorned style, and a small jewel box with four drawers. No ribbons and laces, gloves or fans, dance cards or carefully kept letters, nothing of a young woman poised to begin her life. All was simple, neat, and unremarkable.

She and Bobby were doubtless together tonight, smoking cigars at Bobby's flat, or pretending to enjoy risqué magazines at a gentlemen's gathering place.

I doubted Cynthia would carry the cuttings with her, and

I hoped she'd left them where I could easily find them. She'd have to keep them away from Sara, the upstairs maid who tended her clothes, and the tweeny who cleaned the room. Either maid might mistake the cuttings for unwanted clutter and put them on the rubbish heap.

I turned in a circle in the middle of the room, taking in the bedside tables, the chest at the foot of the bed, the bookcases, the dressing table. The room was large and airy, with a chandelier hanging from the ceiling, gaslights that would cast a bright glow when lit.

My eye fell again on the jewel box on the dressing table. It was a square thing of carved wood with a keyhole above the top drawer.

The jewel box was locked, but a rummage in the dressing table turned up the key, tossed carelessly into a tray inside the middle drawer.

The key fit the jewel box, and I carefully went through it, noting that Cynthia's jewelry was old fashioned and sparse. I'd seen her sister wear some of it, probably handed down from their mother.

In the third drawer down, wrapped in tissue, I found the cuttings. I eased them from their hiding place and closed and locked the jewel box. I returned the key to the dressing table drawer, placing it exactly where I'd found it, then I blew out the lamp and left the room.

Downstairs, I entered the kitchen and spread the cuttings of green leaves before Mr. Li.

"Is this the plant you are looking for?"

I had no idea what tea looked like on the bush—I'd only seen it dried and rolled in a box from the market. These leaves were about the size and shape of bay leaves, but serrated, waxy, and deep green, a bit wilted now.

Mr. Li looked them over carefully and lifted a cutting to his nose.

"All tea comes from the same plant—*Camellia sinensis*," he said, his soft voice taking on the note of a lecturer. "It is the preparation of the tea leaves, and which tea leaves are used, that distinguishes the quality of one tea from another. However, there are a few varieties of the bush that grow in China and nowhere else." He laid the branch on the tissue, his expression sad. "This is not the tea plant stolen from my father."

"Oh," I said in disappointment. "Then why did Mr. Chancellor so covertly take his cutting? He must have been convinced it was the tea."

Mr. Li pushed the leaves toward me. "He was mistaken. But that means, we may thank the gods, that he has not yet found it."

I thought Mr. Li would depart after that, dejected, but neither man seemed in a hurry to rush off, which was to my liking. We shared more of the tea, and Mr. Li told us a little about his life at the emperor's court, which included much formality and etiquette. He told us how he greatly enjoyed visiting his home when he could and spending simple days with his father. From the way he spoke, I gathered that he hadn't seen his family in some time.

At last he and Daniel took their leave, and I went to bed, displeased I hadn't handed Mr. Li an immediate solution. I rose at my usual hour in the morning, washed my hands and face, and went downstairs to begin cooking for the day.

Mrs. Daley entered the kitchen once we had eggs boiling on the stove, while Tess chopped potatoes for bangers and mash for the staff.

"Why don't you step into the larder, Tess?" Mrs. Daley said. "I need to speak to Mrs. Holloway."

Tess utterly ignored her. She continued dicing potatoes, dropping the cut pieces into a large pot of salted water.

"We are very busy just now," I said to Mrs. Daley. "I will speak to you after service."

Mrs. Daley sniffed. "Very well, I will say my piece in front of witnesses, and you may take the consequences. I saw you in Lady Cynthia's bedchamber last night. You rifled her jewel box, and you left the room with something in your hand. What was it you stole?"

Tess looked up in astonishment. Elsie's dish clattering broke off in the scullery, and she craned to look through the doorway, her eyes wide.

"Don't you be accusing Mrs. Holloway like that," Tess began. "You didn't see nuffink, you old—"

"Hush, Tess," I broke in. I looked Mrs. Daley in the eye. "I was in the chamber, yes, but I was fetching something Lady Cynthia asked me to give to Mr. McAdam."

Not exactly the truth, but I knew Lady Cynthia wouldn't have minded me showing the cuttings to Daniel and Mr. Li. In fact, if I'd decided to wait and ask her for them, she'd likely demand to know why I hadn't simply gone into her room and retrieved the blasted things.

Daniel had taken one of the cuttings away with him, and I'd tucked the other into my drawer upstairs, not wanting to enter Lady Cynthia's chamber again last night.

"Mr. McAdam?" Mrs. Daley asked in puzzlement. "You mean that scruffy-looking villain who brings in sacks of potatoes? What on earth could Lady Cynthia want to give *him*? But yes, I know he was here last night, and I know he brought a dirty Chinaman with him, and you let them both right into the kitchen. You served them a cup of tea, of all things. What had the likes of them to do in the mistress's house? And in the middle of the night?"

A woman like Mrs. Daley labeling Mr. Li a "dirty China-man" made my blood boil. The man was worth a hundred of her, and I'd gladly spend weeks listening to his stories than one more day with Mrs. Daley.

I drew myself up, my voice going cold. "Whomever I let into *my* kitchen is my business. And if you'd gone to Lady Cynthia about the matter instead of confronting me with in-sinuations, she would no doubt agree that she had left some-thing for me to give Daniel—I mean, Mr. McAdam. And if I share a cup of tea with gentlemen who work very hard, that is also my business. It was *my* tea—nothing purchased for the house. My personal box." Which was again safely upstairs, hidden with the tea leaves from Sir Jacob's garden.

"But it is not *your* kitchen, is it?" Mrs. Daley said. "Mrs. By-water is mistress of this house, not you. Even Lady Cynthia is a poor relation at best. And where was *she* all night, I ask? Not in her bed, that is for certain. But you knew this, which is why you knew you were safe to rummage about in her chamber."

"For heaven's sake, Mrs. Daley—" I snapped.

"And it ain't your place to go hosting tea parties at mid-night. You are to cook the meals and retire for the night, and that is all. I know your sort, Mrs. Holloway. You think because you have a little skill at cookery, you can put your feet up like a queen and have the lords and ladies bow down to you. *And* entertain your beaus in the night like a hussy. It's *my* place as housekeeper to see that you don't."

I faced her, nose to nose. "It is *your* place to keep the rest of the house running smoothly, while I tend the kitchen. Your place is not to be underfoot while I'm cooking, nor to gather odds and ends the maids didn't put away and shut them in your parlor. Nor to steal the master's brandy. How much did you drink before Mr. Davis noticed it had gone missing?"

Mrs. Daley went brick red. "How *dare* you?"

"How dare you accuse *me* of stealing from Lady Cynthia? What were you doing snooping around the house in the night, in any case? Were you looking for more things to pilfer?"

"I told you why those things were in my room."

"And I told you why I was in Lady Cynthia's chamber."

Mrs. Daley backed a step, but she hadn't finished. "I am certain the mistress would be interested to know that you let a Chinese person into her house, especially after one of those vermin killed the master next door. Was it the same man? Are you hiding him? Perhaps you had a hand in it?"

"Now you are being amazingly ridiculous."

"You are up to something, Mrs. Holloway," Mrs. Daley said with conviction. "You mind your manners with me, or I go to the mistress with it."

"Do you mean to blackmail me into being courteous to you?" I demanded. "If you did your job instead of haranguing me, absconding with the brandy, and reading magazines all day, we might get along nicely."

"If I harangue you, it's for your own good," Mrs. Daley said. "You are wasteful, extravagant, and arrogant—I understood that from the moment I clapped eyes on you. You're far too young and impertinent to be in service. When *I* was a cook, I got the meals on the table without putting on airs, and those upstairs was grateful to get them."

"Which makes me wonder why you are not a cook any longer," I returned. "Mine is not a shameful profession. Perhaps those upstairs couldn't stomach what you made and so you had to change to housekeeping. Which, I must tell you, involves a great deal more than simply bullying the maids and harassing the cook. How did you come by this post, anyway? Are you a special friend of Mrs. Bywater's?"

Her deepening flush told me I'd hit close to the mark. "Mrs. Bywater was happy to have me. I come highly recommended."

"As do I, Mrs. Daley. I have references from some of the best families in England, because I cook very well, never mind how young I am. So I must beg you to leave me to it."

"That does not make you any less arrogant, my girl." Mrs. Daley stepped close to me once again. "I warn you, do not cross me any more than you already have, or you will be out on your ear. Won't be a thing Lady Cynthia can do about it— her lord and lady dad and mum won't be happy when I tell them she's chummy with a cook and gadding about in the small hours with another lady in trousers. Lady Cynthia abets you in lording over the rest of the house, and Mrs. Bywater and I intend to see that it stops."

Rage seared through me, but what I would have said next I do not know, because at that moment, Tess hefted the tub of water and potatoes.

"You shut your gob, you old bitch!" she shouted, and she hurled the contents of the tub at Mrs. Daley.

I screeched and shoved Mrs. Daley out of the way. Mr. Davis came charging in, just as the water, which Tess couldn't stop, poured over me in a great salty, potatoey wave, drenching me from head to foot.

Mr. Davis halted, his patent-leather shoes just shy of the spreading water. Tess dropped the tub and gaped at me, eyes wide in horror. For a moment, all was silent but for the water dripping to the slate floor.

Mrs. Daley grabbed Tess by the ear. "You bloody little

hellion, you get out of this house and back to the street where you belong."

Tess kicked out, twisting in the woman's grasp, her language raw.

"Tess!" I shouted. "Stop! Mrs. Daley, release her at once."

"She's not fit to work in a lady's house," Mrs. Daley said, dragging Tess toward the scullery. Elsie dropped her rag into the dirty dishwater and cringed against the wall.

Mr. Davis skirted the puddle and shoved himself between Mrs. Daley and the scullery door. "Mrs. Daley!" he roared in his most stentorian tones.

Mr. Davis rarely shouted, but when he did, his voice could rattle the windows. Mrs. Daley halted in uncertainty, which gave Tess the opportunity to wrench herself away from her. Tess picked up her skirts and kicked at Mrs. Daley, but missed in her agitation, thank heavens.

Mrs. Daley and Mr. Davis faced each other, Mr. Davis with his head up and shoulders square.

"Keep to your place." Mr. Davis spoke each word slowly then shut his mouth.

While Mr. Davis could be pompous and somewhat absurd, he knew his job and did it very well. He had a natural authority, and Mrs. Daley, under his stern stare, was becoming aware of that authority.

Mr. Davis did not have to say another word. As we watched, Mrs. Daley visibly wilted.

"The mistress will hear of this," she muttered before she swung around and marched from the kitchen.

She attempted to leave with dignity, but she slipped on the wet floor, scrambled to remain upright, and stumbled from the room. We heard her footsteps on the back stairs and then the door slam at the top.

"Run away, you nasty witch," Tess snarled.

"Tess," I said sharply. "Mind your tongue. Mop up this water and throw away the potatoes, and then you scrub and peel another dozen, right quick. And shame on you for that display. You never, ever turn on those above you, and never with brutality. We are not savages on the streets."

Tess planted her hands on her hips. "Well, I weren't trying to hit *you*. Why'd you get in the way, Mrs. H.? She deserved a drenching."

"I did it to save you from being dismissed, you silly girl. Who knows what she might have done had you succeeded? She might even have sent for the police. Now clean this up, and we'll say no more about it."

I wrested off my apron and flung it down. I'd have to change my gown before I could continue—I was soaked through all the way to my petticoats.

Mr. Davis started for the hall as Elsie ran in with a mop to help Tess. Elsie's eyes were shining, and she fought to keep a grin from her face.

I met Mr. Davis in the kitchen doorway, where we faced each other in mutual admiration.

"Thank you, Mr. Davis," I said. "I mean that with great sincerity."

Mr. Davis met my gaze. "Not at all, Mrs. Holloway. I might have just given us all the sack, but it was worth it."

We did not see Mrs. Daley the rest of the day. She remained upstairs for the entire morning, and I did not notice that she'd returned to her parlor until the servants took their tea in the afternoon. She must have slipped in while they gathered noisily in the servants' hall, because I saw that the parlor door was shut tight again—and locked—after that.

"Tea" was a grand name for the meal the servants had in midafternoon, before they waited at table or prepared the ladies for their evening outings. Today, I made sure there was plenty of bread and butter, along with seedcake and leftover rissoles.

Tess and I kept ourselves in the kitchen, not speaking much to each other. She was not at all contrite that she'd thrown the water at Mrs. Daley and was only sorry that it had hit me. I could see I had a long journey ahead to polish her.

On the other hand, I couldn't help my glee that she'd stood right up to Mrs. Daley, especially in my defense. Tess was a brave young woman, and I was pleased to see she'd never be cowed.

Cynthia arrived downstairs as another seedcake was coming out of the oven. She wore her man's clothes and seemed refreshed and sprightly in spite of her night out.

I cut off a large hunk of the warm cake for her. I did not mention the confrontation with Mrs. Daley—I did not want to trouble her with such things or confess I had temporarily lost control of Tess—but I did tell her I had entered her room and taken the tea leaves, to ask Mr. Li about them.

"It's quite all right," she said, sitting down at the kitchen table to partake. "I ought to have given them to you for safekeeping in the first place. What did your Chinaman make of them?"

"He said they were tea," I answered glumly. "Nothing more significant." I did not add the tale of the tea stolen from Mr. Li's family, as the kitchen full of servants was not the place to discuss it.

Cynthia chewed through a large bite of cake. "I'd say

the significant thing is that Mr. Chancellor took some cuttings."

"Yes, I have been wondering why he did, if it was ordinary tea—he'd know that, surely. Tomorrow is my day out. I have a mind to spend it at the gardens at Kew. Perhaps you would care to visit it again?"

Cynthia nodded. "I would. What better place to hide an exotic plant than in a realm of exotic plants?"

I busied myself neatly stacking more slices of bread. "Perhaps Mr. Thanos would join us." I spoke lightly, as though I didn't care one way or the other.

"Perhaps." Cynthia's tone was so nonchalant that I risked a look at her. She was frowning at the seedcake. "But you'll have to keep it a deep, dark secret. That goes for you too, Tess."

I blinked, my butter knife poised over a slice of bread. Tess made the motion of locking her lips and tossing away the key. Cynthia, finished with her cake, pushed back her chair and left the kitchen, boots ringing on the slates.

"That's interestin'," Tess said, sotto voce. "Wonder if the master barred the door to Mr. Thanos? Be a pity if he did—Mr. Thanos is a kind man, even if he is a bit odd. Ooh, I'm gossiping about my betters again, ain't I?" She sent me a grin, in no way worried. "'Course, I'll have to gossip about my betters to tell you the goings-on next door, won't I?"

"Don't be impertinent," I said, but gently. "And yes, I suppose you are right. What have you found out?"

She looked mysterious. "I'm still gathering information. You have your day out, and then I'll tell you all about it."

She serenely continued to sort greens for this evening's meal, and I didn't press her.

The next morning, I rose early to ready myself for my day out. I would fetch Grace and then we'd spend the entire day at Kew. I was in a way relieved Cynthia had discovered Grace's existence, because I could search for Mr. Li's tea with her without having to sacrifice my day with my daughter.

Mrs. Daley hadn't appeared by the time we finished breakfast, and I hurried a bit with my preparations for the rest of the day so I could leave before I encountered her.

Tess filled a large pot with water and placed it on the table then began to peel potatoes. I eyed the pot as I untied my apron.

"You are not to throw that water at Mrs. Daley," I said sternly.

"I won't." Tess kept her gaze on her peeling, but her smile was sly. "But I'll keep it here as a warning."

As I drew breath to admonish her, Mr. Davis, in his shirt-sleeves and waistcoat, strode in waving a newspaper.

"He's been murdered!" he declared.

Tess jumped, a potato slipping from her hands. My apron strings suddenly knotted and my fingers fumbled.

"Who has?" I asked. "You shouldn't shout such things, Mr. Davis."

"Your Chinese man, Mrs. Holloway." Mr. Davis threw the newspaper to the table without apology. "He was found in Kew Gardens, in what they call the Temperate House, strangled in the shrubbery. What a turnup, eh?"

14

Blackness spun before my eyes like sudden night. I staggered and the edge of the table dug into my hip, the only thing holding me upright.

I pictured the serious face of Mr. Li as he described the mountains of his childhood, the precious tea growing there, the theft that had brought him thousands of miles from his home. He was a harmless old man, trying to right a wrong. He didn't deserve to die, nor did his family deserve to be stolen from. Sir Jacob, the Old China Hand, had used his expertise about the country to locate the most precious bits of it, tear them out, and cart them home.

Mr. Li had searched for what had been taken, and now he'd been killed as well. Had Mr. Chancellor done this? Or had one of the others connected to Sir Jacob's household—Mrs. Knowles, Mr. Pasfield, Sheppard—followed Mr. Li, worried, since he'd been near that night, he'd have seen who murdered Sir Jacob? I wished the bloody lot of them at the bottom of the sea.

Mr. Li was supposed to have been confined to his lodgings, with Daniel watching over him. Had he slipped out and gone to Kew Gardens, because he reasoned the tea might be there?

Which led me to the question, where the devil was Daniel?

Tess's touch brought me out of my stupor, her brown eyes filled with worry. "You all right, Mrs. H.?"

I finished tugging my apron strings apart and flung the apron over a kitchen chair. "Yes," I said, breathless. "I'm off."

I snatched my coat from a peg near the door and shrugged it on, only just remembering to snatch off my cook's cap before jamming on my hat. Not until I was out the back door and halfway up the stairs to the street did I realize I hadn't changed out of my gray work dress, but it couldn't be helped. I did not want to take the time to go back now.

Nor did I intend to fetch Grace before I rushed off to Kew Gardens. I did not want her anywhere near where a man had been murdered.

"Wait for me, Mrs. H." Cynthia's light footfalls sounded behind me. I slowed until she fell into step with me, Cynthia clad in trousers and greatcoat. "I saw the newspaper and came downstairs to tell you about the murder, only to see you racing out the door. Let's get a hansom, shall we?"

The cabbies who regularly roved this neighborhood knew Lady Cynthia, and one stopped as she waved him down. "Victoria Station," she ordered. "Quick as you can."

"Yes, my lady." He was more patient than the driver who'd taken Mr. Thanos and me home from Scotland Yard, and held the horse long enough for us to be seated before he set off.

Waves of sorrow and anger poured over me—as soon as

one ebbed, another came. "It isn't fair," I said, feeling hollow. "He'd done nothing."

Cynthia nodded her understanding, her face set in grim lines. I knew I had no absolute proof that Mr. Li hadn't killed Sir Jacob, only my conviction, but my instincts had been correct before.

The ride down Park Lane past the statue of the Duke of Wellington and along Grosvenor Place took what seemed an immensely long time. The cab rolled on past the gardens of Buckingham Palace before we alighted at Victoria Street and hurried into the massive station.

Cynthia purchased the tickets, and we leapt onto the first train departing to the west. She'd procured us seats in a first-class carriage on an aboveground train, and we arrived in an hour at Kew Gardens station, where I had come with Grace on Monday.

The garden wall rose before us, grim and gray, befitting a place that had witnessed a death.

It must witness thousands of deaths, I thought incongruously. Plants lived, thrived, and then died here; some of the flora brought in from other continents perished. Not every living thing could stand the climate of England.

The wind had pushed in clouds up the river, and now rain began. I hadn't brought an umbrella, and neither had Cynthia, but we strode so quickly the drops hardly had time to wet us.

The park was not yet open for the day, but the constable who had been patrolling on my last visit spied us and admitted us. I let him believe Daniel had given the order for him to do so.

All was quiet beyond the gates. Gardeners puttered among the green near the pagoda, but none moved near the great structure of the Temperate House. A constable stood by that house's front door, ready to bar our way.

Before Lady Cynthia or I could demand entrance, the door opened and Daniel emerged. He was dressed in work clothes, hat in place, but his affable look was absent.

"I thought you'd come," he said. "All right, Constable."

The guard did not look happy to admit two ladies, one dressed as a gentleman, the other a domestic, but he obeyed Daniel.

"What happened?" I cried as Daniel led us in out of the rain. "What was Mr. Li doing here?" I lowered my voice. "Do you think he found his tea? Is that why he was killed?"

Daniel frowned. "Mr. Li? No, Kat. The dead man isn't Mr. Li. It is a much younger chap. But I'm afraid McGregor thinks Mr. Li might have killed him as well."

I halted so abruptly that Lady Cynthia ran into me. She steadied us both with a hand on my shoulder, and I dropped the skirts I'd lifted from the damp, my hands suddenly numb.

"Not Mr. Li?" I breathed out, the close, clammy air in the greenhouse making me dizzy. "Thank the Lord. Oh, thank the Lord."

"Forgive me," Daniel said, his voice gentling. "I should have sent word. I didn't realize you'd think it was our friend."

I hadn't–Mr. Davis had said so, and I hadn't looked at the newspaper to make certain.

As I regained my senses, the second thing Daniel said struck me. "But Mr. Li couldn't have killed anyone," I protested. "He's under house arrest, remember? Looked after by you."

"I'm afraid I've lost sight of him," Daniel said, crestfallen. "He wasn't at his boardinghouse last night when I looked in on him. The man he lodges with said he'd gone out not a half hour before I arrived, but Mr. Li never returned while I waited—and I waited a blasted long time. His fellow lodger was tasked to make certain Mr. Li stayed home, but apparently Mr. Li slipped out. I searched the area and never found him. Still haven't. I don't know where he's got to." Fury and frustration filled his words.

"Well, if the dead man isn't Mr. Li, who is it?" Cynthia demanded.

"That is the question," Daniel answered, his mouth a tight line. "I was here when the body was found, but I did not recognize the man. No one did. He's been taken away, but I can show you where he was."

I appreciated that Daniel did not seem at all worried about taking the two of us to where a man had been killed. As we moved down a paved walkway, my relief let me notice the huge greenhouse now, the manor house made of glass.

The ceiling stretched a long way to a lofty pointed roof. Rain pattered on the high windows, rolling to the lower roofs on either side of the enormous room. I could see the heavy clouds clearly, but we were protected in this bubble of glass.

It was cooler here than the tropical Palm House, but we'd left behind the chill of the September morning. Plenty of palm trees lived here as well, but their fronds were different from the ones in the Palm House. I'd had no idea that so many sorts of palms existed.

Shrubs thickly lined the walkways, along with trees with black, gnarled trunks hung with flowers of vibrant colors. Spiral staircases rose in opposite corners to a walkway with a white-painted wrought iron railing under the eaves.

Daniel took us at a quick pace to a corner filled with orange trees in tubs, their swelling fruit still green. Between these a square bed held a clump of bushes with broken limbs, a depression marring the earth in the middle of them.

Cynthia gazed at the ruined shrubs, gloved hands flexing. "How awful. And you don't know who the bloke was?"

Daniel shook his head. "All I know is that he is Asian—from what country, including this one, I couldn't tell you. Mr. Chancellor found the poor chap. He shouted out, and I came running."

"Mr. Chancellor?" I asked in surprise.

"Indeed." Daniel carefully parted the bushes. "That is interesting, is it not? The fellow was lying here, facedown. At first I thought he might have suffocated in the mud, but there was a cord around his neck. A piece of leather, a common enough strap someone might use to hold down a load or secure box. Nothing significant. I had the constable outside fetch the Kew police sergeant. The sergeant in turn sent a telegram to Scotland Yard, and presently McGregor turned up. This all happened at about four this morning."

The newspapers had got hold of it rapidly, but newspapermen did. Newspapers went to press in London very early and were in the hands of readers only a few hours later.

"What were *you* doing here at four in the morning?" I asked.

"Helping Chancellor. He said we had to hand-pollinate a certain mountain flower, which opens only at night, and apparently there is but a small window of time in which to do it. He disappeared from his greenhouse without a word while I was back among the shelves, and I had to follow quickly to keep him in sight. He came here—and not long later found the body. He's back in his greenhouse now, at his trays."

"Coolheaded of him," Cynthia said, peering down the walkway.

"He was most upset," Daniel said. "Panic-stricken, even, but happy to leave the details of the police to me. Sending him back to his plants seemed the kindest thing."

"Hmm," Cynthia said. "At least he didn't flee, which could mean he had nothing to do with the man's death."

"Or he is an obsessive botanist," Daniel said. "More important to pollinate his flowers than run for his life."

"What are these bushes?" I asked, indicating where the man had been found. "Not tea, I think."

"*Laurustinus*," Daniel answered. "They flower in winter, white and pink, Chancellor told me."

"Are there tea bushes here?" Cynthia asked. I had told her Mr. Li's tale as we'd traveled on the train, begging her to keep the secret, and she'd readily agreed, understanding why the secret was important. I hoped Mr. Li would forgive me bringing her into our confidence—if we ever found him.

"In the Temperate House?" Daniel answered. "Yes. But not here. They're on the far side."

"Possibly nothing to do with tea then," Cynthia went on, but she sounded skeptical. "Or Mr. Li."

"Why was the dead man in the Temperate House at all?" I asked. "How did *he* get in, in the middle of the night? I assume the doors are locked, as some of these plants are valuable."

Daniel nodded. "All are valuable, some priceless. Some grow nowhere else but here or in their native home. So, yes, the doors are bolted and guarded."

I gazed upward at all the glass. The windows on the ground floor were tightly closed, but those under the eaves had been propped open for air.

"Could a man scale the walls to the top windows?" I asked. "Did he appear to be athletic?"

"He was slim and lithe, yes," Daniel said. "It would be difficult, but not impossible. But guards look up as well."

"In the dark, on a cloudy night, with the guards unable to look all places at all times . . ."

"As I say, not impossible," Daniel agreed. "But no matter how the man entered, he did, and someone else found him, and killed him."

"Without the guards or constables hearing?" I asked.

"It seems so." Daniel's voice held sadness.

"I wonder if he saw an open window and took a chance," Cynthia mused. "Which brings up the question—did he climb the walls to enter Kew at all, or hide while the gates were shut for the day? Was he hired to steal something specific? Or was he after something for himself?"

None of us could answer.

"May we see the tea bushes?" I asked.

Daniel gave me a nod and led us through the great house. We passed the main entrance, and then went down a shorter walkway to a gathering of green bushes whose leaves were like those of the cuttings Cynthia and I had taken from Sir Jacob's garden. So similar, in fact, that I would never have been able to tell the difference.

"These have been planted from seeds brought back from the Himalayas, from Darjeeling," Daniel said. "And those were originally taken from China. These are the full-grown specimens—they have others they study in smaller greenhouses that are closed to all but botanists."

"Will they let *you* into these greenhouses?" Cynthia asked. "As a botanist's assistant?"

"Only when one needs help carrying heavy objects. The greenhouses are full of growing trays and pots, seedlings and plants too delicate to move. The botanists experiment with light and heat, types of soil, amounts of water and what is in the water, as well as transplanting and grafting. They also dissect the plants to study them, and compare different varieties of the same species."

I took in the greenery around me, the trees reaching for the gray sky. "Why did the man come here instead of breaking into those greenhouses? These plants are large and well rooted."

"Unless he found it easiest to get into this place," Cynthia said. "And didn't know where the special plants were kept. And as Mr. Chancellor did, he could have stolen cuttings."

Daniel nodded. "He might have systematically been working his way through all the greenhouses when he was caught. But we don't know anything except that he slipped inside here. Whether he meant to steal, or meet someone, or just wanted to look about, who is to say?"

"A thief would have to understand that the plants were valuable and which ones to take," I said. "Not everyone would know that."

"They ought to," Cynthia said. "It's blasted in the newspapers whenever they talk about Kew. I'm surprised the place isn't overrun with plant thieves."

Daniel's lips twitched, his face softening. "Not every man knows how to sell such things to the receivers. Your average thief is looking to shift silver candlesticks, fine clothes, pocket watches, handkerchiefs."

"But presumably there are people who deal in stolen plants," I said. "Just as some must specialize in old books or paintings."

"Indeed, there are," Daniel said. "There's a market for everything in London, if you know where to look."

I glanced up at the rain pattering on the roof, the rivulets of water rolling down the glass. "I'd like to speak to Inspector McGregor, to perhaps find out if the dead man has anything to do with Sir Jacob, and Mr. Li's purloined tea."

"We only think so because the newspapers said he was Chinese," Lady Cynthia pointed out. "A tenuous connection."

"Murdered in a place where stolen tea might have been brought by a man who is also now dead," I said. "More than tenuous, I think."

"I understand you, Mrs. H. I was trying not to get your hopes up."

"I have no hope at all of untangling this mess," I said wearily. "I only want the inspector to leave Mr. Li alone."

"Mr. Li might be guilty of this crime, Kat," Daniel reminded me. "I have no idea where he is at the moment, remember."

"*Might*," I said. "I refuse to condemn a man with so little proof."

Daniel studied me, as did Cynthia. Then Daniel gave me an understanding nod and led us to a side door. He procured a large umbrella from a stand near the door and handed it to Cynthia before we went out into the rain.

The umbrella was wide enough for Cynthia to share with me and keep her man's hat from the wet. Daniel didn't bother with one for himself but hunkered into his coat, pulling his cap low.

He took us down the walks to the park constable's house, opening the door to a warm, stuffy room that smelled of boiled tea.

A counter upon which rested piles of papers and a box marked *Lost Property* divided the front of the room from the empty desks behind it. Notices about known thieves and warnings to park goers to mind their pockets hung on the walls.

Daniel walked around the counter and down a narrow hall, knocking on the door at the end.

"What is it?" came the snarl of Inspector McGregor.

Daniel opened the door and ushered us inside. A table had been pulled to the middle of the room, leaving its chairs behind. On top of the table lay an unmoving human being covered by a blanket.

A constable sat at a desk near a window, the young man trying to make himself small and unnoticed, a difficult task because he was so large. He jumped to his feet when we entered, hovering uncertainly.

Inspector McGregor leaned over a desk on the far side of the room, resting his weight on his fists as he studied papers strewn there. He glanced around as we entered and did not hide his dismay.

He managed to give Lady Cynthia a muttered, "Your ladyship," before he glared at me and Daniel. "Not your case, McAdam."

"I've been told to take an interest. I'm sorry, sir. I know it is an annoyance."

"Don't try to talk me 'round. This is enough of a bother without my superiors sending you to put your oar in. And you bring *her*." He pointed a blunt finger at me.

"Mrs. Holloway was distressed," Daniel said before I could speak. "The newspapers only said the dead man was a Chinaman, and she feared Mr. Li had been killed."

"Well, he hasn't been," McGregor growled. "But he might have done the deed. I'll not let you look at that body, Mrs. Holloway. Or you, Lady Cynthia. He's been strangled, which is gruesome and not a sight for ladies."

The constable went a bit green at the mention, and I wondered if he'd ever seen a dead body before.

"He is a young man," Daniel told Lady Cynthia and me. "I'd say twenty at most. Dressed in Chinese-style clothes but topped with a Western coat. All are in need of a wash, but of decent quality. I did not have time to look in his pockets."

"Well, I did," the inspector said in a hard voice.

Cynthia raised her brows. "You sound as though you didn't like what you found, Inspector."

"What *did* you find?" I asked as McGregor closed his mouth again. "Could you discover who he is?"

"I could." The word was short. "He carried papers that let him travel to this country and an introductory letter." He indicated the sheets that lay on the desk. "All are in English. His name, these tell me, was Zhen. Zhen Harkness."

15

⁌ ⁍

"Harkness?" Lady Cynthia exclaimed as my eyes widened. "Good Lord," I said breathlessly.

"Yes." Inspector McGregor looked quite angry. "The letter claims that Sir Jacob Harkness was this young man's natural father and that Sir Jacob looked after him and let him use his name. The young man came to England seeking employment, or so the letter says. The papers indicate he entered the country two weeks ago."

"And then his father was murdered," I said softly.

"That is so, Mrs. Holloway. A Chinese young man comes to England searching for his English father, and not long after that, his father is found dead. Doesn't look good for the wife now, does it?"

"Or another who didn't want this fellow to inherit whatever his father might have left him," Lady Cynthia suggested.

"I had a look at Sir Jacob's will," Daniel said. "It is a public record," he said to McGregor's outraged face. "I saw it yesterday.

No one by the name of Zhen Harkness was mentioned. Any son, for that matter."

"Doesn't let anyone off," McGregor said. "Maybe Sir Jacob was killed before he could change his will and leave part of his vast fortune to a Chinese by-blow. I can imagine the family and friends were incensed by this lad turning up."

"But why murder him now?" I asked. "If he received nothing?"

Daniel spread his hands. "Sir Jacob might have given him something, promised him something, whether it was in his official will or not. He must have been fond of the lad if he'd been willing to accept him and take care of him. I imagine there are plenty of half-caste children all over the Orient whose fathers can't be bothered to acknowledge their existence."

"Britannia rules the waves," McGregor said dryly. "All those sailors need something to do on shore leave. Oh, I beg your pardon, Lady Cynthia."

"No bother," Cynthia said. "You should hear what the sons of the Home Office ministers say at their drinking establishments when they don't realize a woman is near. Far, far worse, believe me."

McGregor scowled at her, his face reddening. "I'd think you'd want to spare yourself that."

Cynthia shrugged, too carelessly. "It's a lark, isn't it?"

McGregor continued to scowl. "In any case, this son came to England looking for his father, and now both he and his father are dead."

He did not like this turn of events—I forbore from telling him that young Zhen likely was even more unhappy with the situation.

"Did Sir Jacob come to meet him, I wonder?" I asked. "The

night he was killed, I mean. He'd been to Kew Gardens for some reason. Perhaps he arranged to meet his son here."

"Possibly," Daniel agreed. "Sir Jacob contributed so much to the garden he likely had the run of the place." He turned to the constable who continued to look nervous in the presence of Inspector McGregor. "Did anyone see Sir Jacob here that night?"

"No, sir." The constable's voice squeaked. "There was such a mist. We patrolled with lanterns as usual, but we could easily have missed someone in the dark."

McGregor's disgust was evident. "I've had words with the sergeant, who is doing penance by searching every inch of this park with the rest of his men."

I'd wondered why the office was so deserted. I felt sudden sympathy for the Kew Gardens constabulary.

Lady Cynthia directed her next question to Daniel. "What did Mr. Chancellor say when he found the body?"

"He did nothing but make distressed noises and lose his breakfast," Daniel answered. "I had to hustle him outside."

The constable made a faint retching sound. "You should have a cup of tea," I told him. "You'll feel better."

"Mr. Chancellor had a cuppa before he fled back to his plants," McGregor growled. "He's being a bit of a woman about things."

"There is nothing wrong with being a woman, Inspector," I said. "We are sensible creatures and know we ought to fortify ourselves when things go wrong."

McGregor's lips pinched. "Quite."

"Thank you, Inspector," Daniel said. "Lady Cynthia and Mrs. Holloway were anxious to help, but we'll take no more of your time. Your ladyship." He gestured to the door, and Cynthia took the hint.

"Good work, Inspector," she said. "Keep it up."

She marched out, putting on her hat and unfurling the umbrella as she hit the rain. McGregor watched stonily as I turned to leave, Daniel following. I took Cynthia's arm, huddling once more under the umbrella with her.

"This puts a different complexion on things," I said to Daniel as he walked beside us. "Why would young Zhen come to Kew last night? Because he knew Sir Jacob's tea was here?"

"He could have been looking for clues to Sir Jacob's murder," Lady Cynthia suggested. "Everything is pointing back to Kew Gardens. Can't imagine the committee, or whoever runs this place, is happy with that."

"We may never know why he came," Daniel said. "Not for certain. Or why he made the long journey from China to find Sir Jacob after all this time. Or if he even knew about the tea."

"It fits though," Cynthia said. "He heard that Sir Jacob absconded from China with a valuable tea plant, one that would make any person thousands of guineas if they sell it to the right buyer. Young Zhen takes ship to find Sir Jacob, perhaps simply to be with his father, but perhaps to learn what became of the plant. They meet at Kew Gardens, deep in the fog. It might have been a happy reunion; it might not have. Families can be hellacious things. Then Sir Jacob is killed, and Zhen searches diligently for the tea or other treasure, the same as everyone else in that house."

"Sir Jacob was very kind to him," I reflected. "Many a man would ignore an illegitimate child, especially a half-caste one. Sir Jacob and Lady Harkness had no children of their own, so perhaps he wanted to leave Zhen as much as he could."

"Zhen couldn't have believed Sir Jacob's family would welcome him with open arms," Cynthia said. "Hence the covert meeting in Kew Gardens—if he was indeed the person Sir

Jacob came to meet. But here's a thought. Perhaps Zhen followed Sir Jacob home, and *he* was the Chinaman Mr. Chancellor saw lurking. He told Inspector McGregor it was Mr. Li,
because Mr. Chancellor either couldn't see well in the dark
and mist or he wanted to block Mr. Li from finding his tea.
What better way than sending him off to Newgate?"

"You are assuming Chancellor knows about the tea." Daniel dodged the spokes of the umbrella. "We don't know that
anyone knew of it, except Mr. Li. The 'treasure' Lady Harkness's housekeeper says the family friends are searching for
might be a Ming vase."

"There are several in his house," Lady Cynthia said. "Piled
next to cheap junk from a souvenir cart." She let out a laugh.
"Not sure Harkness knew the difference."

"He may have purchased any number of valuable pieces,"
I agreed. "But I will wager Mr. Chancellor *was* looking for the
tea, or at least trying to decide what sort of tea is growing in
Sir Jacob's garden. And will it survive London's climate?" I
studied the drenching rain and gray sky, which rendered the
grassy park and bedding plants a deep green in the gloom.

"Tea likes cool mists and rain. It can be cultivated here if
care is taken." Daniel grinned at my surprised look. "I read up
on it."

"Where is Mr. Chancellor's haven?" Cynthia asked. "I'm
getting soaked."

In spite of the umbrella, the breeze blew the rain over us,
and I shivered under my thick coat.

"In another greenhouse," Daniel said. "A warm one. Not
too far now."

Daniel had led us toward the outskirts of the gardens, and
now we reached a much smaller building under a clump of
trees.

Stepping out of the rain into the greenhouse was a welcome relief. I unbuttoned my coat as Cynthia shook out and folded up the umbrella.

Mr. Chancellor sat next to a small metal table, in his shirtsleeves, drinking heartily from a teacup. A long wooden box, such as those used for bedding plants, rested on a table in the middle of the room, holding clumps of large, flat leaves. Plenty of flowering plants in pots and boxes covered more tables and filled shelves along the windows.

When Mr. Chancellor spied us, he leapt to his feet, nearly knocking over the table with his tea, and grabbed his coat, which he shrugged on.

"McAdam, what . . . ?" He stared at Lady Cynthia. "Aren't you her ladyship from Mount Street? Sir Jacob's neighbor?" He turned a bit red, no doubt remembering how she'd scolded him for arguing with Sir Jacob in the middle of Lady Harkness's garden party.

"I am indeed," Cynthia said. "I heard you had a bit of a shock this morning."

"I did." Mr. Chancellor obviously didn't know what to make of Cynthia in her trousers, but he settled his coat and said nothing more.

Mr. Chancellor's beard was as brown and bushy as I remembered, the hair on top of his head thin and graying. He was portly, but more solid than fleshy. An educated gentleman, I assessed him, with a scientific job.

Cynthia scraped a wrought iron chair from the wall and sat upon it, waving Mr. Chancellor back down. "You found the young man this morning."

Daniel fetched a chair for me as well, and Mr. Chancellor did not sit until I had sunk into it, sliding out of my coat in the process. It was quite warm in here.

Mr. Chancellor let out a heavy breath as he resumed his seat. "Yes, as you say, a shock."

"McAdam told us about the night-blooming flower," Cynthia said. "Do you often come in so early for such things? You'd need keys, wouldn't you?"

Daniel seemed to be happy to let her ask the questions. He lounged against an iron beam and quietly waited for Chancellor's answers.

"I have keys to the greenhouses, yes," Mr. Chancellor said. "Though the park constables let me into the grounds. I like to work before the gates are opened to the public. Sometimes the punters interrupt me or ask questions—usually the way to the privies." He snorted a cynical laugh.

"What sort of work do you do?" Cynthia asked, sounding admiring. "Must be fascinating."

Mr. Chancellor looked pleased at her interest. "I examine stamens and pistils, do experiments to see if I can replicate a plant, or make it flourish. It's to do with . . ." He broke off and turned quite red. "Reproduction."

"Ah." Cynthia grinned at him. "A bit less lurid when it's a plant."

Mr. Chancellor opened and closed his mouth, clearly at a loss. "It is absorbing," he managed.

"Must be. So you arrived early to see how your flowers were faring. Where do you do this work?"

"Here." Mr. Chancellor sounded surprised. "These are my plants."

I looked over the bright yellow and red flowers straining upward from their pots and boxes as though seeking the rain they could not reach.

"In that case, why did you go to the Temperate House?" Cynthia asked.

Mr. Chancellor hemmed, cleared his throat, cleared it again. His eyes moved quickly from her to Daniel and back.

"To check on transplants," he said at last, as though happy he'd thought of a plausible reason. "When I finish here, I take plants to beds in the Temperate House, where they are left to thrive, and also to serve as displays."

"Quite lovely they are too," Cynthia said. "So you went to check your plants in the Temperate House, and found the young man facedown in the bushes."

Mr. Chancellor shuddered. "I didn't realize he was dead. I thought he'd fallen—how or why, I couldn't say. I was about to roll him over, when McAdam here reached me. We turned him over together. I was amazed he was Chinese."

"Then what did you do?" Cynthia asked.

"I . . . well, I had a bit of a turn." He gave her a sheepish smile.

"Not a surprise," Cynthia reassured him. "You must have been very upset."

"Yes. Yes, I was." His eyes widened as he regarded her, as though being interrogated by a lady in a man's suit was another part of the madness of a mad day. "Why are you asking me this, your ladyship? Are you assisting the police?"

"Just want to get a clear picture," Cynthia said cheerfully. "The inspector might accuse *you*, you know, and I thought you'd need a friend."

"Ah, I see." Mr. Chancellor gave her a fervent nod. "I am grateful to you, although you might have to recommend a solicitor. I rarely use them."

"Nothing wrong with that. A botanist is not knee-deep in litigation, I presume. Why did you work for Sir Jacob?" she asked as though avidly curious.

"He has interesting specimens." Mr. Chancellor brightened, his fascination with plants cutting through his shock. "He'd brought back much from China and stuck it into his garden, and asked me, as I am an expert on Asian plants, how to take care of them. Had no idea how to grow the things in England." He laughed breathily. "I had to explain that many of the mountain plants might like our wet weather, but they also prefer rocky soil, which drains easily. The roots will rot in our constant dampness." He lifted his cup and took a calm sip.

"Like the tea bushes," Cynthia said.

Mr. Chancellor choked. He dropped the cup to the table, where it rattled and bounced. He continued to cough, and Daniel leapt forward and smacked him on the back.

Cynthia righted the teacup. "You all right, man?" she asked him.

Mr. Chancellor nodded, and Daniel gave him a final pat and backed away. "Down the wrong pipe," Mr. Chancellor wheezed.

"I saw you, you know," Cynthia said. "Taking a cutting from the tea bush in Sir Jacob's garden. Why did you do that, I wonder?"

Mr. Chancellor coughed some more. I did not correct Cynthia's declaration that she'd been the one to see him in the garden—I waited to hear how Mr. Chancellor would explain.

"I must beg you to keep that to yourself, your ladyship," he said, contrite. "I would not like Lady Harkness to believe me a thief. But I was curious. Sir Jacob brought the bush back so carefully, asked me specially how to keep it thriving. I wondered if it was a significant sort of tea. So the morning after his death, I went to the garden and snipped a bit off, to bring it here to study." He looked shamefaced but not guilt stricken.

"And what did you find out?" Cynthia asked. "Is it some exotic species?"

Mr. Chancellor shook his head. "Tea is all one species. Linnaeus believed that green tea and black came from two types of bushes, but we have since learned that they do not. The process of curing the tea is different, that's all. The black is made by frying the leaves in woks and drying—" He broke off. "But that is neither here nor there. The tea was ordinary. I mean, as ordinary as a bush brought back from China can be. But no different from the thousands growing in Darjeeling or here at Kew. This was nothing special."

So Mr. Li had said, his disappointment acute.

I could no longer keep silent. "Why did you tell Inspector McGregor that you had seen Mr. Li outside the house the night Sir Jacob was killed? How did you know it was Mr. Li?"

Mr. Chancellor started. He stared at me, taking in my cook's frock as though uncertain what to make of me, but he answered with conviction.

"I know it was him, madam, because I saw him. I'd met Mr. Li before, when Sir Jacob invited him to his house to consult with him about some pottery—at least, that is what the chap said he was there to do. But I was suspicious, because Sir Jacob had gone out that night—Sir Jacob had given me leave to putter about his garden whether he was there or not. I feared Mr. Li had returned to steal the pottery the night Sir Jacob died. Perhaps he killed Sir Jacob when Sir Jacob stumbled upon him."

"You are certain it was Mr. Li?" I pressed. "Not the young Chinese man you found dead today?"

Mr. Chancellor frowned as though thinking very hard, then he flushed. "Now that you say it, it could have been this young man. It was dark, and I only saw a man in Chinese dress."

I realized as he spoke that Mr. Chancellor was the suggestible sort. I wondered whether someone in Sir Jacob's house had speculated that the Chinaman he'd seen was Mr. Li, and Mr. Chancellor had decided it was a good idea.

"It hardly matters now, does it?" Mr. Chancellor said. "The Chinese chap is dead, and if I saw him outside the house, he probably killed Sir Jacob. So the murderer has already been punished."

He lifted his cup, looking pleased that he'd cleared everything up.

I wondered if it occurred to him that we did not know for certain whether Zhen killed Sir Jacob, nor did we know who'd strangled Zhen, and why, and why the deed had been done inside the closed Temperate House at Kew Gardens.

We left Mr. Chancellor enjoying his tea, much relieved in his mind.

I was anything but. Mr. Li was missing, another man was dead, and Sir Jacob could have done anything with that tea—if it even still existed. I was cold and rain drenched, and I feared catching a chill from moving between warm moist greenhouses and the windy damp.

However, it was still my day out, and I more than ever wanted to see Grace.

Daniel walked with us to the train. The rain slackened as we went, becoming a light mist, but it was cold—autumn had truly arrived.

We reached the station and its relatively empty platform. As Cynthia approached the window to purchase the tickets, Daniel drew me behind a pillar and put his hands on my shoulders.

"Are you well, Kat?"

"As well as can be expected." My words were scratchy. "I must tell Mr. Davis to cease making announcements about murders. I always believe it is one of my friends." I recalled the horror I'd felt not many months ago when the friend I'd thought dead was Daniel.

"I planned to send for you, or at least send word about the whole affair," he said. "I had no time, and then here you were."

"You have no need to look out for me," I said in surprise. "If I draw the wrong conclusions, then it is my fault."

Daniel's fingers tightened. "I do have need. To look out for you, I mean."

Wind stirred his hair around the edges of his cap.

"Really," I said faintly. "I look out for myself."

"I don't agree. You have murders in your house and next door, you give aid to fugitives—I include myself in this number—and you put yourself in danger. You need a guardian angel. Or maybe you have one, a very good one, seeing as you are still alive."

"Quite amusing, Mr. McAdam."

Daniel drew a breath to continue our banter, but then with a jolting suddenness, he dragged me against him and closed his arms around me.

"Damnation, Kat."

Daniel was a strong man—I closed my eyes and leaned onto the solid wall of him, enjoying his warmth. There was something to be said for being held by a very good friend, a knowledge that one wasn't alone in the world.

We stood for a time, sheltered by the roof of the station house, the waning breeze drifting around us. Daniel stroked my back, and I sank into him.

"Go to your daughter," he whispered. "Forget all of this for a day."

Excellent advice, I decided.

"McAdam!" Cynthia strode toward us, her hand full of coins. Daniel released me, but calmly, as though we had nothing to be ashamed of. "You'll have to procure the tickets for us. The damned man at the window wants nothing to do with me."

Cynthia had eased down from her anger by the time we were bumping toward the heart of London, once again in a first-class compartment. Daniel had remained behind at Kew after cheerfully purchasing our tickets with the money Cynthia had shoved at him.

"It's a devil of a thing being a woman," Cynthia sighed as she threw her hat to the seat beside her. "You are to let the men of the family buy the train tickets, or at least have a servant to do it for you. When a woman wants to step outside and do a little sightseeing, she has to arrange it with seven other people first, especially if she has the misfortune to have an earl as a father."

"At one time in this country, you could go to jail for dressing as a man," I pointed out, though I couldn't argue with much conviction. The code of behavior for unmarried ladies was severe. "Times have changed somewhat."

"I probably still could be arrested," Cynthia said. "Bobby gets away with more, because she cuts off her hair and has such a gruff voice, and people don't always realize she's female. She advises me to shave off my locks, but I can't bring myself to do it." Cynthia touched the coiled knot of her very fair hair. "Ridiculous, isn't it?"

"You have lovely hair, and I can understand your reluctance to part with it. I would never cut mine either."

"But you aren't trying to live as a man. And I'm not—not really. I want a man's freedom to dress comfortably and walk where I want to, to travel where I wish, without, as I say, an army to buy the tickets and carry the bags. I prefer to remain a woman, but I want to act, dress, and do as I please."

"A difficult thing," I said in sympathy.

"Dashed difficult." Cynthia leaned back as the open lands gave way to clusters of houses and crowded streets.

"I have been meaning to ask you," I said. "You never showed the tea we took from Sir Jacob's garden to Mr. Thanos. I thought you were off to see him right after we found it."

Cynthia flushed a deep red, still looking out the window. "No," she muttered. "No, I didn't."

"Why not?"

Cynthia turned to me, shame and embarrassment in her blue eyes. "Because I'm a fool, Mrs. H. An idiot of the highest order. Maybe I do need an army to look after me, because I'm making a balls-up of my life myself."

16

⸱—⸱

"Good heavens," I said, as Cynthia continued to look distressed. "Whatever happened?"

The train clattered over points as we turned through Chiswick and headed straight east, and Cynthia heaved a sigh.

"I meant to speak to Mr. Thanos the afternoon we found the plants, yes. In fact, I went to Bedford Square to meet him in the upper room of the pub as I have before. But when I arrived, he was with a friend—that Cambridge man, Professor Sutherland."

"Mr. Sutherland?" I asked in surprised. "Did *he* put you off? I found him polite and courteous, much like Mr. Thanos."

Cynthia let out another breath. "I know, but I was in my trousers, ready to rush in all hearty, as I do. I suddenly felt awkward. Mr. Thanos takes me as I am, but I don't know Mr. Sutherland. I'm afraid I lost my nerve. I bolted into the blue. I feel a fool, but there it is."

"It's not like you to be shy," I said. "Though I believe I understand."

"Do you? Well, I don't. I flout my unconventionality and then fear what people think of me. How silly am I?" Cynthia folded her arms and slid down in her seat.

"You want Mr. Thanos's friends to like you," I said. "It's natural."

"What is natural about it? I either cleave to my convictions, or I abandon this charade."

I decided not to answer. I knew full well why Cynthia feared censure by Mr. Thanos's circle. I longed to tell her that she had no need to worry—Mr. Thanos was well smitten, in my opinion—but then, one never knew. Mr. Thanos admired Mr. Sutherland, and if Mr. Sutherland took against Cynthia, Mr. Thanos would be in a confusing spot.

"He has asked after you," I said. "Mr. Thanos, that is. I'm certain he will want to speak to you about this matter."

"Oh, I'll look him up—when I'm certain we'll be in a deep, dark cellar where none of his friends can see me. Or whenever I conquer my silly trepidation. In any case, that day, I fled to Bobby's flat for a stiff whisky and told her all about the murder and Mr. Chancellor and wondering why he was digging in Sir Jacob's garden. She suggested a journey to Kew, but it was too late that day once I finished my moaning. The next morning, we met at Victoria Station, climbed onto a train, and went there. Which is where I saw you."

"Yes." Now I was the one who felt awkward.

Cynthia's expression softened. "She is a lovely girl, Mrs. H. You have nothing to be ashamed of."

"I am not ashamed of Grace," I said stoutly. "She is, as you say, a beautiful child. I am ashamed of myself, for my lack of judgment. For trusting without any sort of skepticism."

Cynthia sat up. "Why shouldn't you have? You were young and in love, swept off your feet. Is that why you are so careful with McAdam?"

Heat crept into my face. "With Daniel?"

Cynthia's smile flashed. "Well, if you don't know what I mean, then you have a right to think yourself innocent and gullible. The man is damned fond of you. And you of him."

"And I know little about him," I said. "So yes, I am being careful."

The train swayed. Cynthia braced herself on the wall while I pressed my feet into the floor. "If you'd like, I can investigate him," she said. "Find out whether he has several wives tucked away and a few illicit lovers. We know he has a son."

"Whose mother has passed on, I believe."

Cynthia shrugged. "Worth looking into. *I* believe him, but I could set your mind at rest."

"Daniel would not be happy to think we were snooping into his private life."

"Don't agree. He'd understand, possibly approve. Not that I planned to tell him about it." Cynthia crossed one slim leg over the other, her spirits restored. "I have my resources. Speaking of that, Auntie will be out tonight. Some dour party where they discuss improving books. Uncle is at his club again, so the house will be empty. I've invited Lady Harkness and her companions over to take coffee. If you serve that coffee, you can listen in to our conversation."

I wanted very much to hear what Lady Harkness's friends had to say, not forgetting Mrs. Redfern's worries about them, but I was naturally cautious.

"Is it fair to Lady Harkness to corner her? She might truly be grieving."

"An invitation to call is just the thing to take her out of

that awful house and rest her mind. I'm surprised she's not yet bolted back to Liverpool."

"Still putting things in order, I imagine. But Sara serves coffee upstairs, not me. They will wonder why a cook is puttering about the drawing room."

"They'll wonder nothing of the sort. Lady Harkness is not quite certain which servants do what, and she won't know the difference. I'll wager the other two ladies will not either. I want you there because I don't want to get it wrong when I repeat the conversation to you, and you have a wiser head on your shoulders than I do."

I wasn't certain about that, but I followed her reasoning. "I will have to make certain Sara understands why I've taken over her job. She is keenly aware of her status as upstairs maid."

"I'll give her a coin or two and the evening to herself. She won't mind."

"And we must ensure that Mrs. Daley does not interfere."

"Oh Lord, that's true." Cynthia frowned. "I'll tell her some tale, don't worry. She doesn't much like you or Mr. Davis, I'm sorry to say—she complains something horrible about you, so much so that even Auntie grows weary of it. I do hope the woman finds you so intolerable she beetles off. She claims she's running the house more efficiently, but she gives the maids so much work they're wearing themselves out and running into one another trying to get it all done. It's becoming unnerving."

"Meanwhile, she sits in her parlor with her feet up, sipping cordial." I held my tongue about the altercation in the kitchen and her taking the brandy—Mrs. Daley might have done so for the exact reason she told us, and accusing her of stealing could land her in jail. While I did not like the woman, I could not bring myself to have anyone arrested without proof. I knew firsthand the terror of that.

"I told Auntie it was a mistake bringing her on," Cynthia said, idly swinging a booted foot. I recalled Mr. Thanos's besotted face when he'd told me she had the well-fitting boots made for her in Bond Street.

"Where did Mrs. Daley come from?" I asked. "Am I correct that she was already an acquaintance of the mistress?"

Cynthia let out a laugh. "Acquaintance of a sort. Mrs. Daley was cook to one of Auntie's friends in Somerset. When Auntie was asking about for a housekeeper on the cheap, the friend sent Mrs. Daley, likely to be rid of her."

"I see," I said in annoyance.

"I will continue to suggest to Auntie that we dismiss her. Auntie will see reason, especially if the woman costs Auntie any money. You'd never know that Uncle does quite well in the City, the way Auntie wails about expenses."

"It is wise to be frugal," I said, trying to find some virtue in the situation.

Cynthia's next laugh held true mirth. "There is a difference between frugal and cheeseparing, Mrs. H. I have nothing but my small allowance—which, happily, is managed by Papa and not Aunt Isobel—but I refuse to sit in a darkened chamber, counting my coins with trembling fingers, like some character out of Dickens."

I had to smile at this.

Cheered, Cynthia gazed over the rainy city, talking to me about happy times she'd had as a child, before tragedy had struck her family.

We left the train at Victoria Station and went our separate ways, Cynthia to find a hansom to take her home, me to change to the underground to travel on to see Grace as swiftly as I could.

I emerged at the Mansion House station, which was close

to St. Paul's, and walked up to Cheapside as the bells from St. Mary-le-Bow began to chime.

Grace was waiting, impatient and a bit worried. I told her why I was late—I always told my daughter the truth—and then she wanted to know every detail. I took her to tea in a shop near St Paul's and told her most of the story, leaving out the gruesome particulars.

I took Daniel's advice and let my cares drop away, absorbing myself in Grace until my heart healed once more. Daniel was a very wise man.

At eight that evening, I finished boiling the coffee and poured it into a tall silver pot. I arranged a tray with cups and saucers, and placed among them plates of sponge cake and apple tartlets. Tess assisted me readily, as I'd told her exactly what the coffee was for. She demanded, of course, for me to relate to her later all the ladies from next door had to say.

Mrs. Daley did not interfere. I did not know what Cynthia had said to the woman, but she'd stalked into the kitchen upon my return, announced she'd take her supper in her parlor, and stalked out again. Emma, the downstairs maid, served her, and once Emma was out of the parlor again, scurrying as though a dangerous animal was after her, we heard the key turn in the lock.

Mr. Davis entered the kitchen as I lifted the heavy coffee tray.

"Sara should take that up," he said with a frown. "Or one of the footmen."

"I can manage, Mr. Davis," I said without rancor. "Lady Cynthia asked me expressly."

I headed straight for him, and Mr. Davis had to jump aside to let me out without getting smacked with the edge of the tray. A footman ran ahead of me to open the door at the top of the stairs, and I trudged up, carefully balancing my load.

I entered the drawing room to find the ladies from next door already seated. Cynthia wore a dove gray frock trimmed with black piping, a narrow band of lace at her collar and cuffs. The gown was well tailored and subdued, showing Cynthia's modest taste.

Lady Harkness, in contrast, was in heavy mourning, every inch of her covered in black bombazine, her hands in black lace gloves. She'd removed her hat and veils, and one dull jet comb reposed on her graying hair, which again was dressed in a fussy style. Her companions' gowns, also black, were weighted down with yards of braid, grosgrain ribbon, and glittering black buttons.

I surmised that the two companions wore mourning for the show of it, but Lady Harkness's eyes held an emptiness, a bewilderment. I realized with a jolt that in spite of Cynthia claiming the woman hadn't shed many tears, she'd deeply loved her husband. I've seen that look in the truly bereaved before.

Mrs. Knowles hovered around Lady Harkness like a flitting sparrow. The second woman, whom I gathered was Mrs. Tatlock, was middle aged, thin, and quietly dour, where Mrs. Knowles tittered and spoke in breathless bursts. *Dear Julia*, Mrs. Knowles called Mrs. Tatlock. *Dear Millie* was Lady Harkness.

Once they were settled, I presented the coffee, which Cynthia poured out while I passed around the cakes. Lady Harkness ignored the sweets, but she imbibed the beverage as though grateful for it.

"I haven't tasted coffee in an age," Lady Harkness said with a satisfied sigh as she set down her cup. "It is kind of you, Lady Cynthia."

"Because coffee is bad for you, dear Millie," Mrs. Knowles said. "It excites you, and you don't need excitement at the moment." She spied me in the corner and snapped her fingers. "You. Girl. Bring tea as well."

"No," Lady Harkness said sharply. "I don't want any tea. Don't be foolish. It's rude to Lady Cynthia."

I remained rooted by the sideboard and the plates of cake, and Cynthia shrugged. "You can have whatever you like. I ordered coffee because I imagined you'd had your fill of tea, what with living in China."

"Too right," Lady Harkness said, the tones of Liverpool seeping through. "I'd like to never see another cup of tea. Or a Ming bowl, or anything made of lacquer."

I could see Cynthia had been correct when she'd speculated that Lady Harkness would jump at the chance to leave the warehouse next door, if only for a few hours.

"Why don't you sell up?" Cynthia asked her. "Get rid of the lot and go home?"

"I would love to," Lady Harkness said with fervor. "But there are so many matters to settle first, and the police have asked me to remain in London for now."

"Ah yes, the police." Cynthia sent Lady Harkness a sympathetic grimace. "I'd hoped they'd leave you alone, the brutes."

Lady Harkness shook her head. "I don't blame them—they are only doing their job. I do hope Inspector McGregor catches the fiend that did for my Jacob." She bowed her head, tears in her voice.

Mrs. Knowles stroked her shoulder. "Now, don't take on so, Millie. You know we can't rush off right away, no matter what.

So much to sort through. You wouldn't want to lose something valuable."

Lady Harkness raised her head and threw off Mrs. Knowles's hand. "I wish the pile of it to the devil," she said savagely. "Jacob bought everything in sight when we were in the Orient, saying he'd turn it into a pound here, a pound there. Everyone did. But I'd trade all of it to have him back with me." Her voice broke.

"I'm so sorry," Cynthia said in genuine compassion. "It's horrible. I wish I could help."

"Leave her alone, Amelia," Mrs. Tatlock said abruptly. "Millie doesn't like to think of such things."

Lady Harkness pulled away from both her friends and took a gulp of coffee. "I will not be able to leave soon even if I wish it. The police are adamant I stay, and now Sheppard, who was helping me look through my husband's things, has gone missing. Well, perhaps *missing* is going a bit far. He left without giving notice, I should say."

Cynthia's brows went up. "Did he? What did the police say to that?"

"They are most annoyed. As am I."

"What I mean is—do they suspect Sheppard?" Cynthia asked. "Since he's scarpered?"

Lady Harkness blinked in surprise. "Good heavens, *Sheppard* couldn't have killed my husband. I can't imagine it. Sheppard is fearful of everything. He didn't even like going out of the house, but Jacob was prone to roam the city—any city he was in—and insisted Sheppard accompany him everywhere he went."

Worms could turn, I mused. Perhaps Sheppard decided he'd had enough of following Sir Jacob about.

"Valets have murdered their masters before," Cynthia said, echoing my thoughts. "So I've been told. Do the police have a culprit in mind, if not Sheppard? I know they arrested a Chinese man, but then let him go."

"Oh, I don't believe that Chinaman had anything to do with it," Lady Harkness said. "Li Bai Chang was very polite when he came around, well spoken and learned. I talked with him a few minutes, when he was distressed my husband was not at home. Men like Li don't wield knives—they wield pens, writing calligraphy all day long about who knows what. The idea that Chinese men skulk about waiting to murder people at the behest of their warlords is absolute nonsense. Most are ordinary folk, like you and me, going about their business, polite and personable. I never had any trouble dealing with the Chinese."

Mrs. Tatlock rigidly lifted her cup. "What foolishness you talk, Millie. Saying heathens are just like us."

"Well, they are." Lady Harkness's lips pinched. "Mothers look after their children, fathers work to take care of their families. Family is a very important thing in China. I can admire that."

"Which is why missionary work there is so crucial," Mrs. Tatlock went on. "I was so hoping Sir Jacob would give to our cause."

"And *please* cease your prattle about missionaries," Lady Harkness said in irritation. "I can't abide them. Most aren't allowed in China, for good reason. Missionaries can't leave people the devil alone." She broke off, flushing. "I do beg your pardon, Lady Cynthia. It is an old argument."

"Not at all," Cynthia said. "I'm fascinated by foreign parts."

Mrs. Tatlock turned to Cynthia, obsequious. "Perhaps *you* would be interested in funding missionary work, your ladyship."

"Oh yes," Mrs. Knowles joined in. "Dear Julia is doing such wonderful things."

"Dear Julia is always tapping my acquaintances for money," Lady Harkness snapped. "Do not worry, Julia. Jacob left a legacy for your missionaries as he promised to."

Mrs. Tatlock looked mollified, but no less rigid. I remembered Daniel telling us he'd read Sir Jacob's will, but he hadn't revealed the details, except for the fact Sir Jacob's son hadn't been mentioned.

Mrs. Tatlock, at least, had benefited from Sir Jacob's death, it seemed. I wondered how large the legacy was.

Lady Harkness set down her empty cup. "Sheppard doing a bunk has left me in a sad position. It's difficult for me to go through Jacob's things."

Her eyes filled with tears, which she hastily blinked away. Cynthia took up the pot and refilled her cup.

"At least you have dear Mr. Pasfield," Mrs. Knowles pointed out. "He is ever so helpful. Coming 'round at all hours, always on hand to help search for something or carry a load."

"Too much so," Mrs. Tatlock said with disapproval. "He ought to understand that Millie is bereaved and leave her be. His presence is unseemly."

Lady Harkness's fingers tightened in her lace gloves. "If you ladies are implying that Mr. Pasfield is trying to court me, you are both mad. He was Jacob's dearest friend. My Jacob never forgot his roots, your ladyship," she said to Cynthia. "He didn't abandon his friends when he moved up in the world. Mr. Pasfield and he were thick as thieves, always were, ever since we were children in Liverpool. Jacob was so kind to everyone . . ."

She broke off, clattered her cup to the table, and pulled out a black linen square to catch tears that trickled from her eyes. "I beg your pardon, Lady Cynthia."

"Not at all," Cynthia said briskly. "I've lost loved ones. It's a difficult thing. I am glad your husband's friend has been here to lend a hand."

"He has." Lady Harkness dabbed at her cheeks. "I don't know what I would do without dear Leonard's shoulder to lean on. But Julia and Amelia are ridiculous to suggest that his purpose is to marry me. Nothing could be further from his mind. I have no wish to marry again, and Mr. Pasfield knows this. He is a *friend*."

Her annoyance made me believe her. She was surprised at the idea, not flushing and trying to brush it aside. If Mr. Pasfield was always underfoot, it was not to get in good with the widow—or at least, not in Lady Harkness's opinion.

"What will you do with the Chinese items?" Cynthia asked. "Can you sell them? Or were they willed out of your hands?"

"Jacob made small bequests," Lady Harkness said, returning to the comfort of her coffee. "To servants, to Julia's missionary fund—mainly because she harped at him for months about it."

"It's for a good cause, Millie," Mrs. Tatlock said in answer to Lady Harkness's withering look. "Not for me personally."

"So she states, every day. Do not worry, Julia. I will not contest the will. Jacob had no heirs—we had no children." Lady Harkness's voice became sorrowful. "We were not blessed. The whole lot comes to me after the bequests, and then yes, I'll sell up. Mr. Pasfield is helping me separate what is valuable from the silly souvenirs Jacob tended to bring home. I imagine some antiques merchant would like to get his hands on the Ming pottery."

"But there is no hurry," Mrs. Knowles said quickly. "It's too soon to part with your husband's things."

I saw worry in Mrs. Knowles's eyes, as well as Mrs. Tatlock's quelling look at her. Mrs. Knowles caught the glance, and she gulped and closed her mouth.

"My Jacob was what I call an optimistic collector," Lady Harkness said with a faint smile. "He'd have no idea of the value of an item, only that he liked it and hoped it would make money sooner or later."

"Still, he found many lovely things," Cynthia said. "So I've seen."

"Yes, but it grows wearying." Lady Harkness sighed. "Though I wouldn't be surprised if a few of the gewgaws are worth small fortunes. Jacob was a dab hand at turning a penny into a pound," she finished proudly.

"A skill many of us would like to have," Cynthia said. "More coffee, Lady Harkness?"

The ladies departed within the hour. After she saw them off, Cynthia helped me gather plates and cups and carry them out. Ignoring my protests, she led the way down to the kitchen and lugged her load into the scullery. Brushing off her skirt, she sat at the kitchen table and helped herself to the remains of the sponge cake.

"What did you think, Mrs. H.?"

I finished setting the dishes next to the scullery sink and then poured myself tea and sat down across from her. The kitchen and servants' hall were quite empty—Tess must have gone up to bed with the rest of the staff.

"I gathered Lady Harkness is not as slow witted as her two friends wish her to be," I said. "She realizes they're hanging on to her skirts for what they can get."

"I must say I do have a little more respect for her now." Cynthia dunked her cake into the remains of her cold coffee and took a large bite. "Decent grub," she said around crumbs. "Coffee excellent too."

"Thank you." I gave her a nod. "They wished her to believe Mr. Pasfield is smitten with her, but her adamancy that he is not was genuine. She would know him better than they, if he lived in China with her and Sir Jacob."

"I caught that. I do wonder though if Pasfield is in cahoots with the companions, trying to steer Lady Harkness into marriage with him. Perhaps Pasfield has promised Mistresses Knowles and Tatlock loot if he marries the wealthy Lady Harkness."

"I think marriage to Mr. Pasfield is their own idea," I mused. "A way to keep Lady Harkness in London a while longer. I wonder if Lady Harkness will drop the acquaintance once she is home in Liverpool with family and old friends."

"I'd like to speak to the lady away from her two leeches," Cynthia said decidedly. "They are very keen to make certain she doesn't simply sell up and bolt."

"I wish I knew whether they were looking for Mr. Li's tea specifically. Or are they simply after anything that could turn a profit?"

"Difficult to say. I imagine they'll fall upon whatever they can sell. I also wonder if Mrs. Tatlock is truly gathering money for her missionaries, and if they exist at all."

"That would be easy to discover," I said. "Find out which group she claims to be affiliated with and ask them."

"I can do that. Auntie knows all the institutions for the less fortunate, and she'll be chuffed I'm taking an interest. I also had a thought—I can send Bobby to follow Mr. Pasfield about. She's keen to help."

"Is she?" I asked in surprise.

"She says so, and she's not dim. Bobby can follow Pasfield, or even hunt up Sheppard. She knows a lot of blokes and their valets."

"If she doesn't mind," I said, trying not to sound too eager.

"No, indeed. Bobby is weary of the tedium of life. Why do you think she's trying to leave her gender behind? Sitting and embroidering would kill her. She finds more freedom as a man, but she admits that even they fall into their routines. Luncheon and newspapers at the club, whisky and women at the gaming hells, then back home to the wife and children, pretending to be virtuous gentlemen."

"Not all men behave so," I said quickly.

"You are thinking of Mr. Thanos," Cynthia said, reddening. "We are fortunate to be acquainted with exceptional gentlemen. Bobby is uncertain what to do with herself. She can't literally become a man, and she refuses to remain a woman—that is, marrying and setting up a nursery as her father wants her to. She's at a bit of a loose end."

"I would welcome her help," I said in some sympathy. "As long as she is discreet."

"She's dressed and lived as a man for years in a world that would condemn her for it. I'd say she's learned to be discreet."

"Then please ask her." I took a fortifying sip of tea. "Tess has said she's finding out some things next door, which worries me a bit."

"You'll keep her calm, Mrs. H. You've already done wonders with her."

I wasn't certain about that, but before I could respond, someone banged on the back door. It wasn't Daniel's knock, and I wasn't expecting him, but I hurried out to lift the bolt.

"Mrs. Finnegan," I said in surprise. That lady stood in the

doorway in her cook's apron and cap, both garments soaked by the fine rain sleeting down.

"Mrs. Redfern sent me running over, Mrs. Holloway," she said, her eyes wide in her wet face. "The mistress has taken sore ill. Mrs. Redfern says she's been poisoned!"

17

❦

I snatched up a shawl and hurried out after the distraught Mrs. Finnegan, Lady Cynthia on my heels.

"She were right as rain when she came home," Mrs. Finnegan said to me as we hastened along to the house next door. "She went straight to bed. As soon as she lay down, she came over sick. Barely was able to ring the bell to summon help. Mrs. Redfern is with her now."

She led us down the stairs and into the Harkness kitchen. Cynthia's gray gown was spotted with rain, as she'd not taken the time to fetch a shawl or coat.

The kitchen had been cleaned for the night, but Mrs. Knowles stood near the table, facing a tight-lipped Griffin, the lady's maid. Griffin held a basin of water, and Mrs. Knowles was trying to take it away from her. The battle had resulted in most of the water splashing to the slates and down the front of both women's dresses.

Mrs. Finnegan stopped and wrung her hands, doing nothing useful, but Cynthia stepped briskly forward. "Ladies, please! If you're fighting over who takes up the water, *I'll* do it."

She held out her hands. Mrs. Knowles backed away, red faced, and Griffin straightened her back. "No need, your ladyship," she said coldly, before she turned and marched out with the basin.

Cynthia motioned me to accompany her, and I followed her and Griffin upstairs, Mrs. Knowles trailing behind us.

Lady Harkness's bedchamber was on the second floor, and as full of Oriental clutter as the rest of the house. The bedstead was a fantastic latticed creation of rosewood with heavy carved feet and hangings of red velvet.

Lady Harkness lay in the bed in a dressing gown, her face yellow-green with illness. Mrs. Redfern stood like a sentry at the head of the bed, Mrs. Tatlock at the window as though she'd been banished there. Another maid tearfully emptied the contents of a washbasin into the slop pail.

Griffin replaced the soiled basin with the one she'd brought from the kitchen. She wrung out a rag in the clean water and went to the bed, where she patted the damp cloth to Lady Harkness's brow as tenderly as a mother.

Mrs. Redfern lifted a glass from the night table and came to us, thrusting the glass under my nose. "What is in that?" she demanded. "Mrs. Finnegan had no idea."

I took it and sniffed. The glass was empty, but I smelled the faint remnants of its contents. "Mustard." I sniffed again. "And lobelia."

"I smelled the mustard," Mrs. Finnegan said behind me. "Ain't no poison in that."

"But mustard can be an emetic," I answered, returning the glass to Mrs. Redfern. "Lobelia is certainly a powerful one. Similar to ipecac."

"I am trying to discover which of them gave it to her," Mrs. Redfern said.

Mrs. Knowles raised her hands. "I poured out the glass from the bottle and had her drink it. I didn't know what was in it, I promise you. I thought her tonic."

"Tonic," Mrs. Tatlock sneered from the window. "I saw you dump that vial into the glass before you handed it to her."

"I thought it was her tonic!" Mrs. Knowles wailed. "I couldn't smell. My nose is all plugged tonight." She sniffled as though to prove it.

Mrs. Redfern eyed the ladies coldly. "I must ask you both to leave this house. Whether done on purpose or not, her ladyship is quite ill. I am prepared to call the constable to escort you out if you do not leave on your own."

Mrs. Tatlock's scowl deepened. Mrs. Knowles drew herself up, though she couldn't quite meet Mrs. Redfern's eye. "Well, I never. When dear Millie is better, she'll sack you for this."

On the bed, Lady Harkness groaned. I could not say whether she understood their words, but it was the moan of a woman in distress.

"Come along, ladies," Lady Cynthia said. "I'll see you downstairs."

She shooed the two women toward the door. Mrs. Tatlock went at once, leaving in chilly silence. Mrs. Knowles continued to fret, but she at last fled the room, Cynthia herding her.

The front door slammed not long later. I hoped we hadn't just let a murderer out into the rainy night.

I remained in the bedchamber awhile longer, though it was clear I could do nothing but suggest they have Lady Harkness drink a great deal of water and weak tea. If the dose had been only a purge, it should not kill her. Tea, and much later, a bit of bread, should settle her stomach.

I left Lady Harkness in the charge of her dragons Griffin and Redfern and returned below stairs. There Mrs. Finnegan bustled about making tea while I sank wearily to the table in the empty servants' hall.

"Poor woman," Mrs. Finnegan said, carrying in a teapot and cups on a large tray. "Better to have no friends at all than companions like those."

I had to agree. As I sipped the tea Mrs. Finnegan poured, I thought over the tangle of events and what they could mean.

Sir Jacob had been murdered after being left in his bedroom alone, Sheppard the valet finishing with him at nine o'clock in the evening. Mr. Chancellor, departing the house after learning Sir Jacob had retired for the night, had spied a Chinaman in the street. He'd assumed it was Mr. Li, whom he'd met before, but I now believed it was the young man called Zhen, who'd presumably come to try to see his father.

If Zhen was the person Sir Jacob had gone to meet at Kew earlier that evening, perhaps they'd quarreled, and Zhen had followed Sir Jacob home. To continue the quarrel? To beg for money? To murder him?

The afternoon of the day Sir Jacob had been found dead, Mr. Chancellor had gone through the garden digging at tea bushes and taking a few shoots. Lady Harkness's companions had begun rooting through the house, claiming they were "helping" Lady Harkness have a clear-out. Mr. Pasfield, it seems, was assisting them.

Mr. Li, having traveled from China in search of the man who'd stolen his father's tea, *had* been in the vicinity of this house several times before Sir Jacob's death, including the night he'd had the appointment with Sir Jacob. I had to be honest with myself. Even though I hadn't noted Mr. Li until I'd run into him the day of the garden party, he could have come to Mount Street many times.

Because of his proficiency with English, Mr. Li had been able to obtain a post as a translator once he'd reached London, and then found work assisting Mr. Sutherland. Mr. Li had convinced Mr. Sutherland to contact Sir Jacob and suggest that Mr. Li help translate the markings on some very ancient pottery Sir Jacob had collected. An excuse, I now knew, Mr. Li had invented to get himself into Sir Jacob's home or garden where he could search for the purloined tea.

Mr. Li turned up for his appointment only to find the man out. Had Sir Jacob decided he had better things to do that evening, or had he not been informed of the appointment at all?

I wondered who had read the letter from Mr. Sutherland suggesting the meeting between Sir Jacob and Mr. Li—did Sheppard go through his master's correspondence? Lady Cynthia said Sir Jacob expected Sheppard to be always by his side. Sheppard had, in fact, accompanied Sir Jacob to Kew Gardens on the fateful night.

Perhaps Sheppard, all along, had planned to kill his master, and seized the opportunity of a foreign stranger wanting to call a few weeks before the murder. He suppressed the letter from Mr. Sutherland asking Sir Jacob for the appointment with Mr. Li, and suggested that Sir Jacob go out the night of the meeting. Then Sheppard could claim that Mr. Li had simply turned up and tried to gain admittance—most suspicious. The result was that Inspector McGregor had focused on Mr. Li right away.

Mr. Li or Mr. Sutherland might be able to produce a letter from Sir Jacob fixing the time, but if Sheppard had written the letter, purporting to be Sir Jacob, everyone could rightly say that Sir Jacob had never penned it.

Sheppard, also, had been the only one to see Sir Jacob in Kew Gardens the night of the murder—he could have invented the fact that Sir Jacob disappeared into the mist for a bit, making us believe Sir Jacob met a villain who might have followed him home and killed him.

Or perhaps Lady Harkness had hidden the letter making the appointment, for the same purpose. She too would have access to her husband's papers, might have acted as his secretary—Mrs. Redfern would know. Lady Harkness seemed truly grieved at her husband's death, but perhaps she hadn't realized, until the deed was done, how much she loved him. I'd seen a husband who'd beaten his wife to death in a horrible temper weep and wonder how he'd live without her.

Mrs. Redfern too could have intercepted the letter and lured Mr. Li here to be a convenient scapegoat. She made no secret of her dislike for Sir Jacob.

Whatever the reason, Mr. Li had turned up on the night of his appointment to find Sir Jacob out.

There was always the unhappy possibility that Mr. Li *had* done the murder, despite my convictions. He'd been on the spot—what were the chances that he'd chosen the very night of the murder to bring me the box of tea? He might have done the murder beforehand and nipped around to be innocently standing in the shadows, waiting for me.

I'd seen no blood on his clothes, no telltale signs of agitation on his face, but it had been dark, and at the time, I'd been unaware of Sir Jacob's death.

Had Mr. Li afterward sought out and killed Zhen? And why? Perhaps Zhen *had* followed Sir Jacob home that night, and had seen Mr. Li going into or coming out of the house.

Where was Mr. Li now? Hiding? Or was he dead and we simply hadn't found him? I closed my eyes on the thought, praying he was well.

"Hey ho," a rumbling voice said. "Mrs. Finnegan? You sleeping at the table again? Hold up—who's this . . . ?"

I opened my eyes to find a small, portly man with a large mustache peering into my face. Mrs. Finnegan flushed, her eyes starry, and creaked to her feet.

"Cup of tea, dear?" She fetched a cup and saucer from the dresser as the man seated himself at the end of the table.

"Don't mind if I do." The gentleman continued to study me, then he snapped his fingers. "I know where I've seen you. You work next door."

"This is Mrs. Holloway," Mrs. Finnegan said as she poured out the tea. She measured in two lumps of sugar without asking and shoved the cup at him. "She's Lady Cynthia's cook."

"Ah, serving aristocracy." He winked at me. "Moving up in the world, are you?"

I did not enjoy being winked at by men I did not know, so I sat up straight and gave him a cool stare. "I am afraid you have me at a disadvantage, sir."

"Don't take on so, Mrs. Holloway," Mrs. Finnegan said, smiling happily as she sat down again. "This is Mr. Pasfield, the master's great friend."

I hadn't met or seen Mr. Pasfield, the friend who'd traveled the Orient with Sir Jacob. Lady Harkness had scoffed at the notion that Mr. Pasfield was smitten with her, and glancing between Mr. Pasfield and Mrs. Finnegan, I understood her conviction.

"Bit of a row upstairs, what?" Mr. Pasfield took a loud sip of tea. "Excellent as always, Mrs. Finnegan."

Mrs. Finnegan blushed like a girl. "Now, Mr. Pasfield, it's only tea."

I sat back on my stool, taking a sip of overly strong and tepid tea, new ideas in my head.

"I guess you're surprised to see me downstairs, eh, Mrs. Holloway?" Mr. Pasfield grinned at me over his cup. "Never was comfortable upstairs—neither was Jake, no matter that he slept on a pile of money and could put a lofty 'Sir' in front of his name. We was the same starting out, he and me. Hauled coal scuttles for those what would pay us, or we swept the streets. We got hired on at a warehouse full of Oriental goods, and you might say it piqued our interest. Seemed a man, any man, could ship himself off to China and return rich as a king. But it had to be done the right way, of course. Jake was a genius at it. Got us posts with merchants—sort of errand boys who'd do anything—and eventually we became clerks. Jake scared up books and started teaching himself and me Chinese, and when these men went on a trading expedition, they took us because we knew the language. Well . . . Jake knew it, and I faked it." Mr. Pasfield chuckled. "I found it much easier to learn when I arrived in China and fell in with the natives. Jake, lucky fellow, met a lass willing to teach him all she knew." He chortled and winked again.

Mrs. Finnegan gave his hand a playful slap. "Now, don't be naughty, Leonard. I imagine you were one with the ladies when you were a young fellow."

"Not really," Mr. Pasfield said cheerfully. "Jake had them running after him, I can tell you, but I was always the hanger-on. Not many ladies noticed a short cove like myself— even when I was twenty-three." He laughed some more, his eyes crinkling with good humor.

I had the feeling he was downplaying his interactions with women for Mrs. Finnegan's benefit, but I kept these thoughts to myself. I imagined the two young men, far from home, off to seek their fortunes and sow their share of wild oats.

"When did Sir Jacob meet Lady Harkness?" I asked in curiosity. "If I can persuade you to gossip."

"Oh, I'm an old gossip, me. Not good for much more these days."

"Dear Leonard," Mrs. Finnegan said. "Such a tease, you are."

"Millie and Jake, they knew each other always," Mr. Pasfield answered. "She lived on the same backstreet where he grew up, and they became attached at a young age. Jake, Millie, and me—inseparable. Jake told her about his dreams to move up in the world, and Millie believed in him. I think they had an understanding even before we went off the first time—that he'd make his fortune and come back for her. She waited, bless the girl. Very loyal, is Millie."

"And they married," I said. "Obviously."

"Made for each other." Mr. Pasfield nodded. "Me and Jake, we came back from our first venture in a couple of years. Not with the money he has now, of course, but we didn't do poorly. We'd moved up in the company—Jake faster than me. He had all the ambition, and pulled me along for the ride. He and Millie married—I was groomsman—and not a year later, we were off to China again, Millie with us this time, and old Jake grew even richer. He could turn a turd into gold—begging your pardon, ladies."

Mrs. Finnegan only nodded. I had the feeling she'd forgive him anything.

"Not at all," I said. "Lady Harkness said Sir Jacob had a gift for acquiring wealth. Mrs. Finnegan, the teapot is empty. Can I trouble you? Or perhaps I should . . ."

I rose as though ready to move to the kitchen and leave

the lovebirds alone, but Mrs. Finnegan forestalled me. "No trouble at all. Won't be a tick."

I waited until I heard her voice raised in faulty tune in the next room before I addressed Mr. Pasfield.

"I don't doubt Sir Jacob's devotion to his wife, but I recently learned that he had a son," I said in a whisper. "A Chinese son."

Mr. Pasfield nodded without worry. "He did. It were before he married Millie. He was as devoted to Millie in marriage as she was to him. But before . . . Well, now, we were very young, excited, and full of the devil, if you understand what I mean. The world was laid before us, and we took it." He shook his head in nostalgia.

"Does Lady Harkness know?" I asked.

Mr. Pasfield shook his head. "No, she don't."

Mrs. Finnegan returned with the teapot and set it on its trivet. "Goodness, everything went quiet. Now, what were you two talking over?"

"Jake's by-blow," Mr. Pasfield said. "Don't look shocked, Mrs. Holloway. Finny knows all about it. As I say, I gossip too much."

Mrs. Finnegan resumed her seat and poured me more tea. "Leonard knows it's safe to talk to *me*. Who will I blab to while I'm up to my elbows in dough? But we don't tell Mrs. Redfern. She'd take umbrage, and also tell the mistress."

"I understand." I borrowed Tess's gesture of locking my lips and throwing away the key. Mrs. Finnegan and Mr. Pasfield looked pleased with me.

"Not my business, so I keep out of it," Mr. Pasfield said. "How did *you* learn of it, Mrs. Holloway?"

I sipped my tea, which was bitter, as Mrs. Finnegan hadn't changed out the leaves.

"I am afraid he's been killed," I said, unhappy now that I'd broached the subject. "He was found in Kew Gardens."

Both looked dazed, Mr. Pasfield's exuberance fading. "That was *Zhen*? Jove. The poor chap. I never liked the boy much, but—What is the world coming to these days? Was he robbed? Or was it because he was Chinese? Horrible what people do."

"I saw the story in the newspapers," Mrs. Finnegan chimed in. "But it only said he were a Chinaman. What was the lad doing in England?"

"Looking for his pa, I wouldn't wonder." Mr. Pasfield seemed more nonplussed than grieved. "Jake was tender-hearted to Zhen, though the boy wasn't always grateful. Jake gave him a job in his warehouse in China, even let him use Jake's name, which would make it easier for him to travel to Britain if he wished. Jake never told anyone about the son but me, but he was good to him. Proud of the lad. He and Millie never had little ones of their own."

So Lady Harkness had said. I sat in silence, not certain how to respond. Mr. Pasfield was open enough about his friend's indiscretion but did not appear moved by Zhen's death apart from surprise.

Mr. Pasfield's tale of the three as friends together in the old days explained some of Lady Harkness's grief. If she and Sir Jacob had been sweethearts from babyhood, their marriage inevitable, her loss would indeed be deep.

Mr. Pasfield appeared happy enough to return to his roots, courting a cook below stairs. I wasn't certain if his blithe acceptance that his friend Jake had been better than he at acquiring riches was the truth, but Mr. Pasfield looked contented enough at this moment. He took up his tea, giving Mrs. Finnegan a fond look as he sipped.

I wished them well. I also very much wanted to speak to Daniel.

I departed and encountered Lady Cynthia on the street.

"I put both the old biddies into a hansom and sent them off home," she said. "They room together in Pimlico—isn't that interesting? Then I went back up to see how Lady Harkness was faring. She'll recover, I think, but she'll be weak for a time, poor woman."

"I suspect Mrs. Knowles really did dose the tonic," I said. "Or Mrs. Tatlock did and tried to throw suspicion on Mrs. Knowles. I'm not certain they were trying to kill her."

"No," Cynthia agreed. "I wager they got the wind up when I encouraged dear Millie to sell everything and go back to Liverpool. If she's ill, she can't travel, can she?"

I shivered and pulled my shawl close. "It's good of you to look after Lady Harkness."

Cynthia shrugged. "She's not as bad as I pegged her. Fish out of water. She has my sympathy on that score."

"We need to pool our knowledge," I said. "I started looking into the matter to help Mr. Li, but this killer must be stopped. I want to ensure that Mr. Li is well and then tell what we know to Inspector McGregor."

"McGregor?" Cynthia's brows arched. "Good Lord, you *are* worried."

"Will you send word to Mr. Thanos?" I asked. "The four of us need to gather. And Tess. She keeps hinting she has things to report."

"Of course I will." Cynthia pressed her hand to her heart. "Gracious, an unmarried lady writing to a gentleman. Oh, the scandal."

She laughed, throwing her head back in the misting rain as she made for the front door of our house.

I hurried down the stairs to the back door, wanting warmth and my familiar place, to be met by Mr. Davis waiting in the center of the kitchen.

"There you are. Come with me."

Mr. Davis knew I disliked him giving me orders, so I concluded he was much upset. I followed him without question down the narrow passage to the housekeeper's parlor. Mr. Davis took out his keys and unlocked and opened the door.

Lying in a heap on the floor was Mrs. Daley. I started forward in alarm when I saw that beside her lay the master's decanter of brandy, the remains of its contents a pungent golden stain on the carpet.

18

"Good . . . heavens." The words jerked from my mouth. "Is she all right?"

"Shall we haul her up and see?"

Mr. Davis headed purposefully for Mrs. Daley, and I quickly joined him, worried what he would do in his temper.

Mr. Davis grasped her under one arm, and I took the other. We lifted her to the Belter chair, which was the largest and softest. Mrs. Daley didn't wake during this procedure—her head lolled, and she let out a snore.

"Mrs. Daley." Mr. Davis patted her cheek, rather more firmly than necessary. "Wake up, now." His next pat was almost a slap.

I seized his arm. "I'll wake her. You get the brandy off the floor."

Mr. Davis scowled at me, but he bent to fetch the decanter. "She's been at this and several of the wine bottles. I drew a line on each of them, and sure enough, the levels have been inching downward. She doesn't take much from any one, but has a go at them all."

I moved to the washbasin, which had a finger's width of water in the bottom, wet my handkerchief, and used this to swab Mrs. Daley's flushed cheeks. After a moment, she groggily opened her eyes.

"Mrs. Holloway?" she asked in puzzlement, her words slurred. Then she saw Mr. Davis with the decanter and sucked in a breath. "Mr. Davis! Whatever are you doing with that?"

"Hadn't you better get up to bed, Mrs. Daley?" I suggested in my no-nonsense voice. "I'll help you."

Mrs. Daley pushed away my hands. "I'm fine. I fell asleep is all." She gained strength as she spoke. "Why are you in my parlor?"

"I heard you fall off the chair." Mr. Davis waved the decanter. "Found this on the floor next to you. You're a drunk, Mrs. Daley."

"I am *not* drunk." The slur had faded but not disappeared. "I fell asleep is all." Mrs. Daley's eyes narrowed. "It was that Tess. The bloody girl came in here and left the decanter next to me. I'll stake money on it."

"Tess doesn't have a key to this room," I said.

"She doesn't need one, does she? She picked the lock. She's a thief, and you know it. Bad blood."

"Utter tripe," Mr. Davis said in a hard voice. "There wasn't time for her to sneak in here after I heard you fall off the chair. You've been pinching the wine and brandy, and I'm going to the master about it."

Mrs. Daley rose to her feet. Though she reeked of drink, she was remarkably steady.

"You do that, Mr. Davis. Then I will tell him all about Tess, and about you, and about *you*." Her finger went from Mr. Davis to end up pointing at me.

"What about me?" Mr. Davis squared his shoulders. "Or Mrs. Holloway? We have nothing to be ashamed of. We're not drunken thieves."

"No? But *you*, Davis, are less than a man—yes, I've heard all about you. And Mrs. Holloway has a daughter she keeps hidden. No wonder she needs so many days out."

My mouth went dry. The damp handkerchief fell from my nerveless fingers, leaving a wet patch on my gown on its way to the carpet.

"*That* old chestnut?" Mr. Davis scoffed. "An idiotic young man who misunderstood me. And Mrs. Holloway hasn't got . . ."

He trailed off as I stood woodenly, my face so hot I must be red as glowing coal.

"Mrs. Holloway?" Mr. Davis stared at me in puzzlement. "You were married?"

"A long time ago," I said faintly.

"The mistress don't know anything about it." Mrs. Daley's eyes were slits. "And she never has to, if you take my meaning."

I stood motionless, anger and fear battling inside me until I was nearly ill. Mr. Davis gaped a moment before he snapped his mouth shut.

"What does it matter?" he asked Mrs. Daley. "A widow working to keep a daughter is a damn sight better than a woman who has no idea how to run a household, but plenty of ideas on how to steal from it."

"A widow?" Mrs. Daley said with a sneer. "Is that what you think? No better than she ought to be, that's what's said in the streets where Mrs. Holloway is from."

I relaxed, but only a fraction. While I had my detractors, no one from my old haunts knew my marriage had been a sham. *I* hadn't known until my husband had died and I'd seen his will—which was public record. Had Mrs. Daley gone to Somerset House, where records were stockpiled, to investigate me?

But no. Holloway was my maiden name, which I'd used again after my husband's death. Mrs. Daley knew me by no other. I'd moved after my marriage to south London, where my husband had come from, living there while he'd gone to sea—I was willing to wager none in the streets where I grew up remembered his name either.

I faced her with more confidence. "Are you telling me you went to the middle of London and asked all about me, Mrs. Daley? Why don't you use that zeal to keep house instead?"

"I like to know about people," Mrs. Daley said. "Keeps them from spreading rumors about *me*." She looked down her nose as she spoke, every inch the haughty housekeeper.

Unfortunately for her, I now knew she was a fraud. Mrs. Bywater's friend had foisted the woman on us, probably happy to have the blackmailing cook who drank her way through the master's wine cellar out of her house. Mrs. Bywater must be much indebted to this friend.

"Mrs. Holloway?" Mr. Davis looked back and forth between us, bewildered.

"She knows nothing," I said quickly. "My husband drowned. He never saw his daughter, who now boards with my friends. They look after her while I work."

My firm words belied my fears. If Mrs. Daley circulated stories that I was a hussy with a by-blow daughter, whether she had proof or not, Mrs. Bywater might turn me out, and even those who wanted my excellent cooking would think twice before hiring me. As I'd reflected when Cynthia had

discovered I had Grace, all mistresses were sticklers for pro-
priety among their servants, especially the female ones.

In this world, when a master of the house tumbled a maid,
it was the maid who was turned out with a stain on her character. Servants were expected to be impeccable, no matter
what the goings-on above stairs.

Mr. Davis gave me a look of sympathy, but Mrs. Daley
gazed at me in exultation. She'd won. Or so she thought.

"Go ahead and tell the master about the wine, Mr. Davis,"
I said, my voice cool. "I doubt it will do any good. Mrs. Bywater will simply find a way to keep her on."

"That is so," Mrs. Daley said with confidence.

Mr. Davis's lip curled. "You are no doubt correct, Mrs. Holloway. But I will be watching *you*." He pointed at Mrs. Daley.
"You take another sip of the master's brandy, and I will write
to Lord Rankin. *He* laid down this cellar, and he'll be less
than pleased to learn a trumped-up servant is draining it for
him." He turned his back and strode away.

Mrs. Daley watched him go, and smiled.

"And you will leave Tess out of your machinations," I said
to her. "If you say anything to get her the sack, I will make
certain you regret it. Deeply."

Mrs. Daley trained her too-confident gaze on me. "Why? Is
she your daughter too?"

I gave her a disparaging look. "Oh, for heaven's sake."

I followed Mr. Davis's example and stalked haughtily from
the room. Behind me, the parlor door slammed and the lock
clicked.

Mr. Davis, who had returned to his pantry across the hall,
beckoned me inside and shut the door.

"What are we to do?" he asked in a quiet voice. "We must
do *something*."

"Leave it to me, Mr. Davis." I already had a few ideas in my head.

Mr. Davis obviously longed to ask me what, but he refrained. "Why didn't you tell me about your daughter?" He sounded hurt.

"Fear, Mr. Davis. Pure and simple."

Mr. Davis sighed. "Ah well, I know about that. Facing down your enemies is usually best. I understand your caution, but be ready for the knowledge to come out. Don't trust that woman to keep her silence."

I shivered but nodded. He spoke wisely.

I wondered very much about the skeleton in Mr. Davis's closet, the one he'd called "that old chestnut," but now was not the time to ask.

I thanked him, said good night, and left him muttering about the wine cellar.

The next afternoon, after luncheon was served and before I had to prepare for tea and the evening meal, Tess and I went with Lady Cynthia to visit Bobby. It was Tess's day out, so she'd already left the house, and we met at the hansom Lady Cynthia had procured.

Bobby lived in a flat of rooms in Duchess Street, a narrow lane that opened a little past where Regent Street curved around All Souls at Langham Place. The rooms were modern, with polished paneled walls, simple but comfortable furniture, and a glowing stove to keep us warm.

Lady Roberta was delighted at our invasion. She produced a folding table from a back room and Cynthia and I helped her pull various chairs to it.

I had warned Tess to mind her manners, and I wondered if she'd be intimidated by sitting down with Bobby—she was comfortable with Cynthia, but she didn't know Bobby. Tess, however, looked perfectly at ease as she assisted with the chairs. Bobby might be highborn, but she was eccentric, which I supposed made her easier to take.

Mr. Thanos arrived not long after we did, with Daniel in tow. I saw James nowhere, and I assumed he was working at his odd jobs.

"I invited Sutherland," Mr. Thanos said after he'd greeted us all. "But he's lecturing today. It's a paying crowd at the museum, so he couldn't bunk out."

"Does he have anything for us?" Daniel asked.

Daniel held my chair for me, settling me gallantly before he took his seat. Cynthia, in a gentleman's suit once more, thwarted Mr. Thanos's attempt to hold her chair by turning said chair around and straddling it. Bobby tipped herself back in another chair and regarded us in enjoyment.

"Nothing more than he's already told us." Mr. Thanos gave up trying to assist Cynthia and sat down. "He's worried about Mr. Li."

"As am I," I said. "Daniel, have you heard from him?"

Daniel shook his head. "Not at all. McGregor is not happy with me for having lost track of him. McGregor hasn't yet accused me of smuggling the man out of the country, but he's strongly hinted at it."

"Why should you?" Bobby asked. "Unless you were in cahoots with this Chinaman."

"Exactly what McGregor thinks," Daniel answered. "He is always itching to arrest me."

"Not very gracious of him," I said. "With all the help you've given him."

"McGregor is not a gracious man." Daniel smiled his dry smile.

"Quiet now." Lady Cynthia raised her hands. "Mrs. Holloway brought us here for a reason. She's found out some things."

"So have I," Tess said. "Oh, have I."

"Mrs. H. first," Lady Cynthia said. "Then Tess."

Tess readily fell silent, which made me worry a bit. I launched into my tale of Lady Cynthia's chat with Lady Harkness and companions, then told of Lady Harkness falling ill, most likely dosed with an emetic by one of the companions, and finally, my conversation with Mr. Pasfield.

When I finished, there was a silence.

"Mrs. Finnegan is a deep one, ain't she?" Tess said in awe. "If she marries Mr. Pasfield, she'll be in clover. He has money, I hear—not as much as Sir Jacob, but he's plenty comfortable."

"Mr. Pasfield confessed it was his habit to go below stairs to find someone to talk to," I said. "He said he wasn't a gentleman and never would be. If he and Mrs. Finnegan make a match, I wish them happy."

"As long as neither is a murderer," Mr. Thanos put in. "Mr. Pasfield had the run of the house without anyone questioning it. And Mrs. Finnegan could have let him in the back door on the night of the murder."

"I have not ruled it out," I said. "I admit they both had good opportunity. And I suppose their motive would be the same as everyone else's—to take what was valuable from Sir Jacob's collection. But Tess is ready to burst. Do tell us what you know, Tess."

Tess sent us a mysterious look and then plopped her elbows on the table and launched into her tale. "As I told ya, Mrs. H., I have my ways of getting information. One of the footmen fancies me, so he'll tell me much, but there's also a constable who walks the beat on Mount Street, and he was patrolling the night of the murder."

I was impressed she'd made friends with the constable—Tess who feared and loathed the police. "And what do these two resourceful young men have to say?" I asked.

"Well, Caleb, the constable, says that when he was walking his beat, he swears the window at the Harkness house weren't open at nine o'clock—the one everyone says *was* open. That window would be hard to climb through, he says, as it's behind the railings and high off the ground. The burglar would need rope and hooks and such, and there was no sign of that. Caleb didn't notice it open until half past ten that night, but he never saw anyone coming or going through it."

"Jove," Mr. Thanos said, looking excited. "A blind."

"No, it has curtains," Tess said, and laughed out loud. "Just teasing ya, Mr. Thanos. Looks like someone opened the window to make us *think* the killer came in and left that way."

"Which means he—or she—was admitted to the house through a door, and likely remained after Sir Jacob was killed," I concluded. I'd always thought the window must have been opened to suggest a burglar, but it was nice to have my theory confirmed.

"And no one ever used the window," Daniel said, the satisfaction in his eyes matching mine.

"But the drawing room was a wreck," Cynthia said. "I saw it. Tables overturned, drapes torn . . ."

"Which could also have been done deliberately," Mr. Thanos said, his cheeks growing red as Cynthia turned to him.

"Anyone in the house that night could have killed Sir Jacob," I said, touching my fingers as I listed names. "Lady Harkness, Mrs. Knowles, Mrs. Finnegan—the rest of the servants as well, including Mrs. Redfern and Sheppard. Mr. Chancellor arrived, but claimed he departed once he learned Sir Jacob was abed. Did the servants see him go?"

"No one saw him but Sheppard, so the footman told me," Tess said. "Caleb watched Mr. Chancellor go in, but never saw him come out. Though Mr. Chancellor could have left when Caleb was around the corner."

"And what the devil has become of Sheppard?" Cynthia asked.

"A reasonable question," Daniel said. "Mr. Pasfield might also have been at the house that night, let in by Mrs. Finnegan. He was on the spot quickly in the morning."

"Very quickly," Tess agreed. "Within the hour of Sir Jacob being found, according to the footman. But no one saw him arrive."

"There you are, then," Cynthia said. "It was Pasfield. Had to be."

"There's one other," I said slowly. "Two, really."

"Zhen Harkness," Daniel said, catching my eye.

"And Mr. Li," I finished. "I do not want it to be him. But he came to see me, was on the street, and I don't know where he went after he disappeared into the mist toward Berkeley Square. I swore to Inspector McGregor that he never returned to Mount Street, but I can't know that, can I? If we speculate that the window wasn't the means of entry, Sheppard or Sir Jacob himself might have let Mr. Li in through the front door after I went back to my kitchen. Mr. Li could have quarreled with Sir Jacob and killed him, opened the window and lay down the furniture to make it look as though a burglary had been committed, then slipped out another way."

I ceased speaking, sorrow in my heart.

19

Daniel squeezed my hand, his voice gentle. "The same can be said for Zhen, Kat. Sir Jacob would have admitted him—his son—possibly himself, to not draw attention to the lad. Or else Sheppard was sworn to secrecy. Zhen was young and athletic—he could have left by the window even if he didn't enter by it."

"Sir Jacob often *did* answer the door himself," Tess said, eager to return to her report. "So footman says. Drove Mrs. Redfern spare. Footman says Sir Jacob had several visitors that day, but as Sir Jacob admitted them himself, he doesn't know who they were."

"Sheppard would know, presumably," I said. "A good manservant is a gentleman's shadow, always on hand to provide coffee or brandy or a hat, anticipating his master's every need. He'd see who came and went. Probably why he's missing," I finished glumly. "Unless he did the deed himself."

Cynthia broke in. "Hang on, now. You're saying a chap

visited Sir Jacob earlier in the evening, waited around until he went to bed, stabbed him to death, then crawled out a window—or out a door after opening the window to throw the police off the scent—and toddled off home."

"It's possible," Daniel said.

"Or a woman did it." Tess rested her chin on her clasped hands. "Mrs. Knowles was there. She could have rushed down and opened the window and knocked things about. Caleb, the constable, says he tried to tell the sergeant the window weren't open at nine or even shortly after, when Sir Jacob was getting himself killed, but the sergeant wouldn't listen. And Caleb weren't allowed to speak to Inspector McGregor."

"Foolish," I said. "But I cannot be surprised. Those with a small amount of power are inclined to abuse it."

Mr. Thanos peered about morosely. He'd not put on his spectacles, probably because Cynthia was there, and he rather squinted at us. "So we are back to the fact that anyone connected with Sir Jacob could have done it. Only Mrs. Tatlock was not in residence, correct?" he asked Tess.

"No, she were there," Tess said with confidence. "She came with Mrs. Knowles. Said she had a headache and could she lie down in a spare bedchamber? Was asleep when all the ruckus happened, and missed it, so she says. She departed quietly later in the night."

"Oh." Mr. Thanos looked even more crestfallen. "And I haven't helped at all with this case. Though I could have a look at Sir Jacob's pottery with the inscriptions, see if there is anything in that. Mr. Li might have found something worth killing for, even if he didn't do the killing himself."

I gazed at my hands resting on the tabletop, work worn, with one finger pink where I'd brushed it against a hot roasting pan a few days ago. Mr. Thanos was close to the mark, but I did not want to mention the stolen tea in front of Bobby.

"I think Zhen was killed because he saw whoever it was come out the window . . . or out of the house by other means," I said. "I believe he did come from China to find his father, whether to ask for money or help, or just to speak to him, we will never know. I wager it was he Sir Jacob went to Kew Gardens to meet that night, perhaps to keep Zhen from the house—or perhaps Zhen wanted to meet there for some reason. But Zhen followed Sir Jacob home. He arrived between nine and half past ten and saw the killer going in or out. Zhen might have understood what he saw, or he might not have. Either way, he was tracked down and killed."

"At the Temperate House in Kew Gardens in the middle of the night," Mr. Thanos said. "Interesting place for a murder."

"He'd know his way about if he met his father there," Daniel said. "He and Sir Jacob might have rendezvoused at Kew more than once. The murderer could have lured him there, promising him money for silence, or to try to explain away what Zhen saw."

Or Zhen could have been searching for Mr. Li's tea, I mused. If he'd learned of its existence, he'd realize it would be worth a fortune.

"Murdering Zhen at Kew points to the Chancellor fellow," Cynthia said. "He'd have access to the Temperate House. Not everyone in London has a key."

"Locks can be picked," Daniel said. "But yes, Chancellor looks very suspicious. Of course, the murderer might have chosen the place to point to him."

Bobby, who'd listened in silence, sipping a large glass of port, now said, "What a mess. This Zhen chappie is dead because he saw something. Sheppard is missing, probably for the same reason, as very likely is your Mr. Li. Sounds like the murderer is picking off any witnesses. Lady Harkness will be next, I'll wager. How can the killer be certain *she* saw nothing?"

"She takes a tonic," I said. "Before bed. It's a sleeping draught. I saw the bottle on the night table, from an apothecary. She'd have been fast asleep, as she claims."

"Her friends are dosing her," Tess said abruptly.

We turned to her, Tess waiting for our attention.

"Dosing?" I prompted.

"Giving her something to make her tired and compliant. Like laudanum. Would that be in a sleeping draught?"

"Not necessarily," I said. "Chamomile and lavender can soothe one to sleep. But laudanum would make her tired all the time, yes, and eventually some grow to depend on it."

"There you are, then." Tess looked pleased. "The footman had it from the upstairs maid that she's seen Mrs. Tatlock put drops of something in the tonic quite often. The two ladies have been heard talking about it, how they have planned for—oh—two years now to make her leave everything to them in her will."

Lady Cynthia's eyes widened. "They talked of this openly? Are they mad?"

"In secret, so they thought. But there's ways to hear."

"Jove, I ought to look out what I say in *my* house," Cynthia said, half in jest. "But they'd know servants hear everything, wouldn't they? I can't imagine them being so careless."

"Oh, a *servant* didn't hear that." Tess's grin widened. "I had a secret informant. Name of James McAdam."

Daniel went very still. "Oh?"

"He were happy to help. He's been hired on for odd jobs up and down the street, so it were easy to convince the groom or

Mrs. Redfern to bring him in from time to time to haul coal or clean out the garden shed or brush the horses. Mrs. Knowles and Mrs. Tatlock liked to have their chats in the garden, and James could be in the shed or on the other side of the wall. Those two planned to take her for everything she had."

Cynthia's eyes widened in shock. "They said so? That blatantly?"

"They did. Mrs. Tatlock is always on her ladyship to hand over money for her missionaries, though her ladyship has resisted so far. The charitable cause is her own pocket, *I'd* say. Mrs. Knowles touches her ladyship for a little bit here, a little bit there, even invented a niece who needs money for looking after. Ain't no such person."

"Ah." Cynthia rested her boot on her chair and hooked her arm around her slim leg. "So I'm right that when I prodded Lady Harkness to sell up and go home, and she made clear she'd take my advice, they *did* make her sick so she couldn't."

"The harpies," I said angrily. I always believed in speaking respectfully of my betters, but as Tess had pointed out, not everyone above one's station in life is necessarily *better*. "I believe I will present all this to Mrs. Redfern, and she can tell Lady Harkness. Perhaps you could be there when she breaks the news, Lady Cynthia, to give it even more credence. Well done, Tess."

Tess beamed under my praise, eyes sparkling.

"I wondered why I hadn't seen much of James lately," Daniel said in a mild tone. "Now I find he's been snooping about a house in which a murder occurred, where, if Lady Roberta is correct, the witnesses are being killed or put out of the way."

"James weren't there when the murder happened," Tess said quickly. "I didn't ask him until days after. And it's no different from what you do."

"I am aware of that." Daniel's voice was dry. "But I believe I'll have a chat with James. Please, tell him not to go back to the house for a bit."

Tess looked downcast. "'Ere, I didn't mean to get him into trouble. He were happy to help."

"Oh, I have no doubt he was most eager." Daniel gave her a pointed look. "All the same."

Tess scowled, but nodded. "I'll tell 'im."

I curled my hands on the table. "I've become very, very anxious for Mr. Li. Perhaps one of the two ladies—or both of them—were talking of plans to rob Lady Harkness when Mr. Li arrived for his appointment with Sir Jacob, and he heard them. Part of the plot may have been to kill Sir Jacob so they could more easily go through his things. Or perhaps . . ." I grew more thoughtful. "*Sir Jacob* learned that the two women were trying to siphon everything from his wife and confronted them, and they killed him. If Mr. Li heard anything of this, the ladies would want to find him and silence him too. If they could murder robust Sir Jacob, they'd have no trouble with Mr. Li. Mrs. Tatlock is quite wiry."

"Damnation." The explosion came from Mr. Thanos, who immediately looked contrite. "I do beg your pardon, ladies. But I've just thought—if Mr. Li heard plotting when he turned up to visit, so did Sutherland. He might be in danger, and at this moment, he's happily lecturing to a crowd at a museum."

"I doubt this killer will throw a knife at him in front of an audience," Daniel said, raising a calming hand. "He or she likes secrecy. But I take your point. He will have to come off the podium at some time."

Mr. Thanos leapt to his feet. "I must go." He glanced at Lady Cynthia, his brow furrowed. "Er, would you . . . That is . . . Perhaps . . . ?"

"I believe he's asking you to accompany him, Cyn," Bobby said, merriment in her eyes.

Cynthia flushed. I remembered what she'd told me about losing her nerve at appearing before Thanos's friends in her men's clothing.

"Perhaps Professor Sutherland will understand," I suggested, with a pointed look at Cynthia's suit.

"Eh?" Mr. Thanos blinked at me then Cynthia, who'd unfolded herself from the chair. "Yes, Sutherland understands about all that. I've told him about you. He wants to meet you."

Cynthia's flush deepened. "Wants a look at an oddity, does he?"

"Pardon? No, indeed. Sutherland is a rather open-minded man. He finds you refreshing." Mr. Thanos grew as red as Cynthia. "Not that I speak of you at length. Please don't misunderstand." He began to splutter.

"For God's sake, Elgin," Daniel said, having risen when Cynthia did. "Argue about it on the way. Stand watch over the man until we can decide whether he is in danger."

Mr. Thanos cleared his throat, wound his hands together, and glanced nervously at his hat hanging near the door.

Cynthia put an end to the debate. "Come on, Thanos. This is no time for us to prevaricate. I will give your friend a chance, and if we have to save his life to do it, so be it."

She seized her hat and Mr. Thanos's as well, thrusting it at him as she led the way out.

Bobby, still in her chair, applauded as they went. We heard the door slam below. "Poor things. Do you think they'll realize it one day?"

I was pleased to see her interest in the dance between Cynthia and Mr. Thanos. Cynthia had been unhappy she'd hurt Bobby when she'd turned aside Bobby's amorousness. However, Bobby seemed to have reconciled herself to the fact that she and Cynthia would never be anything more than friends.

I got to my feet. "Thank you for your hospitality, my lady."

"Not at all. Great fun. Can I help look for the missing chappies? Besides the valet, I mean. Already have inquiries going about him." Bobby had a robust energy that went with her rather masculine face, the sharpness of it emphasized by her cropped hair. "What about this Chinese bloke? Where do you begin the hunt for a Chinaman? Chinatown, presumably."

"Which will be my lookout," Daniel said quickly. "I know my way around there."

He sent me a quelling glance, as though he expected I'd leap on a train and take myself on an instant to Limehouse.

Truth to tell, I wanted to. I was very worried about Mr. Li. But I decided to let Daniel have his way, while I returned to Mount Street to begin the search a little closer to home.

It was still Tess's day out, and I determined she'd have it, so upon arriving home I scrambled to prepare the evening meal on my own. Mr. Davis said nothing about my absence, greeting me serenely and going about his business. Neither did he speak about Mrs. Daley, to my relief. The lady did not appear to be in the house at all, but I did not have time to inquire where she'd gone.

Friday suppers were not as involved as those on Sundays, but I prided myself on not simply slapping down cold meat left over from earlier in the week and having done.

I thought about the noodle dish I had tasted in Covent Garden and spent a little time trying to replicate it—not to serve upstairs but to taste for myself. I gave the Bywaters roasted pork with a sauce of apples, brown sugar, and cloves; mashed potatoes; and a salad of greens and walnuts. I'd found some good damsons, plump and purple, in the market, and sent up a bowl of those, dusted with sugar, for pudding.

The noodles, from what I remembered, had a soupy sauce containing finely diced chicken, a bit of ginger and garlic, and a few more complex flavors. The young man had told me fish "essence," star anise, and peppers. The peppers had been red, possibly something like cayenne.

I decided that the dark, salty flavor I'd tasted had come from soy. It was difficult to find a good sauce of soy that hadn't been watered down, oversalted, or treated with molasses to make it darker, but I had one or two merchants in mind whom I could trust for imported foods.

I put together an indifferent copy of the noodles, which was not terrible, but it wasn't the same. I'd have to visit a Chinese market and see if I could find better ingredients. Perhaps when we found Mr. Li—if we did, and he was alive and well—he could advise me.

I busied myself to keep my worry about Mr. Li at bay. It was true that any of the household, including Mr. Chancellor, could have heard or seen what they should not and be in danger. Daniel was right to say James should have nothing more to do with it, and I would tell Tess the same. She'd run off to look in on her brother after we departed from Bobby's flat, so I at least hoped she wouldn't be investigating today.

I chafed at my confinement in the kitchen, but cooking is tedious and time-consuming work if it is to be done well. Even boiling an egg takes a certain skill.

Tess returned in time to eat supper with the staff. She looked relaxed and refreshed from her day out and helped me finish off my noodles, remarking in surprise that she liked them.

Lady Cynthia had not returned home by the time I went to bed, and I heard nothing from Daniel. I hoped I would not have to worry about them as well.

Saturday dawned, and that morning Mr. Davis declared he'd take his day out.

I regarded him in astonishment as I sautéed onions and leftover peppers to go into omelets. "You never take a day out, Mr. Davis."

"Well, I will today." He'd dressed in a dark suit and overcoat and now pressed a bowler hat to his head. "I will return in time to serve the evening meal. Good morning, Mrs. Holloway."

Tess, Elsie, Charlie, and I all stared at him as he walked out of the kitchen and lightly up the outside stairs to the street.

"He's an odd one, to be sure," Tess said. I did not respond, but I wondered very much.

Tess said little about what she'd done the day before, except to report happily that her brother was well. Neither of us mentioned Mr. Li, Sir Jacob, the murder, or anything of that nature.

I did not have time to, in any case. I had to direct the maids and footmen in their duties as no one knew what had become of Mrs. Daley.

Truth to tell, the house felt lighter without her in it. The maids were less harried, the footmen joking and laughing—they exhibited more high spirits than they ought to have, but I could not bring myself to admonish them.

The day proceeded as usual for a Saturday. Mr. Bywater departed for his club, and Paul the footman brought down a message that Mr. Bywater would dine there and not be home for supper. The master had spent much more time at his club lately, and I wondered if this was significant.

Not five minutes after Mrs. Bywater went out on her daily calls, Sara appeared and told me Cynthia had sent for me.

Cynthia wore a gentleman's suit, but she'd not dressed to go out. She barged about the small sitting room in the rear of the house in beaded slippers that were incongruous with her trousers, waistcoat, and frock coat.

"There you are, Mrs. H, Auntie's gone, and this confounded house is empty. Where is everyone?"

"Working away downstairs," I said. "Pleased that Mrs. Daley is not here."

Cynthia halted in midpace, and shot me a grin with a lightning-swift change of mood. "I persuaded Auntie to tell me why she won't sack Mrs. Daley. I told her Mrs. D. is a bully and excellent at getting everyone but herself to do work, and that she needed to be sacked. Auntie agreed, to my surprise. Auntie's friend, who'd had Mrs. Daley as a cook, is holding some sort of obligation over Auntie. She wouldn't tell me what, no matter how much I prodded. But the bargain is, she takes the awful Mrs. Daley and Auntie's friend considers the obligation fulfilled."

"Is blackmail the fashion these days?" I asked sourly. "Mrs. Bywater is being coerced to employ Mrs. Daley, who in turn is trying to blackmail me about Grace's existence, which she found out about by snooping at my old digs. She threatened Mr. Davis as well, though I'm not certain what she believes she has on him."

"Oh, *that*." Cynthia waved it aside, mirroring Mr. Davis's reaction. "There was some talk of Mr. Davis and a footman, long, long ago. Mr. Davis says it's all nonsense and a misinterpretation, and I believe him. If Mr. Davis was an unnatural, there'd be much more talk about him than that one incident. Men—don't matter whether they prefer the female sex or the male—can't help but be libertines. So if it did continue, he has been impossibly discreet."

"Mr. Davis never shows much interest in women," I said, thinking it through. "Men either, for that matter."

Cynthia shrugged. "Some folks don't have any interest one way or another. I'm not sure why *that's* not called 'unnatural' instead of preferring one's own sex. It's hard to imagine not wanting anyone, ever."

"Desires of the flesh can be wearying," I said, rather envying those who had dispensed with them.

I'd once thought myself finished with passion forever. It was a distraction, and really, I had no time for it. Then Daniel McAdam had made a delivery to a kitchen, and the cocoon I'd woven around myself had begun to crack.

"I wouldn't know how wearying they are," Cynthia said, her mirth gone. "I'm not likely to know either, unless I marry one of the idiots Uncle parades before me. I can't think of a greater deterrent to desire than those popinjays."

I had to agree. "You did not invite me upstairs to talk about desire," I said. "Although we can have that discussion if you like."

"Ha. I am restless and need something to do. I meant to tell you about yesterday. Mr. Thanos and I rushed to Sutherland's lecture at the British Museum, elbowed our way to the front, and stood watch. Absolutely no one tried to assassinate him, though a know-all did attempt to trip him up over a question on ancient China—in the Warring States period, I think it was. Sutherland skewered him. Metaphorically, of course. We escorted Sutherland home and told him why. He said he'd seen and heard nothing unusual the night he took Mr. Li to Sir Jacob's, so he believes he's perfectly safe, but he was concerned we'd lost Mr. Li."

I twined my fingers together. "I have the terrible feeling that when we find Mr. Li, it will be awful. He'll either be dead or a murderer."

"Don't give way, Mrs. H." Cynthia gave my shoulder a pat. "We've been in tighter spots."

"At great cost." I recalled the explosion on the river between Devonshire and Cornwall, the calm viciousness of the criminal called Pilcher as he talked over how to kill us, and the horror of seeing James run down by a wagon.

"Inspector McGregor is scouring the metropolis for Mr. Li," Cynthia said. "Thanos and I went to Mr. Li's rooms and found constables all over the street looking for the man, and on watch in case he returns."

"He will never return if constables are surrounding the place. Mr. Li is no fool."

"Another reason not to worry too much about him," Cynthia said, trying to comfort me. "He's taken care of himself this long."

That was true, but I no longer trusted my convictions.

"Thanos went to stay with Sutherland," Cynthia went on. "He said that two spindly academics were better than one. Sutherland's opinion is that Mr. Li went back to China once his existence became complicated by police and murders. He's an important man in his circle and will be warmly welcomed home."

I could hope Mr. Li was on his way home, and safe, but I knew in my heart he hadn't departed these shores. He'd not leave England until he found out what had become of his father's tea.

I'd thought very hard about what had become of the tea, and I believed I knew the answer, but I kept it to myself for now. I'd need Mr. Li to confirm it.

"Did you find Mr. Sutherland acceptable on this occasion?" I asked her. "The last time you saw him with Mr. Thanos, you rushed away. I am pleased you settled your mind."

Cynthia looked abashed. "Don't cast up my shortcomings to me, Mrs. H. I was understandably nervous. Thanos has always spoken highly of Mr. Sutherland, and if Sutherland didn't like me . . ."

"But he did?"

Cynthia blew out a breath. "He seemed to approve of my unconventionality. But he's an oddity himself, he said, preferring the intellectual life to that of politics, or sport, or chasing money and women as gentlemen are supposed to. Even so . . ."

"Even so?"

She shrugged. "Mr. Thanos is curious about me and my ways, but in a friendly fashion. Mr. Sutherland was plenty friendly, but in a different way. As though he was curious about why I wore men's clothing but not interested in *me*, if you understand what I mean."

"A scholar through and through," I suggested.

"Something like that. But he did not condemn me or embarrass Mr. Thanos, so all is well."

I was happy to hear it.

Cynthia abruptly changed the subject. "Any word from McAdam?"

"Not a blessed one. Or James, though Tess says Mrs. Redfern is looking for him to run more errands for her. She likes him."

"James is a good lad." Cynthia stuck her hands into her pockets. "I haven't heard from Bobby either. I suppose she's enjoying herself."

"She seems to have recovered from you not wishing to live with her," I said.

"I *do* want to live with her, but we have it clear now on

what terms. Bobby's not the sentimental type, fortunately, so when I explained things to her, she was disappointed but happily turned her attentions elsewhere. I suspect she had her eye on the other lady the whole time, hedging her bets. I'm not sure whether to be offended or relieved."

I did laugh this time. It felt good to laugh. "Relieved is the correct choice. You felt guilty for not being able to be what she wanted."

"We're still great friends—that's the best thing. It's good to have a friend, Mrs. H."

I agreed. My friendship with Joanna Millburn was one of the joys of my life. I wanted to count Lady Cynthia as such a friend, though I knew it was not the way of the world for a cook to be great chums with an earl's daughter.

Cynthia waved her hands. "I must go out and do something or I'll perish here. I'll put on a frock and visit Lady Harkness. Make sure she's well."

"It's good of you."

"Poor woman has been through hell. I'll let you know if anything interesting turns up."

We let it go at that.

I returned below stairs, looked over the dough Tess had rolled out for a meat pie, and declared it well done. Pastry was difficult to master, but she was coming along. Tess looked pleased with my praise, and I left her to it to step next door myself.

Mrs. Finnegan was busy in her kitchen, also making pastry but for an apricot tart. At her insistence, I sampled some of the filling bubbling on the stove and advised her to put in much more sugar and maybe a touch of cinnamon. Then I turned to why I'd come.

"Mrs. Finnegan," I began. "I believe I will need your help."

20

---◆-----◆---

By the time I returned home after my conference with Mrs. Finnegan, Daniel was there, delivering a heavy sack of flour I hadn't ordered. I remembered my conversation with Cynthia about passion and deliberately turned to my work table to help Tess with the pies.

Daniel began to heave the sack off his shoulders. "Don't set it there," I said. "You'll just have to move it again. Put it in the larder."

He gave me a good-natured grin and hauled the bag through the kitchen and into the narrow passageway. "Whoops," he said as he nearly ran down Emma on her way in. She flushed but did not look displeased.

When Daniel returned from the larder, he snatched up a piece of peppered beef ready for the pies and popped it into his mouth. "I love a good steak and kidney. Save me a slice, Tess. I know it's useless to ask Mrs. Holloway."

"Right you are," Tess said with a wink.

"Why are you so cheery?" I asked him. "Did something happen?"

Daniel waited until Emma had gone and Elsie was clattering dishes in the scullery. "No, unfortunately. But I like to keep my spirits up." He filched another piece of beef before I could stop him. "I'm sorry, Kat. I haven't found Mr. Li."

I nodded as I folded the dough to put into its pan. "You'd have said so right away if you had."

"I went to Limehouse and other places where Chinese families live. I asked about. No one has seen him—few had even heard of him."

"Did you make your inquiries in Chinese?" Tess asked. "Maybe they didn't understand you."

"My grasp of the language is rudimentary, I admit," Daniel said. "But I know men in Chinatown who interpret for me."

"Of course you do," I said. "Daniel has all of London in the palm of his hand."

"Don't make fun of me, Kat." He spoke teasingly, but his expression was somber. "I did learn a few details about Zhen, however. He'd boarded with a family in Limehouse, and while he didn't tell them much about his business, they put things together. They discerned that he'd journeyed to London to find his father—whether they knew that father was an Englishman, I don't know, and I didn't mention it. They said he went out one evening and never returned. They were not terribly surprised when I told them he was dead." He reached into his coat. "They let me take his things."

He spread out a knotted handkerchief to reveal a pitifully sparse collection—a few English coins, a paper written in Chinese, and a piece of card, very dirty, but I saw the word *Kew* on it.

I lifted the card. It was flimsy, a souvenir from Kew Gardens with a drawing of plants and the pagoda. The card had been folded and unfolded several times, worn around the edges and the fold.

"So he did go to Kew," I said. "Before the night he was killed, I mean, or he wouldn't have this. To meet Sir Jacob? We still do not know for certain why Sir Jacob went there the evening of his murder."

"Or someone sent this to Zhen as a message, luring him to Kew to be killed."

"I wonder why Zhen did turn up that night," I said thoughtfully. "Was he looking for . . ." I trailed off, choosing my words, as there were too many ears in the room. "Sir Jacob's plants? Or did he arrange to meet the killer? Perhaps Zhen knew who killed his father and was demanding money for his silence." More blackmail.

"Don't matter know, does it?" Tess asked. "Whatever he believed, whoever he met, they did him over."

"Poor lad." I touched the kerchief. Along with the clothes on his back and the letters Inspector McGregor had found in his pockets, this had been all he'd had, or at least all Zhen had brought with him from his faraway home.

"I hope Mr. Li hasn't met the same fate," Daniel said.

As did I. "Mr. Li strikes me as a man who's been down a few streets," I said. "He wouldn't fall for someone luring him to Kew in the middle of the night, even if they did claim they had valuable knowledge for him."

"No, but someone could have set a trap of a different kind," Daniel said quietly.

"Or Mr. Li might have done the luring," Tess said.

"I know." I was not happy about that. "But my first instincts told me he was innocent, and those instincts usually aren't wrong."

"I trust them." Daniel's eyes held warmth. Before I could respond, he turned away. "I must get my hands on James. Things I need him to do."

"You won't be able to order him about much longer," I warned him. "He'll be a man soon."

"I have a little bit of time." Daniel stole another tidbit of beef. "I must make use of it. Good afternoon, ladies."

He tipped his cap to Elsie as he went through the scullery and ran up the outer stairs with a spring in his step.

"I'm right that you need to marry him," Tess said to me decidedly. "That man needs looking after."

I longed to answer her with a quelling witticism, but absolutely none came to mind. I could only frown at her and tell her to go back to work.

M r. Davis returned at five o'clock, just as I sent up tea to Mrs. Bywater, who was home from her calls.

Cynthia also returned, entering through the kitchen to report to me. Lady Harkness was recovering, she said, and neither Mrs. Knowles nor Mrs. Tatlock had been seen since the night Cynthia had sent them away.

"Did you have a fine day out, Mr. Davis?" I asked him after Cynthia had gone to join her aunt for tea.

"Yes, yes. Most productive." Mr. Davis removed his hat, used two fingers to straighten his hairpiece, and continued down the hall toward the butler's pantry.

I stepped into the passage to watch him shrug out of his coat and hang it and hat on a peg inside the pantry's doorway. He made no move to tell me anything further, so I returned to preparing for supper.

I was searing breadcrumb-encrusted sole filets in my

frying pan, the scent of baking meat pies seeping from the oven, when James came rushing into the kitchen. "Mrs. H.— where did my dad get to?"

Tess paused her chopping in concern, but I could not look up from shaking the fish around the buttered pan, lest it burn.

"Has something happened?" I asked over my shoulder. I was not unduly concerned, as James was wont to rush about excitedly, and often asked after his father here.

"Mr. Thanos has a message for him." James fished a folded paper from his pocket. "I think it's very important."

"Don't you know?" Tess reached garlicky fingers for it, but James held it back.

"I can't read it, can I?"

"Well, I can," Tess said impatiently. "Give it here."

"No, no. I mean, I know my letters. But this ain't them."

I scooped the filets from the pan and set them on a plate— they were so thin they were already done. I wiped my hands as I approached James, whose face was red with windburn and worry.

He handed me the paper, which hadn't been sealed in any way, only folded into quarters. I opened it and looked over the contents in perplexity.

The single page was covered with numbers—a few letters poked their way in here and there, but they looked like Greek writing.

"Mathematical formulas, I believe," I said. "What they mean, I have no idea. Would your father?"

James shrugged his large shoulders. "Maybe. Mr. Thanos said I was to get it to Dad, and he'd know what to do. You haven't seen him?"

"Much earlier, and he went off looking for you."

"He found me *then*. Not since?"

"No." I studied the strings of numbers, my worry rising. "I wish I knew what these meant."

"That Mr. Sutherland might," Tess said. "He and Mr. Thanos have the same book learning, don't they?"

"Mr. Sutherland is the gent what gave this to me," James said. "Dad sent me to be a lookout for him and Mr. Thanos today, in case the killer goes hunting for them. Mr. Sutherland comes out and says Mr. Thanos is in a bother about getting these numbers to a fellow who's giving a lecture tonight—the chap is using some of Mr. Thanos's theories, he says, and Mr. Thanos was supposed to assist, but he don't want to leave Mr. Sutherland alone. So he asked me to take the formulas to Dad to give to this bloke. Mr. Sutherland said *he* couldn't understand them, as he knows languages, not mathematics, but they looked important to him."

I scanned the paper once again, but I could see nothing more than I had before. The letters spelled out no messages that I could discern.

"Why didn't Mr. Thanos instruct you to go directly to the lecturer?" I asked.

"Don't know. Maybe Mr. Thanos thought the lecture hall wouldn't let in a scruffy lad like me." He sounded more concerned than offended. "Mr. Thanos's message was to give these to Dad, and Dad would know where to take them."

"Then I say that we must find your father." I gave James a sharp look. "But the person who would most likely know where he is, is you."

James scrubbed his hair. "He ain't in his usual places, and he ain't at home. That's why I thought he might have come to see you again."

"Blast the man." I thought rapidly, and then untied my apron strings with quick tugs. "Tess, finish supper. Have Mr. Davis help you if need be. It's simple tonight—just the fish and the pies, and fruit for pudding."

Tess glared indignantly. "You're rushing off to have adventures, just like that, are you? *I* can help look for Mr. McAdam."

"I do not intend to search for Daniel—a needle in a haystack that would be. You stay here so if he arrives, you can tell him where I've gone. James, you and I are off to speak to Mr. Thanos and Mr. Sutherland. I do believe they are in grave danger."

J ames guided me to Howland Street, a lane off Tottenham Court Road. The houses on this road were plain brick affairs, the sort to house rooms for gentlemen who studied at the nearby British Museum and other places of learning.

Mr. Sutherland had taken lodgings in a house in the middle of the row. A woman with narrow shoulders and large hands opened the door to our knock and gave us an inquiring look.

"Mr. Thanos still here?" James asked hurriedly.

"Mr. Thanos?" The woman blinked baleful eyes, clearly not recognizing the name.

"A guest of Professor Sutherland," I told her.

Her expression cleared. "Oh, the two university gents. No, dear, they went out."

"Out?" I repeated faintly.

I knew in my bones that Mr. Thanos's message had been a plea for help. Whether or not the formulas meant anything, Mr. Thanos had used them as an excuse to send James running for Daniel. Mr. Sutherland had taken the paper to James in the street, because it wouldn't be unusual for a man who lived in this house to summon an errand boy, and a page full of mathematics would have been innocuous had James been waylaid and searched.

The two gentlemen had been taken somewhere, I firmly believed. The ploy was not as effective as Mr. Thanos had hoped.

"Where did they go?" I asked the landlady in desperation.

"Don't know, dear. A hansom came 'round."

"Did you hear where they told the driver to take them? Please, it's very important."

The woman shook her head. "The world of academics must be an exciting place, I'm sure. Lots of arguing and hasty talk upstairs all last night and throughout today—I didn't understand a word of it." She considered, too slowly for my taste. "Now, let me think. One of them said something about a garden. Maybe they wanted a look at Regent's Park. Or maybe Kensington Gardens."

I was off as soon as she said the word *garden*, the rest of her speech fading into the darkening afternoon.

James sprinted next to me, his youthful gait easily keeping up with mine. "Where are we going, Mrs. H.?"

"I need a cab to the nearest Metropolitan station. You run back to Mount Street and find Lady Cynthia and tell her what's happened. Then hunt down your father, no matter what you have to do to find him."

I waved my arms at a hansom, which in no way slowed for me. James rushed at another, nearly grabbing the horse's bridle before the growling cabbie halted his rig. I scrambled aboard, and told the cabbie where I wanted to go.

He started the horse, and I shouted around the door. "Tell

Lady Cynthia to take herself to Kew Gardens, at once. And find your blasted father!"

The cab slid around a corner, heading for the underground stop at Portland Road. I saw James leap into the air, yelling, "Right you are, Mrs. H.!" before he came down at a run and was gone.

21

◆—◆

The journey to Kew Gardens took far longer than I liked. I had to change my train at Notting Hill Gate, and then I bumped westward, sometimes in tunnels, sometimes mercifully aboveground, but at last the train slid to a halt at Kew Gardens station.

It was growing dark, and the gates to the gardens would be closing soon. I ran for them, dodging through the crowd flowing out.

"Mrs. H.!" Lady Cynthia materialized out of the shadows, dressed in trousers and greatcoat. "What has happened? James came barreling in as I was readying myself to go to Bobby's and told me to dash to Kew as fast as I could. Mr. Thanos is *here*? And Sutherland? Why?"

"Because Sir Jacob and his son were murdered," I said hurriedly. "And the search for the tea continues. We must run."

I caught her hand and dragged her along toward the Temperate House. Cynthia, bewildered, jogged beside me.

"The tea truly is here? And why didn't Thanos simply send for us?"

"Because the killer would not let him. I've thought it through—we have a man fluent in Chinese, together with a man who knows exactly what the stolen tea is worth, because it belongs to his family. What else is needed? A botanist, perhaps? One who knows where the tea would be kept at Kew Gardens."

"Mr. Chancellor?" Lady Cynthia gazed at me in surprise. "Good Lord—*he* is behind this? But what about Mr. Li? Is he here too?"

"He is, if I am not mistaken. Mr. Thanos, unfortunately, has been caught up in the madness."

Cynthia shot me a frightened look. "We must rescue him, then."

"Exactly why we are here," I said then saved my breath as we hurried down the muddy path.

The Temperate House had sprung first to my mind when Mr. Sutherland's landlady mentioned a garden. Young Zhen had been killed there, and I had the feeling he'd been searching for Sir Jacob's tea plants. Sir Jacob might not have left anything in his will to his illegitimate son, but he could have told Zhen about the stolen tea, giving him the secret to vast wealth. The murderer had either found Zhen or lured him here, perhaps pretending to help.

I led Cynthia to the side door of the Temperate House, where Daniel had let us out the day Zhen had been found. It was unlocked.

Wouldn't they bolt the side doors first before closing up for the night? I wondered dimly. *To shunt any stragglers out the front door?*

Whatever decisions those in charge of the gardens had made, they hadn't yet secured the door. I did not pause long to worry—I simply stepped inside.

No rain beat upon the roofs this time, and one chance ray of the setting sun flared against the glass. The walls and ceiling blazed like a sheet of diamonds, so bright I screwed my eyes shut.

When I opened them again, the light had winked out, dusk falling quickly.

Shadows made the arching trees seem to sway, and palms reached black fingers across the glass sky. A stiff breeze sprang up the walkway and then cut off, as though a door somewhere had been opened and slammed shut.

I did not want to look at the spot where Zhen had been found, but I couldn't help myself. The crushed bushes had been trimmed back. The setting was as lush as ever, the scent of night-blooming flowers heady.

The place was deathly silent. Cynthia shivered and pulled her coat close.

We moved to the main hall, its enormity breathtaking but equally silent. I thought we'd find the caretakers or perhaps a lingering botanist caught up in his research, but we saw no one.

I pointed to the corner where a spiral staircase ran up to the railed gallery along the high windows. From there we could look over the greenhouse and see if anyone lurked.

Cynthia would not let me go first. She didn't speak but rather firmly pushed past me and began the ascent, making sure her boots made no noise on the metal steps. I gathered my skirts and followed her, holding hard to the railing with my gloved hand.

Once we reached the top, we looked down on greenery, succulents, flower beds, and trees, many of which grew taller than the gallery. The wide, main walkway below bisected the hall, and several other walks met it at right angles.

The greenery whispered and moved, and I saw that a few top windows were open, likely to regulate the temperature inside. It was warm in here, though not much warmer than a fine spring day.

Two men came down the main walk from the north end of the building. Cynthia drew a breath to call out, but I stilled her with a hand on her wrist.

"Is he here?" Mr. Thanos asked the taller man at his side. "Jove, we need to find him. What's this way?" He pointed down a side path.

"I don't know. More shrubbery, it looks like."

"If we find him, what then?" Mr. Thanos sounded worried.

"Let us concentrate on locating the fellow first."

They took the path, voices drifting away. I tiptoed along the gallery to keep them in sight, Cynthia nearly treading on me to keep up.

She whispered into my ear, "Why aren't we going to them? Helping?"

I held up my finger to hush her. We reached the spot where the two men had left the main walk, and I clasped the rail and looked down.

The two gentlemen wandered along the side path, the taller and the shorter in nearly identical suits. Black hair and red showed below their tall hats. They looked about for a moment then returned to the main walk, moving to the next intersecting path. Cynthia and I followed like ghosts above them.

"There you are!" Mr. Sutherland cried suddenly. He struck

out with a walking stick, right into a stand of palms. "Come out of there, blast you."

A man unfolded from the greenery, giving the stick a wide berth. The last of the dusky light showed me a wispy beard against a dark silk robe.

Mr. Li.

I wanted to gasp and rush down the stairs. Mr. Li was alive and well—and Mr. Sutherland looked to be afraid of him. He kept the tip of the walking stick pointing at Mr. Li's chest.

"Well?" Mr. Sutherland said. "Did you find it?"

"No." Mr. Li's voice was calm. "I did not."

"I don't believe you, old chap. Where is the botanist?"

"Mr. Chancellor has gone."

"Eh?" Mr. Sutherland said. "Why? I thought . . ."

"I sent him away," Mr. Li said. "So he would be safe."

"Well." Mr. Thanos breathed out. "I guess that's that."

"No." Sutherland's affable voice turned hard. "*This* man is a murderer. I don't believe he sent Chancellor away at all. He must have killed him as well, to keep his cherished secrets."

"The tea is not here," Mr. Li said without heat. "I have looked."

"Good for you, my friend," Mr. Sutherland returned. "Forgive me if I don't believe you. We'll have the police here, and that will be the end of it."

Mr. Li laughed. Not the evil laugh of a stage villain, but an amused chuckle. "Yes, I would like the police."

"They'll take you away in shackles. They took you once, and foolishly let you go. I'll be there again, to interpret, and tell them what you've done."

I'd heard enough. I no longer cared for the danger—Cynthia and I were strong young women, and Mr. Thanos would readily assist us.

I ran down the gallery, not worrying about noise, Cynthia directly behind me. The men looked up in amazement, and at that moment, Mr. Thanos struck.

He seized Mr. Sutherland's walking stick with both hands, trying to yank it from him. Mr. Sutherland, taken unawares, lost his balance but regained it with surprising speed. He jerked the stick from Mr. Thanos's grasp and slammed it across the young man's back.

Mr. Thanos yelped and raised his arms as another blow came down. Mr. Li stooped, coming up with handfuls of dirt, which he flung at Mr. Sutherland.

Mr. Sutherland left off beating Mr. Thanos and swung on Mr. Li. Mr. Li sensibly fled.

By that time, I'd reached the bottom of the stairs. Holding my skirts out of my way, I raced down the walk, cutting to the right to intercept Mr. Li. Cynthia ran straight for Mr. Thanos.

Out of the corner of my eye, I saw Mr. Sutherland produce a long-bladed knife, and Mr. Thanos fling himself frantically between him and Cynthia. I could not stop to see what happened, as I desperately needed to reach Mr. Li.

Mr. Li ran along the outer wall, behind wrought iron pillars that supported the gallery. I gave chase, calling his name. When we were almost to the end of the greenhouse, Mr. Li at last halted, sagging against a white-painted iron column.

"Forgive me," he wailed. "I am a coward. I have left your friend—"

Behind us, Cynthia was cursing like a sailor, Mr. Thanos yelling for Sutherland to put away that knife, for God's sake.

"Don't be silly," I said to Mr. Li. "What can you do against a strong and armed young man? Come with me."

I grasped the sleeve of his robe and tugged him along as I

ran to the door through which we'd entered and threw it open to the chill of the night.

"Constable!" I shouted. "Come quick. Murder! Help!"

To my relief, two young men materialized out of the darkness and ran toward me, probably more worried about me trespassing than anything else. It was truly dark now, and the constables' lanterns bobbed like fireflies.

"You all right, missus?" the young man who'd first admitted me to the park asked when they reached me. He scowled at Mr. Li. "'Ere, you. Leave her be."

The constable began to pull Mr. Li from me, but I shoved his hand away. "Stop that. Mr. Li is perfectly innocent. But my friends are being attacked. In there. Please hurry!"

Without waiting, I turned and dashed back inside, making for the place I'd left Cynthia and Mr. Thanos battling Mr. Sutherland. The constables pounded past me, and I heard Mr. Li wheezing as he tried to keep up.

One constable split off from the other so the two could surround the combatants. I followed their lanterns, but it was very dark. I blundered into branches and once headlong into a bush before I convinced myself to pick my way carefully along. I reflected that Mr. Sutherland must have brought a lantern to light his way the night he'd killed Zhen.

I nearly ran into Cynthia before I saw her. She caught me in a sturdy grip. "He's run for it," she said, her voice shaking. "Thanos went after him, the fool. I've lost them in the dark."

"The constables will find them," I assured her, trying to catch my breath. "They know this place better than we do."

"Sutherland moves like the wind, blast the man. I knew there was something I didn't like about him."

Mr. Li staggered toward us. He'd lost his cap, and the top of his shaved head glinted in the shadowy darkness.

"Did you see Mr. Sutherland the night Sir Jacob was killed?" I asked him. "Is that why you disappeared from your house arrest? Why didn't you tell us?"

"No, I did not see him," Mr. Li said, shaking his head. "I did go to Sir Jacob's house after I gave you my gift that night, I admit it, but Sir Jacob was already dead. I meant to speak to him, to explain to him what taking the tea would do to my family, the villagers. Or perhaps I wanted to wrest the whereabouts of the tea from him—I am not certain now. I took you the box as an excuse to be in that area in case anyone saw me. I am sorry. I found the kitchen door unlocked and slipped inside and upstairs, but Sir Jacob was dead, as I say. I fled."

"Bloody hell," Cynthia broke in. "So Chancellor really *did* see you in the street."

"They will not catch him," Mr. Li said, watching the constables' lanterns flit to and fro. "Your friend Mr. Thanos is in great danger."

"He is, damn him," Cynthia said. "Thanos!" she shouted. "Run this way!"

Mr. Li watched for a moment then turned and faded into the darkness.

The front doors crashed open. Men ran inside, lanterns swinging, Daniel, grim faced, leading them. Behind him came more constables and Inspector McGregor, along with James and Tess, both of whom it seemed had refused to remain sensibly at home.

The men spread out, searching. They shone lights in all corners, but nowhere did I see Mr. Thanos or Mr. Sutherland. They could easily have slipped out the far door while the constables were banging their way in the front.

I imagined Sutherland plunging the knife into Mr. Thanos

before he flung the body aside, much as he'd done with Zhen and Sir Jacob, and fear squeezed me.

I heard a faint step overhead and jerked my head up. "There!" I cried, pointing.

Mr. Sutherland was racing along the top gallery, pulling Mr. Thanos with him. Mr. Thanos fought and twisted but was unable to break the man's hold.

Daniel charged up the spiral staircase, McGregor and a few constables after him.

"Stop!" Sutherland roared. In the glimmer of the rising moon, I saw his knife at Mr. Thanos's neck. "Back away, or I slice his throat."

Mr. Thanos continued to struggle, but Sutherland's raw, long-armed strength defeated him.

Daniel halted, breathing hard. "If you hurt him," he said evenly, "I won't be able to stop myself from killing you."

"Threats of murder in front of the police?" Mr. Sutherland shoved Mr. Thanos gut-first into the rail. "Leave now, or his dead body goes over."

"Rot it," Thanos said, voice hoarse. "I admired you, you cretin. I suppose overweening ambition corrupts the soul."

"I'm not after plaudits, my old friend. I'm after the money. That tea is worth more by weight than gold. I'm going to go find it, and you are coming with me, Thanos, to protect me."

He wrenched Mr. Thanos from the railing and dragged him along the gallery. Constables fanned to the far side of the greenhouse to intercept him when he came down, but Sutherland, as Cynthia said, was quick. He'd reach the other set of stairs before they did.

I saw a flurry of robes behind Sutherland, and then Sutherland staggered under a blow to his back. Mr. Li, likely ashamed of his earlier flight from danger, had crept behind Sutherland and struck him with his fists.

Not hard enough, unfortunately. Sutherland stumbled and went down on one knee, but he was up again with amazing rapidity, his knife now slashing at Mr. Li.

Mr. Thanos tried to tackle Sutherland as Daniel raced toward them. Sutherland abandoned Mr. Li for the more formidable threats of Mr. Thanos and Daniel—Mr. Li sagged to the floor of the narrow gallery and was still.

Sutherland fought off Thanos, his knife flashing. Cynthia ran for the staircase—I couldn't stop her.

Mr. Thanos gave a great cry, then cursed, and then toppled over the wrought iron railing. I watched as he tumbled down in a flurry of limbs, heard the crash of brush as he landed in the dark.

"Elgin!" Cynthia shouted. She hurtled back down the spiral staircase, and rushed toward the place he'd fallen, slashing priceless plants out of her way in her haste.

A groan sounded. Cynthia fell to her knees in mud and water, gathering Mr. Thanos to her where he lay in a tangle.

I reached them, my breath coming too fast. "Lie still," I gasped at Mr. Thanos as he tried to sit up. "Cynthia, we should check him for broken bones."

Cynthia, not noticing I'd put no honorific before her name, competently ran her hands over Mr. Thanos's shoulders, arms, wrists, ribs. Thanos lay quietly, his dark eyes clouded with pain.

"It's a doctor for you, man," Cynthia said. "You feel whole, but who knows what you broke open inside."

"Hell." Mr. Thanos let his head loll against Cynthia's shoulder, unembarrassed for now. "First, I am poisoned with ar-

senic, then I fall thirty feet and land in a great lot of bushes.
McAdam has much to answer for."

"Hush," I said gently. "You are a hero, Mr. Thanos."

"For falling over? Jove, I've been a hero all my life then."

"Stop talking, dear idiot." Cynthia pressed her cheek to his
dark hair.

She said nothing more, and Mr. Thanos closed his eyes,
something like peace settling over him.

22

I left Mr. Thanos in Cynthia's care and climbed the large staircase to assist Mr. Li.

The constables had surrounded and trounced Mr. Sutherland. He continued to struggle but was dragged down the gallery by several robust young policemen, followed by a hard-faced Inspector McGregor.

I stepped well aside so the constables could take their captive down the stairs. McGregor stiffened when he spied me then let out a resigned sigh and descended after them.

Daniel had an arm around Mr. Li and was helping him to his feet. I lifted a lantern one of the constables had left behind and went to them.

"Very brave of you," I told Mr. Li. "But foolish. How did you get up here so quickly?" I eyed Mr. Li's slight frame and shaking limbs doubtfully.

He gave me a tremulous smile. "There was a ladder against

one of the trees, very near the railings, and I was quite a climber as a lad. Not as much now."

"I saw you knock him over," I said. "Do not tell me that was not an athletic endeavor."

"More luck than any skill," Mr. Li said modestly. "Mr. Thanos already had him nicely off balance. Is Mr. Thanos all right? That young man saved my life."

"I hope so." I clutched the lantern's handle more tightly. "He's with Lady Cynthia, who will take him to a physician. A good one."

"Which I will pay for," Daniel said. "Thanos will have the best—as usual."

I flashed the light upon him. "He is a bit put out with you."

"*I* am a bit put out with me. I was too slow, Kat, and not paying attention." Daniel's expression darkened, and I took pity on him and moved the light away.

We started down the stairs, taking Mr. Li slowly around each turn. A spiral staircase might look graceful and airy, but it can be an unwieldy thing to get up and down.

At the bottom, we sat Mr. Li on the nearest bench, and I sank wearily next to him.

Daniel gazed down at me, the lantern at our feet playing shadows over his face. "As always, Kat, you are where the danger is, and I nearly didn't reach *you* in time—again. Please busy yourself with pastry and cease putting yourself in peril."

"There are few places more dangerous than a kitchen," I argued. "Sharp knives, fire, burning fat . . . I won't be safe in there, my friend."

"A bookshop, then," Daniel said. "Become a seller of books and do nothing more dangerous than brew tea."

"Books are weighty things," Mr. Li said, his dark eyes twinkling. "They can crush one. I know this from experience."

Daniel gave an impatient growl and turned away to seek Mr. Thanos. Tess and James had joined Cynthia in ministering to him, and their voices filled the hall.

McGregor and Sutherland were already gone. Sutherland had not acknowledged me as the constables had hustled him past me, and I'd heard him snarling invective at McGregor, threatening lawsuits and worse, as they'd dragged him away.

"Dear lady." Mr. Li's soothing voice brought my attention back to him. "Danger draws you, like a light draws a moth. Your friend Mr. McAdam is right to worry about you."

"Goodness, I worry far more about him," I said. "He chases bad men right and left, and expects me to stay behind and feed him scones upon his return."

"It is the way of the world, Mrs. Holloway."

"It is a silly way," I said decidedly. "But you must tell me everything. Where have you been hiding? I feared your demise. How did Mr. Sutherland know you would be here?"

Mr. Li shook his head. "He did not follow me—he brought me. I have been a captive in his house these last days."

I stared at him in shock. "But how could you have been? Mr. Thanos and Cynthia escorted Mr. Sutherland home from a lecture. They would have seen you, surely."

Mr. Li lifted his thin hands, which were still shaky. "I was locked in a room high in the house and they did not come there. I was foolish, dear lady. I sought refuge with Mr. Sutherland, believing I would be safe with him. I do not trust your police, and I worried the murderer would find me. Mr. Sutherland welcomed me, but within an hour of conversing with him, it became clear that *he* had killed Sir Jacob, because he wanted my tea. I do not know how he found out about the tea, but when I worked for him, he came to my lodgings—perhaps he found the letter from my father among my things. Mr.

Sutherland is well literate in Chinese characters, of course. When I tried to flee Mr. Sutherland's house, he imprisoned me, badgered me to tell him where the tea was, and even began to torture me. Yesterday, Mr. Thanos paid an unexpected call, to make sure all was well, and found Mr. Sutherland beating me in his back bedroom. And so Mr. Thanos was imprisoned too."

I listened in dismay, imagining Mr. Thanos's bewilderment, surprise coupled with Mr. Sutherland's strength allowing Mr. Thanos to be locked away.

The lantern's flicker brushed Mr. Li's face, shadowing lines of so much weariness that I put a hand on his thin shoulder. "You have nothing more to fear. I will take you home and get some nourishment into you, and then you will rest."

Mr. Li shook his head, his look one of shame. "I have failed my father. I have searched high and low—and Mr. Sutherland made me search this place when we arrived—but I have not found the tea."

"That's quite all right too," I said, with a lightness I hadn't felt in days. "I know where the tea is. At least, I believe I do. I will return it to you, and as the saying goes—all shall be well, and all shall be well, and all manner of things shall be well."

I wanted to see to Mr. Thanos before we went home. Cynthia had become brusque and commanding, and she had the Kew constables running for a hired carriage. Not a hansom, but a landau with wide seats, plenty of room, and shelter from the weather.

Daniel and James half carried, half supported Mr. Thanos out of the Temperate House, and I followed, the cold wind cutting after the stillness of the greenhouse. Cynthia and

Daniel bundled Mr. Thanos into the landau, while I watched, feeling ineffective.

"I've got him," Cynthia told me from where she sat beside him. "You go on, Mrs. H. Help Mr. Li. And don't let Sutherland use his position to weasel his way out of things."

Daniel gave the driver directions, but waved them on, remaining with me. "Not leaving your side until you're home," he told me with a scowl.

"Very well," I said meekly.

Daniel gazed at me in sudden suspicion. "What are you up to, Kat?"

"Not a thing. I believe we should return to Mount Street. And take Mr. Li with us."

"The police will need to speak to him."

"I don't doubt. They can do so later. This is important."

Daniel gave up. He hired another carriage for us, again a rather luxurious landau, and soon Daniel, Mr. Li, Tess, James, and I rolled through the dark roads toward Mayfair. Anyone peering into the coach would be astonished to see a man-of-all-work in dusty clothes, a cook in a soil-splotched frock, an errand boy, a kitchen maid, and a Chinaman.

Tess made the most of it. "Ooh, ain't I the Queen of England." She made a motion of pouring out into an imaginary teacup. "More tea, Madame?" she asked me in an exaggerated upper-class drawl.

James laughed out loud. Daniel smiled tolerantly, his hand twined through mine. Mr. Li must not have known what to make of us, but he looked on with polite amusement.

When we alighted at Mount Street, Tess started for the scullery stairs to our kitchen, but I grasped Mr. Li's arm. "Come with me. Please," I added, not wanting to sound sharp.

Tess hurried back to us, not wanting to miss anything. I

led the way to the house next door and down the steps, where I knocked on the kitchen door. A curious scullery maid opened it, and Mrs. Finnegan craned from her stove to see us. Mrs. Redfern came out of the servants' hall, keys clinking, eyes widening in surprise when she beheld our party.

"Mrs. Redfern, will you allow us upstairs?" I asked her. "It is very important, but I do not wish to disturb your mistress. How does she fare?"

"Much better," Mrs. Redfern said, her relief apparent. "She et a bit of supper with no trouble, and says she'll leave her bed in the morning. She's taking Lady Cynthia's advice to return to Liverpool. To her people, as she puts it."

"Will you go with her?" I asked as she led us up the back stairs.

"No, indeed. The household will be broken up. I'm out a place, but it's just as well. London is my home, and I don't wish to leave it."

At the top of the stairs, Mrs. Redfern opened the green baize door and admitted us into the main hall filled with the mishmash of screens, tables, lacquerware, settees, and cushions.

"What is it you intend to do, Mrs. Holloway?" Mrs. Redfern asked, clearly not about to let us any farther without explanation.

"I'd like a look into the front drawing room, please. I believe we won't need to go anywhere else."

Mrs. Redfern raised her brows but moved to the pocket doors and slid them open. She lit the gas sconces inside, lighting the cluttered room.

I beckoned to Mr. Li as I walked to the collection of Wardian cases near the front window.

"Is this the tea?" I asked, pointing to a case that stood on a table with straight, white-painted legs. The small plants inside had leaves very like what Mr. Chancellor had cut from the back garden.

Mr. Li stared at the cases, and for a moment he ceased breathing. I caught him as he swayed, but he waved me off and seized the top of one case. It didn't budge.

"They're sealed with lead," I said quickly. "Daniel, can you help?"

Daniel came forward, James behind him, with Tess hovering near, Mrs. Redfern curious in the background.

James removed a stout folding knife from his pocket and handed it to Daniel. Daniel knelt beside the table and worked the knife under the edges of the case. Very slowly, he peeled the lead from the wood, loosening the case from its base.

The small case was very much like the Temperate House in miniature, white-painted beams around which glass was fitted. Daniel went painstakingly slowly, not wanting to mar the plants inside. Mr. Li shifted in some agitation, and my own patience began to wear thin.

At long last, Daniel and James lifted off the heavy cover. Mr. Li's hand shot in, and he uprooted a handful of the tea plants.

He sniffed them, held them to the light, ran his fingers over the leaves, sniffed them again, then reached out his tongue and tasted one.

"Yes!" His word was a cry of joy, his weariness falling away. "These are the plants from my father's garden. Mrs. Holloway, you are, as your people say, a worker of miracles."

"Well." I tried to keep my smile modest. "I've had a while to think it through, ever since I saw the cases knocked about the day after Sir Jacob was murdered."

Mr. Li made a low bow to me, his face stretched with his smile. "I have no words to say how much I thank you."

Tess leaned to gaze at the plants in the case. "They don't look like much. Little bitty things."

"It takes time to grow a full tea bush," I said. "I should have thought of that when—"

I broke off as Mr. Li strode to the fireplace, poked the glowing coals to life, and dropped the tea plants into the growing flames. Without a word, he headed back to the Wardian case.

"No!" Tess cried. She leapt in front of the case then dodged out of the way, eyeing the poker Mr. Li still carried. "I heard Mr. Sutherland say this tea is worth more than gold."

"That is true," Mr. Li said calmly. He reached past her and took another fistful of plants, hobbling back to the fire to thrust them in.

"But don't ya want to be rich?" Tess protested. "Mrs. Holloway, what's he doing?"

"I understand," I said quietly. I gathered a handful of plants—the case was quite full of them—and carried them to the fire. Mr. Li sent me a grateful look.

"Well, I don't," Tess said in anguish.

Daniel answered for me. "Because if these plants are propagated and replicated here, then those growing in the remote mountains of Wuyi will be next to worthless. No one would pay to ship that tea all the way from China—they wouldn't need to. And so Mr. Li's family and everyone who makes their livelihood from the tea will go hungry."

"Why will they?" Tess's brow wrinkled. "The Chinese people will still buy it, won't they?"

"Some." Daniel pulled out a tea plant, gazed at it with regret, and handed it to Mr. Li who'd returned for another load. "But that won't be enough. It is what happened when Chinese tea was stolen nearly forty years ago and taken to India to be cultivated. The market for exported tea from China shriveled, and many tea growers were ruined. The man who sneaked the tea from China in 1848 worked for Kew Gardens—or at least was hired by men employed there."

Tess listened, watched Mr. Li and me burning the tea, and shook her head. "I still don't understand. I'll stick to cooking, me."

Daniel lifted the Wardian case and carried it to the fire so we wouldn't have to make back-and-forth trips. James joined us, and he and Daniel, Mr. Li and I, emptied the small greenhouse of its contents. Mrs. Redfern watched but didn't stop us as we burned the lot. The aroma from the flames was heavenly.

When the case was empty, Daniel brushed out even the soil and sent it into the fire.

"Poor things," Tess said over my shoulder.

I agreed, but I understood Mr. Li's great fear. A work of art was unique, worth much in cash and simply for existing—pictures stamped out at a factory by the thousands were not.

We checked all the other cases, but found no more tea. Flowers, exotic and strange, yes. Tea, no. I wondered how rare and precious the flowers were, and if lives would be ruined because of *them*.

Mrs. Redfern let us search the other rooms, and Daniel and I went quietly to Sir Jacob's bedchamber itself, but we found no more Wardian cases in the house.

Mr. Li waited for us downstairs, his expression a mixture of sorrow and satisfaction. "Thank you, Mrs. Holloway. You have saved my family."

"Not at all," I said. "You were kind to me, and I do feel sorry for you, so far from home. You will go back now, won't you?"

"As soon as I can arrange it. Though I believe I will check at your Kew Gardens again, thoroughly, and make very sure Sir Jacob did not give them any tea to plant there."

"I'll help you," Daniel said. "I already know my way around the place, and I've discovered I like gardening. Maybe I'll take up the post permanently."

"You?" I asked, my brows arching. "The peripatetic Mr. McAdam?"

"I'm not as much a wanderer as you might think, my dear Mrs. Holloway. Mr. Li, the police will want to question you, I am afraid. But again, I will help you, and so will Mr. Thanos."

"Not tonight," I said briskly. "We have done plenty for now, and I am about to drop off my pins. Thank you, Mrs. Redfern. I believe we should all return to my kitchen and have a nice cup of tea."

I wasn't to be allowed to drink my tea in peace after I poured cups all around in the servants' hall. It was plain tea from the shop, nothing fancy, but no one seemed to mind.

When I sat down, the others demanded I explain how I'd worked out the killer's identity and where the tea plants had been hidden. At least Daniel, Tess, and James demanded. Mr. Li sat in quiet satisfaction.

"I didn't discover a thing," I protested.

Daniel rested his elbows on the table and regarded me skeptically. "It looked to *me* that you'd cornered a murderer and told my son to make sure I ran in with constables just in time to take him away."

"Exactly," James said, and Tess nodded beside him.

Mr. Li only calmly sipped his tea, as though he had no more interest in the mystery.

"I wasn't certain of anything until Mr. Thanos sent that note," I said. "James knew there was something fishy about it, and fortunately, he came to *me* when he couldn't find you, Daniel. I had to wonder why Mr. Thanos would send someone a sheet of formulas with no explanation. I suppose another mathematician would understand it, and I realized that if he needed to send out a note of distress, he must do it in a way that whomever was with him wouldn't realize it was indeed a call for help."

"But why'd Mr. Sutherland let him send anything?" Tess asked. "If he were holding Mr. Thanos prisoner, why would he want anyone to know he was there?"

"Because *we* knew Mr. Thanos had been stopping in to make certain Mr. Sutherland was well," I said. "No doubt Mr. Thanos, once he realized he was in danger, made sure to tell him we knew about his visits. Mr. Sutherland couldn't let on that Mr. Thanos was there for any other reason. If Mr. Thanos truly was supposed to help another mathematician with a lecture, and he *didn't* send the notes, an inquiry would be made—at the very least someone would be sent to find the notes. Mr. Sutherland looked over the paper to be certain Mr. Thanos wasn't sending a letter begging to be rescued, but there was nothing but mathematics on it." I looked at Daniel. "Did the note contain a message? A code?"

Daniel shrugged. "I have no idea what any of it meant. I think they are Maxwell's equations he's constantly working on. But I knew good and well Thanos wasn't assisting at a lecture tonight. I would guess he spied James in the street and took a chance to tell him—and me—that he was in trouble. You understood that as well, Kat, and ran to his aid."

"A bit too late," I said dejectedly.

"But you knew they went to Kew Gardens," Tess pointed out.

"Only because the landlady overheard them give directions

to the hansom driver. She never said the word *Kew*, but that was the only place that made sense."

Mr. Li lifted his attention from his cup. "Mr. Sutherland was quite certain I knew where the tea was. I told him Kew Gardens. I thought if I got him there, in a place with people and constables, we could flee him. But he kept a knife on Mr. Thanos the whole time, and I could not risk Mr. Sutherland would not stab him."

"As he stabbed Sir Jacob," I said. "I always thought it odd that Sir Jacob wasn't at home for his appointment with Mr. Li. He liked showing off his Chinese things, which was why his wife held all those garden parties. What if Mr. Sutherland, realizing what a valuable thing Mr. Li was looking for, deliberately told Mr. Li the appointment was on a different day—or perhaps he didn't set an appointment at all. Mr. Sutherland had secretly learned of the tea and didn't want to give Mr. Li a chance to find it before he could. I believe he set up an appointment with Sir Jacob for himself alone on the night of Sir Jacob's death."

"He is a demon," Mr. Li said. "They can take the guise of humans, and smile at you until you believe them."

"You have to look for the cloven hooves," Tess put in. "That's what my mum always said. Or—if they're wearing shoes—a tail."

Mr. Li considered this seriously. "A good thing to remember."

"As I say, Mr. Sutherland must have set an appointment for himself that night," I went on, pretending to ignore Tess. "Unbeknownst to him, Sir Jacob had yet another appointment that evening, at Kew Gardens, most likely with his son. Though we'll never know unless we find someone who happened to see them both there."

"Sheppard," Daniel said. "It should be safe for him to come forward now, if he is alive."

"We will hope for the best," I said. "And continue searching if Lady Roberta finds nothing."

"We certainly will," Daniel agreed. "Please continue, Kat."

I turned my cup absently on the table. "What I think happened is this: Mr. Sutherland turned up sometime after nine, after Sheppard had left Sir Jacob for the night. Sir Jacob, I suspect, let Mr. Sutherland in himself. He had the habit of admitting callers he knew were for him, even if he was already in his dressing gown. Sir Jacob wasn't raised as a gentleman—a wellborn man with plenty of servants wouldn't dream of answering his own front door.

"Mr. Sutherland came to interrogate Sir Jacob about the tea. Perhaps he argued with Sir Jacob, or he wanted to search the house and garden himself, and Sir Jacob tried to stop him. Mr. Sutherland is quite strong, and Sir Jacob was a smallish man, getting on in years. The police say Sir Jacob was killed in the bed, which was already turned down for him by Sheppard, so perhaps Sutherland, in their struggle, forced him down on the bed and stabbed him through the heart, probably with that knife he was so easily waving about." I paused to shudder.

"Mr. Sutherland risked a look about the house but found nothing," I continued. "He opened the window in the drawing room, to suggest a burglary, and slipped out. He's tall enough and robust enough that climbing out the window wouldn't have been difficult for him. That would explain why Caleb, the constable walking his beat, didn't see the window open until half past ten—Mr. Sutherland likely waited until Caleb had gone around the corner before he left, and was far away by the time Caleb walked by again."

"So Caleb was right," Tess said, sounding proud.

"Mr. Sutherland had quietly set a few tables on their sides

to make it look as though a burglar came and went through the drawing room in a hurry," I said. "No one in the house heard any crashing about, I realized, so how did those things get knocked over without making a sound? The funny thing is, he had to move the Wardian cases with the tea in them so he could reach the window. Never noticing the very thing he'd come to steal. I imagine he didn't know, like many of us, what growing tea looks like."

Mr. Li nodded. "It was the right thing to happen."

Ironic, I suppose he meant. "Anyway, Mr. Li decided that night to enter the house himself and look around, finding the kitchen door unlocked—likely Mrs. Finnegan left it open for Mr. Pasfield. Mr. Li saw Sir Jacob murdered in his bed, and fled."

"I did." Mr. Li bowed his head. "I am ashamed. I should have run for help. I did not notice the tea either in my haste, which is my punishment."

"The police would only have arrested you," I said. "If you hadn't run off, you'd be this moment at Newgate, or perhaps even already hanged for the murder."

"I never suspected Mr. Sutherland," Mr. Li said, downcast. "He'd seemed a good man, a fellow scholar. I suppose I grew fond of him because he spoke my language. That can be a comforting thing."

"It must be," I said. "Probably why all the Englishmen live together in foreign parts."

"Fear has something to do with that," Daniel said. "And a knowledge that the natives don't necessarily want them there."

"Perhaps, but I understand what Mr. Li means. Same reason so many Chinese live in Chinatown."

"It is true," Mr. Li said. "But Mr. Sutherland did not only

speak Chinese—he spoke the language of the court. The men in Limehouse are laborers from what you call Canton, which might as well be another world."

"So he was a dab hand at languages," Tess said. "But a bad man all the same. I always knew too much book learning weren't good for you."

"In any case—" I cut firmly through Tess's speech. "Mr. Chancellor, probably the only person that night not paying a call for a nefarious reason, made a fuss about seeing a China-man. Mr. Sutherland might have thought at first it was you, Mr. Li, but he also knew about Sir Jacob's son. Perhaps Sir Jacob told him; or Mr. Sutherland, as a scholar, thoroughly researched his mark. Fearing Zhen might have seen him, Mr. Sutherland found Zhen and lured him to the gardens, kill-ing him there. This would not only silence a witness but pre-vent Zhen from laying claim to the tea as Sir Jacob's son. Doing the murder at Kew would throw suspicion onto Mr. Chancellor, and possibly even Daniel, Mr. Thanos's friend who wormed his way into a post at Kew and asked so many questions."

Daniel pursed his lips. "I hadn't thought of that."

I sent him a smile. "Perhaps you should consider that next time you are so eager to help the police."

"I could say the same for you, Kat," Daniel said. "But Chan-cellor did have a nefarious purpose. The next day he was crawling through Sir Jacob's garden stealing cuttings of a tea bush."

"True," I said. "But he might have been helping himself to *anything* Sir Jacob brought back, either to propagate and sell, or simply from scientific curiosity. If he was after Mr. Li's tea, he was disappointed."

"The price of obsession." Daniel grinned. "I will have to

ask him what he was about, to satisfy my own curiosity. But finish your story, please."

I gave him a deprecating look. Daniel had gall to say *my* inquisitiveness led me into trouble. His was just as dangerous.

"Very well—this is what I believe happened next. Mr. Sutherland heard Mr. Thanos was searching high and low for a learned Chinese man called Mr. Li, so Mr. Sutherland produced him, or at least told Mr. Thanos about him. It would look odd if Mr. Thanos discovered that his old friend knew Mr. Li and never mentioned him. That same day, Mr. Li was arrested. I wouldn't be surprised if Mr. Sutherland betrayed his whereabouts to the police, anonymously, of course, hoping Mr. Li would be blamed for the murder. And that would be that."

"Mr. Sutherland must have decided to pretend to help you through the questioning," Daniel said to Mr. Li. "He couldn't have foreseen that Kat would speak up for you so stoutly. But being the helpful friend worked to his advantage. When you were released by the police and grew afraid the killer would hunt you down, as many now knew where you lodged, you turned naturally to Mr. Sutherland, the fellow scholar, one of the first people in London to befriend you."

"I am a fool," Mr. Li said. "My father always says so."

"Does he?" I asked in surprise. "But you took those very difficult exams, and did so well at them that you work in the house of the emperor."

"All to prove to my father I was not stupid," Mr. Li said bitterly. "One reason I came here to find the stolen tea was to show him I am worthy of his praise." He gave me a sad smile. "He is past seventy-five years old. I am drawing close to sixty. And still I am wishing for my father's approval."

"Huh," James said. "I know exactly what you mean, Mr. Li."

Daniel gently swiped his hand over the back of James's head, and we laughed.

It was not so much James's joke that made us laugh, but relief. A gruesome murderer had been caught, Mr. Li exonerated, and his tea found.

I'd known Mr. Li had been innocent all along. Men may scoff at women's intuition, but it is a powerful thing, and usually correct.

23

The next morning I was a bit sandy eyed, and so was Tess, but we turned our hands to getting breakfast on the table.

Mr. Davis entered with his newspaper, whistling.

"You are in a fine mood this morning, Mr. Davis," I said, somewhat crossly.

"I am indeed, Mrs. Holloway. The effect of an improving day out. I believe I will take them more often."

A knock sounded on the scullery door, and Elsie pulled it open. She flinched when she saw a constable standing there, but Tess dusted off her hands and came forward in welcome.

"Good morning to ya, Caleb."

I studied her bright eyes and flushed face while the young constable stood a little straighter. *Well, well.*

"Good morning, Tess—er, Miss Parsons. Mrs. Holloway. I'm here to make an arrest."

"An arrest?" I asked in confusion and some alarm. I thought

of Cynthia and me tearing up precious plants in the Temperate House trying to get to Mr. Thanos. I'd also helped Mr. Li destroy priceless tea, which the police would consider had belonged to Sir Jacob, and now to Lady Harkness.

"Yes, ma'am," Caleb said then turned to Mr. Davis. "She here?"

"Right this way, Constable." Mr. Davis laid his newspaper on the table and motioned for Caleb to follow him.

Tess and I exchanged a startled look then set down knives and spoons and hurried after them. Elsie abandoned her sink and followed us.

Mr. Davis unlocked the door of the housekeeper's parlor, opening it as the rest of us reached it. Inside, Mrs. Daley sat at her table with a magazine, a cup of tea in hand. She jerked her head up when the door banged open, her mouth open to harangue.

Next to her teapot lay the carved wooden box Mr. Li had given me, gaping open.

"Mrs. Daley!" I shrieked, running to it.

The blasted woman had drunk half the tea left inside, and even now, she took a long gulp from her cup.

I seized the box, snapping the lid closed. "You took this from my bedchamber. How *dare* you?"

Mrs. Daley sent me a complacent look. "Cook has no business keeping secret stashes from the larder. I saw you carry it upstairs. I only brought it back down."

The constable had no interest in the tea. He walked to the bookcase and picked up a bowl of cut flowers, lifting the flowers out, water from the stems dripping to the rug. "Is this it, Mr. Davis?"

Mrs. Daley rose hastily, knocking over her teacup in the

process. The precious tea spread in a puddle across the table. "That's mine!"

The constable held up the bowl, sunlight from a high window catching on translucent porcelain decorated with a dragon chasing its tail.

"I hardly think so," I said when I found my breath. "It's Ming, I believe. From Sir Jacob's collection next door."

"It is indeed, Mrs. Holloway," Mr. Davis said, exultant. "I am certain Lady Harkness can identify it as such. Or Mrs. Redfern, the housekeeper."

"Mrs. Finnegan let you in to visit?" I asked Mrs. Daley with a smile. I had requested that Mrs. Finnegan do so when I found a ruse to send Mrs. Daley next door, and to allow her upstairs, so that her thieving hands might light upon something they shouldn't. I hadn't put the plan into motion, as I'd been so busy with murders and finding a crop of tea, but Mr. Davis must have had a similar idea.

"Mrs. Redfern did," Mr. Davis said.

He closed his mouth, but I saw the mirth in his eyes.

So that was what he had done with his day out, and why he'd said it had been effective. He hadn't visited old friends—he'd spent the time trying to rid us of Mrs. Daley.

I felt humbled.

Caleb was ready with his handcuffs. Another constable had entered the house as we'd cornered Mrs. Daley, and he and Caleb led her off. Mr. Davis carried out the Ming bowl, handling it gingerly before he wrapped it in part of his newspaper and gave it to Caleb to take as evidence.

Mrs. Daley cursed and struggled as the constables pushed her out. She shot Mr. Davis and me a venomous glare, before the constables more or less dragged her up the stairs to the waiting police van. The van rumbled away under the delighted gazes of the neighbors' servants and passing draymen.

Elsie closed the door, and Mr. Davis rubbed his palms together and chuckled.

"Well, ain't you a close one," Tess said admiringly.

Mr. Davis slid off his butler's coat, sat down at the table, and spread out the remains of his newspaper.

"I decided that if Mrs. Daley could scrape up dirt on our pasts, I could scrape some up on hers," he said. "Apparently, she's known to the police. Has stolen from her employers before, but they couldn't prove it. Mrs. Redfern was indignant on our behalf, and agreed to help."

"I'd thought of a similar scheme," I said. "But you beat me to it, Mr. Davis."

"Ah well, you had your hands full assisting the police and fending off Mr. McAdam." He leaned his elbows on the table, lifting the paper to begin reading.

"Fending off Mr. McAdam?" I repeated. "Are you disparaging my character, Mr. Davis?"

"No, indeed, Mrs. Holloway," Mr. Davis said, not raising his eyes from the paper. "You can't help that he's smitten with you."

"Smitten," I muttered, turning away.

Mr. Davis ignored me. I poured him a cup of thick, rich coffee that he liked and set a crumpet dripping with butter next to him. I followed that with a large slice of seedcake.

He deserved it, bless the man.

I did not have to worry about fending off Mr. McAdam, because I did not see him until late that evening. Lady Cynthia returned just after supper, visiting the kitchen to tell me lightheartedly that Mr. Thanos was well.

"Never met a heartier chap," Cynthia said. "I stayed with him at the doctor's and set him up with a nurse at his lodgings, but he'll be walking about in a day or so. Now I'm going to heave myself into bed and sleep for many hours. I want you to tell me everything when I wake up. Oh—by the bye, Bobby found Sheppard. He's valeting for a bloke in Windsor. Seems he was terrified that the killer would think he witnessed the murder, and fled. Wise man. Ah well, good night."

She helped herself to seedcake, her favorite, and disappeared upstairs.

At least that mystery held a happy ending. I wished Sheppard well.

An hour later, as I sat alone in the kitchen—which seemed a peaceful place tonight—Daniel came calling.

I again shared Mr. Li's tea with him—what was left of it—and told him about Mrs. Daley. He laughed loud and long.

"Good on Mr. Davis. I've always admired him. Don't worry about the tea, Kat. I'm sure Mr. Li can be convinced to part with more before he takes ship."

I sighed. "I want Mr. Li to return home and be happy, but I will miss him."

Daniel rested his hand on mine. "I know you will. You're a good woman, Kat Holloway."

"So you've said."

"Mr. Li was very lucky you ran into him that day." Daniel sent me a teasing look. "I know I am easily knocked from my feet by you."

"Don't be daft," I said, but gently. "Mr. Li was trying to find a way into Sir Jacob's house or at least his garden that afternoon. So, indeed, it was lucky. Running into me no doubt made him abandon the idea, or he might have been caught and arrested at once."

"Indeed he might have. Being stuck in jail would have cleared him of Sir Jacob's murder, but who knows what they would have done to the chap merely for trespassing?"

I nodded. It didn't bear thinking about. Mr. Li must go home, where he'd be safer.

I let my fingers twine through Daniel's. "Now that the puzzle of Mr. Li has been solved, I've returned to the puzzle of you."

"That sounds worrying." Daniel smiled, but his eyes held uneasiness.

"Yes. I think I know—or partly know—who you work for."

"Mmm." The uneasiness increased. "Do tell."

"I have noticed a pattern." I caressed his fingers as I spoke. "When our kitchen maid was killed, and the Fenians were likely involved, you began to investigate. Then you were sent to Scotland, a journey about which you have told me little. Next you were put into place when antiquities from foreign lands went missing. Now you are commanding constables again, and the country in question is China. In other words, you are given resources whenever the tangle involves someplace outside England." I paused, watching him. "Ergo, I conclude you work for the Foreign Office."

Daniel relaxed. "Not . . . quite."

"But my guess is near the mark."

"The devil of it is, Kat, I can't tell you whether it is or not."

I stroked his thumb. "It no longer matters. I am fairly good at deciphering puzzles. I will learn all about you in time."

He leaned closer. "When you do—and I have no doubt you will—please keep it to yourself. It's very important. Life and death is no exaggeration."

"You have nothing to worry about from me," I said in a quiet voice. It was only the truth.

"Thank you, Kat."

We sat in silence a moment before Daniel said, "I do believe you should cease doing that."

I frowned. "Doing what?"

He trapped my moving thumb. "That. I am not made of stone."

I let my hand go limp, and Daniel untwined our fingers. Cool air touched my palm, making my hand feel even more empty.

"I have no idea what you are talking about," I said softly.

Daniel spoke into my ear. "When you are close to me, there is danger that I might want to seduce you."

I thought about this, his breath warming me pleasantly. "I see. But perhaps I would not mind."

His eyes flickered, some of the emotion in them surprise. He had not thought I'd say that.

"In that case, I had better depart."

Daniel pressed a kiss to my lips, a long one, and tender, before he rose to his feet. He gazed down at me for a time, while I remained seated, my legs too weak to let me rise.

"Good night, Kat."

He leaned and kissed my cheek, so softly that my thoughts went to seduction once more, but with me as seducer.

Daniel's grin made his eyes twinkle, and he left me alone, banging the door as he went.

Quite right that he should go. A kitchen was no place for passion.

In the morning after breakfast, Mrs. Redfern came to visit. I ushered her into the housekeeper's parlor and brought in a pot of tea, pushing aside the clutter Mrs. Daley had left. I'd have to clear out the entire room.

"I'm finished next door when the month is out," Mrs. Redfern said, a note of sadness in her voice. "Lady Harkness will journey north at the end of this week, and the staff not going with her will pack up the house and then be done. Except Mrs. Finnegan. She is going to marry Mr. Pasfield."

"Ah," I said, unsurprised. "I believe they'll make a fine match."

Mrs. Redfern nodded. "Yes, they swim along quite well." She sipped tea then let out a sigh. "I have come to you with hat in hand, Mrs. Holloway. I know you are out a housekeeper."

"Such as she was." I grimaced, and then nodded. "I think it a brilliant idea, Mrs. Redfern. I know Mr. Davis will approve. I will put it to Lady Cynthia, and she will persuade her aunt. Lord Rankin pays the staff—which is a mercy—but Mrs. Bywater has the authority to hire. I warn you, she can be a bit . . . difficult . . . about money."

"That does not worry me," Mrs. Redfern said staunchly. "I am expert at managing household budgets. And employers."

I clicked my cup to hers. "Then I look forward to it."

"As do I." Mrs. Redfern looked happier as she lifted the pot. "May I pour you more tea, Mrs. Holloway?"

"An excellent idea," I said, holding out my cup. "Thank you, Mrs. Redfern."

Don't miss the next book
in the Below Stairs Mysteries.

Coming soon from
Berkley Prime Crime!

Photo by Silvio Portrait Design

Jennifer Ashley is the *New York Times* and *USA Today* bestselling author of the Below Stairs Mysteries, including *Scandal Above Stairs* and *Death Below Stairs,* and winner of a Romance Writers of America RITA Award. She also writes as national bestselling and award-winning author Allyson James and bestselling author Ashley Gardner. She lives in the Southwest with her husband and cats, and she spends most of her time in the wonderful worlds of her stories.

You can contact her online at jenniferashley.com and visit her at facebook.com/JenniferAshleyAllysonJamesAshleyGardner and twitter.com/JennAllyson.

Ready to find
your next great read?

Let us help.

Visit prh.com/nextread